1

To Janet,
thank you for be
with one! I hope you
enjoyed the book as well)
enjoyed to write !!!

The Three Ladies

amazonpublishing

The Three Ladies

Claudia Cortez

Spanish title
Las Tres Damas

Translated from Spanish
Lloyd McLaren

Published by:
Amazon Publishing, Amazon Media EU
January 2024

First paper edition 2024
ISBN: 9798877670914

My God, how lonely
The dead remain!
Does dust return to dust?
Does the soul fly to heaven?
Everything is vile matter,
Rot and ooze?
I do not know, but there is something,
What to explain I can not
That at the same time infuses us,
disgust and mourning,
leaving so sad,
Only the dead!

Gustavo Adolfo Bécquer

I

She had to keep moving, it was only a matter of time before they found her and took her life. She couldn't allow her mind to dwell on such matters, she could not allow fear to dictate her choices so she had to push on.

Short, sharp breaths became visible as they hit the cold winter air. Her heart raced to its limit, not solely from her exertion but also from the pervading feeling that danger was close; the same feeling that kept her constantly looking over her shoulder.

Her face, a mask of placidity, belied the turmoil of emotion beneath, and in that moment, no observer could have suspected what she had done or was about to do. Her eyes betrayed the desperation of one who has run out of options and her face displayed the serenity of one who has nothing left to lose.

She knew the forest like the back of her hand but now, in the rapidly fading light all the trees had begun to look the same and her path was no longer clear to her. She stopped for a moment at the base of an ancient beech tree, surrounding herself with its undergrowth, to catch her breath and get her bearings. Once she had re-oriented herself and made herself certain that her pursuers were nowhere in sight then she re-emerged to continue her journey.

She ran a winding path through the trees only stopping when she reached the door of the dilapidated hut, she scanned the woods once more before entering. Once inside, she secured the door with trembling hands using a piece of heavy wood that served as a latch. The inside of the cabin presented no better than its outside, the long abandoned cobwebs that adorned corners of the room and the layer of dust which carpeted the bare wooden floor testified to the ravages of time and neglect. The cabin consisted of a single sparsely furnished room which was illuminated by the inadequate flame of a single candle resting on a small table at the centre and an open fire which cast a warm orange glow into the room making the shadows dance. An old and tattered armchair was situated next to the fire and within arms reach of a child's cradle. Brushing a tear from her cheek she moved toward it, her determination overpowering her trepidation she gingerly pulled back the worn and tattered blankets. A little girl with black curly hair lay within, her cheeks plump but all too pale, rested on a rag doll whose pearly eyes glowed in sympathy with the flames burning in the fireplace. She looked at the child with tenderness as she removed her cloak.

Clutching the leather bag concealed beneath her clothing she lifted the strap over her head, with some difficulty, until she was free of its weight. She then pulled the chair closer to the fire. After rekindling the flames she proceeded to carefully untie the straps. She allowed the bag to fall to the floor and ran her fingers almost reverently over the intricately carved leather bound book as it lay in her lap. The expertly embossed tome appeared to have weathered centuries of time. Opening it with great care,

She poured over page after page, looking for written text but it seemed to be filled only with drawings. After some searching at last she found what she was looking for, though her elation soon dissolved into disappointment when she realised that the text was impossible to read. The strange runes populating the rustic page were completely alien to her.

She continued feverishly turning the pages one by one until finally she found a drawing occupying the centre of one of the pages, which depicted a beautiful woman in intricate detail. The woman held a chalice from which a dark substance resembling blood poured. Beneath the drawing, in clear text, read *The Price of a Soul.*

She continued to stare at the pages carefully. Her first attempts to make sense of the runes ended in failure but after a short while words began to form, like some kind of magical optical illusion. She began to recognise them as the ones her father had taught to her when she was younger. The runes had somehow transformed themselves into a language that she could understand.

The gloom of the room forced her to move closer to the firelight and slowly with some difficulty she began to read. She gained in speed and confidence skipping paragraphs which seemed to hold no interest for her. She continued for almost a minute when something in the corner of her eye drew her attention away. It was then she realised that she was not alone.

She sprung from the chair, the book falling at her feet. She felt the heat of the flames as she took an involuntary step backward, closer to the fire and away from the newcomers.

There were two of them. Both women possessed a strangely hypnotic beauty that made it difficult to avert one's eyes, both well dressed, head to toe in black but the similarities ended with their hair, one possessed a mane of flaxen gold and other wore tresses of fiery red.

"What were you looking for in The Sacred Book?" asked the red-haired one.

The girl responded only with wide eyed silence.

The other interloper walked a few paces and approached the cradle. She carelessly pushed aside the blanket covering the child and bent over her.

"She's dead," said the girl, coming out of her silence.

The blonde woman turned her face towards the child and sucked in a loud breath.

She straightened up and looked at her.

"When did she die?" she asked.

"Yesterday."

The red-haired woman moved closer until she was only a few steps away. She bent down and picked up the book from the floor without breaking eye-contact with the girl.

"What are you looking for here?" she asked again as she walked over to the table. She sat down on the chair and rested the book on the table in front of her.

She locked her eyes on the girl; a stare of such intensity that it rooted her to the spot, unable to move. She could feel the fear growing in her stomach. It began to spread throughout her body, sapping her strength, slowing her thought.

The redhead began to tap a long fingernail on the table in precisely spaced intervals like the ticking of a clock, leaving the girl with the foreboding feeling that her time was running out.

That feeling was confirmed when the tapping stopped and the redhead said in a dispassionate tone, "Sister, destroy her."

The blonde's face contorted into a smile dripping with malice and began to move toward the girl.

"Bring her back to life," she ejected, on the edge of panic.

The other stopped in her tracks a few paces away.

"Why would I do that?" asked the redhead.

"Because I will serve you forever, please bring her back."

"Is that what you wanted? To bring her back to life?"

"Don't listen to her, sister, let me deal with her." The blond woman took another step toward the girl but stopped as the redhead commanded by way of a quick gesture.

She regarded the girl with curiosity and the girl returned the gaze, her eyes now blazing with defiance. The redhead smiled with amusement, this young woman was obviously terrified but in the face of fear she displayed a courage that she had rarely seen. This girl was different, perhaps her bravery should be rewarded.

She stood up and approached the cradle contemplating the child.

"I will do as you ask, but she will also be my slave."

"No!" cried the girl.

A threatening look halted her involuntary advance.

"Please," she begged. "Take me, only me…"

"You? No, I want her."

The girl gathered her resolve and leapt forward to take the baby in her arms, but before she could make contact with the child, the redhead reached out a hand and casually passed her long fingernails across her throat.

The girl slumped lifelessly at the feet of the witch, a dark pool forming around her. The blonde witch gave her a cursory glance then moved her attention back to the cradle.

She brushed her fingers across the pale cheek of the sleeping child, leaving a reddish trace on the immaculate skin. She then returned her gaze to the fallen girl beside her and noted that she too displayed the child like serenity.

"People are far less complicated when they're dead," she thought.

She knelt over the girl and pushed the hair aside to expose her lifeless features and noticed that something was hanging around her neck. She pulled at the thick chain until it gave way. The other started to approach but froze when she saw the pendant.

"How in the nine circles of hell did she get hold of that?" she whispered.

Without answering her sister, she twirled the amulet in her fingers. Despite its size it was light, and seemed to be made of some unfamiliar type of metal.

The design of the pendant was extremely intricate. A number of interconnected runes surrounded a central eye from which fell a tear in the form of a tiny violet gem.

She looked up.

"Perhaps she was not just a simple peasant," she said.

Then she tucked the blanket around the little girl's body and lifted her up.

"What are you doing? Said the blonde.

"Fulfilling her late mother's last wish," she said, and headed through the door with the child resting against her chest.

II

'She is dead,' said Dopey, as a robust tear slid down his cheek.

'Is not true,' shouted Grumpy, pushing him out of the way to get closer to the girl. He kneeled beside her and took her delicate white hand.

'Is not true,' he repeated while bowing his head, in anguish. So, they stayed, the seven kneeling around the lifeless body until the sun began to set.

Doc finally broke the silence.

'We should bury her.'

'No! We won't leave her underground!' Grumpy exclaimed, drying his eyes.

'Let's make her a crystal coffin,' suggested Bashful. 'We will put it in the woods, so we can visit her every day.'

They all agreed and got down to business that same night.

The sound of gentle snoring caused me to pause my reading and look at Adela. She was stretched beside me, asleep. I carefully began to close the book, trying not to make any sudden movements, then she opened her eyes.

"Read a little longer," she babbled, adjusting her pillows.

"It's too late, we'll finish it tomorrow..."

"No..." She protested, sleepily.

"Yes," I said firmly, "You will find out what happened to Snow White, tomorrow."

She smiled widely.

"I know she is not dead; she is just pretending."

"Oh, really?"

She pulled a face of exaggerated smugness, she was too smart to be tricked by simple fairy tales.

"She is playing, just like daddy does sometimes."

I smiled adoringly, she had grown up so fast!

"Well, we'll see." I said, fixing the blankets as I stood up. "We will know tomorrow."

After a little more complaining, I moved her four favourite teddies closer, and she made herself comfortable and fell quiet.

"I love you," I said, kissing her chubby cheeks. "Sleep tight."

I couldn't resist giving her another kiss.

I turned off the lights and went to the door.

"Should I keep it open?"

She shook her head.

"No, mommy always closes it," she yawned sleepily.

She rolled over.

As I walked down the long corridor and looked back, I couldn't help wondering how my sister could leave her there: all alone, when she was so small, and with the door shut.

Reaching the staircase, I turned on the lights and went down. I walked through the enormous room, dodging, the sofas, chairs, tables, and stools as I went; and then entered the kitchen.

"Uh! I do more exercise in this house than in the gym!" I said, sitting beside Lucía.

"Did she fall asleep?" she asked.

"Yes. Aren't you scared of leaving her there all alone? She is so far away. What if something happens?"

"What could happen?"

"I don't know... this house is so big and creepy... everything is so dark."

My sister laughed, she got up and turned the coffee machine on.

"We have been living here six years, she was born here! This is her home."

I looked at her, unconvinced.

"One day she'll get lost, and you won't be able to find her."

"Don't talk nonsense. How will she get lost?"

"What if she gets into a secret passage? Wouldn't be surprised if there were one of those around here..."

"Actually, there's more than one. We have walked through them together several times."

My jaw dropped, I couldn't help it.

"Is that a joke?"

My brother-in-law came into the sound of Lucía laughing at me. He stretched and leaned on the antique marble worktop seemingly amused at the scene.

"Anyway," Lucía continued, "it's the perfect place for a talented writer. Isn't that right, darling?" She added, looking lovingly at her husband.

He nodded in agreement as he yawned widely.

"Yep. In fact, today I had a very productive day."

Lucía poured him a cup of coffee and another one for me. She reached up to kiss him. I certainly loved the big man, he was like a brother to me too; those three were my only family.

I had to admit, I loved being in their house; though I would have preferred it if they lived in a simple apartment in the city, instead of that enormous mansion in the middle of the woods. But they were happy there.

Samuel had received the house as part of his inheritance when he was still single, and for years the house had remained uninhabited, almost abandoned. When they decided to get married and began looking for a place to live, he mentioned that house. Lucía wanted to see it, and she fell in love with the old mansion the moment she walked through the doors. It was as if she couldn't see the floor full of leaves and dirt, and the dusty walls, she decided that was the ideal place to live. Of course, Samuel dared not contradict her.

So, they expended a lot of effort renovating the house, investing all her time and almost all his savings. A year later, they were able to move in and start their life together.

The antiquated house was constructed in the nineteenth century. It had high windows with wooden blinds, a black terrazzo roof, and mossy walls of undefined colour. It had that tenebrous beauty of a classic suspense movie, and truly the perfect environment for a horror novelist like Samuel.

His trilogy 'The Three Ladies' brought him out of obscurity and gave him the financial stability to spend his time doing what he loved most. He had published fifteen books, which was no small number. Of course, I had read them all; after all, not everyone had the privilege of having a writer in the family. And even though horror was not my favourite genre, I liked his style since he was able to make something very real from the most implausible situations.

"When are you coming to live with us?" asked Samuel, after sipping his coffee.

"Never."

"Julia is scared of the house..." Lucía said.

"Oh, really?" He asked, smiling. Both started laughing.

"You are so dumb!" I said standing up and leaving the cup in the sink. "I am not scared, it's just..." I grimaced, looking for the right word "...spooky."

Samuel nodded.

"Spookiness is part of its beauty."

"And damp, and cold, and dark," I added.

He came closer to the table with his cup and sat in front of me, Lucía snuggled close to him.

"I understand, and that is the perfect excuse to not move in with us."

I shook my head.

"No, it is not an excuse. I can't leave my job."

"No one talked about quitting your job. It only takes twenty minutes to arrive at your practice on the motorway. Come on, Julia! You only work three days a week." He looked at me smiling, "You know the girls would love that."

I smiled. Of course, he was referring to Lucía and Adela.

"I only work three days, but I have a life in the city. I'd have to be crazy to live in this solitary wilderness! What would I do on the weekends? Be indoors all day?"

Lucía looked at me frowning.

"Right, we forgot about your exciting social life... Remind me, why is it that you are still single?"

I looked at her with mock hatred, she smiled.

I was the older of the two, and at twenty eight I didn't have a boyfriend, a partner, or marriage plans. But that didn't mean I didn't have friends, nor that I didn't enjoy my weekends with them. I loved everything the big city had to offer, concerts, talks, art, cinema, good restaurants and -my biggest weakness- good fashion stores.

"I am still single because I've been mature enough not to get hooked on the first idiot who came up to me," I looked at Samuel. "No offence" I said.

"None taken." He replied, drinking his coffee.

Lucía stood up and opened the fridge, she took out a plate with the leftover dessert from dinner and sat down again.

"Don't worry, love. She wanted to offend me," she said, passing me a spoon.

"I wasn't talking about you; I was talking about me." I explained.

Samuel cleared his throat.

"Ladies, you always end up in an argument, but we never get to anything concrete." He put his elbows on the table and clasped his hands.

"Julia, look at me," I looked at him, "tell me honestly, why don't you live with us?"

As he said, we had talked about the subject several times, they started asking me since Adela was born. And I always refused, either by joking around or giving excuses. I savoured a bite of chocolate cake with whipped cream and caramel, while I thought about what to say.

"Honestly," he repeated.

"I don't want to be a burden," I said finally. Samuel frowned, confused. Lucía sat upright on the chair.

"A burden?"

"Yes, an emotional burden," I specified.

They stared at me.

"And what does that mean?"

"Let's see... you guys have a family, a beautiful family, responsibilities, and a daughter to raise. You must do it together, peacefully, without an extra someone complicating everything."

"You are not 'an extra' , you are our sister," said Lucía, getting serious. I knew she didn't like it.

"Julia, our baby is growing, and you are missing the best parts...."

"I come to see her almost every week."

"That's not true. It has been more than a month since the last time. But that's not the point. We want you to live with us because you and Lucía were all alone for a long time, now we are four, which still isn't much, but we must stick together," Samuel took my hand, "We want you to live with us because we love you."

I bowed my head and sank my spoon back into the cake, trying to hide my wet eyes.

"All right," I said, "I will think about it."

III

I prepared myself for sleep even though I knew it would elude me. It was past midnight; our chatter about various things had allowed time to sneak up on us like an unwelcome visitor.

They were in the habit of going to bed early mainly because Samuel was an early riser. He would always say that his "creative neurons" made the best connections in the morning. Though that night, he had gotten excited reading us a scene from the book he was writing, and we flooded him with ideas and suggestions. Of course, he never listened to us, but at least we felt like we were part of his creative process, part of his success.

While still in my pyjamas I approached the window. I could see the trees that stood on the edge of the garden like leafy sentries marking the beginning of the forest. The rain came in light waves cleansing the plants and healing the earth. The light cast by the old lamp posts that bordered the gardens of the house appeared blurred and pale through the damp haze.

I returned to the warmth of my bed. As I lay down, I heard the protesting creak of wood against the footfall of someone on the floor above. The upper floor consisted of the library, Samuel's study, a large hall, and the guest rooms, which were rarely used. I stopped to listen, but all was still once again.

I turned off the light and settled into the welcoming warmth of the thick quilt. Steps again. I opened my eyes and sat up, nervous. I was sure that Samuel and Lucía were in their room only a few metres from mine. Admittedly, houses of the age of this one are usually full of unexplained random noises, but there was no mistaking the presence of someone in the room above.

As I got out of bed and walked to the door, I knew that the shiver that ran through me was not only due to the cold. I opened it slowly, careful to maintain the silence.

Once in the hallway I made my way quickly to Adela's room. I stopped at the door to listen. Nothing.

The room was in darkness when I cracked open the door, it was difficult to make out if Adela was still in bed. She was so slight and I knew she liked to sleep curled up in a ball in her huge bed.

A whisper close to my ear made me jump. I spun to see Lucía's pallid face in the dim of the night, only centimetres from mine.

"Did she wake up?" she asked and passed by me and entered the room.

"No, I came to see if she was okay."

"Can't you sleep?" she asked, tucking the blankets around the girl.

I didn't respond. She kissed the little girl's head gently and approached me again.

"Come on, it's late."

When we reached my room, she stopped.

"Try to sleep. Do you want some warm milk?"

"No, thank you. Goodnight."

I opened my door and turned around.

"Is Samuel working upstairs?"

"No, he's sleeping. He passed out as soon as we went up," she said, smiling.

I opened my mouth to say something, but I decided against it.

"Goodnight."

"Rest well," she said, walking away.

I quickly got into bed, partly because of the cold and partly because I felt a little exposed. I disliked this house with its damp walls, dark hallways, and... strange noises.

The next day came early. I took a sip of hot coffee as I stared out of the kitchen window at the cold overcast morning. I saw Pedro, the gardener, working on some flower beds at one end of the garden, near the old gazebo.

Without much thought I walked outside, my hands wrapped around the warm cup. I wandered across the lawn until I reached the building, which was truly a work of art. Each column was adorned with clusters of roses and leaves intricately carved from stone. The roof was simply a set of beams, joined in the centre by a kind of ball with a low glass cover. I passed the surprised Pedro and sat at the end of one of the two stone benches inside the gazebo.

"What a beautiful place! Can you believe it's the first time I've been here?" I said, taking a sip of my coffee.

He had returned to his work, replanting some primroses.

"Yes, I can believe that," he said.

"You take good care of this place," I exclaimed, touching the bench with my free hand. "It looks much newer than the house."

Indeed, the walls of the house had been blackened by damp, while the gazebo was completely clean, as if it were a recent construction.

He straightened up slowly and wiped his forehead with the back of his hand.

"It's new," he clarified. "It's only about six years old."

I looked at him in astonishment.

"Really?"

He nodded and walked away towards the wheelbarrow, holding several small pots in his hands.

I stood and walked around the gazebo. It was about four metres in diameter, and on the outside, it was besieged by a colourful arrangement of narcissus flowers. There were two arches with three steps each that led to the interior, and two semicircular benches, one on each side. As I climbed up through the entrance at the back, which faced the forest, I was surprised to see an inscription on one of the floor slabs. It was just a date: 1805-1835.

I leaned over to get a better look and took a step back when I realised it was a tombstone.

"Is someone buried here?" I asked, turning my head.

Pedro didn't even look at me.

"It seems so."

"Who?"

He shrugged. Being a man of few words I didn't think he was going to add anything else.

"We discovered the tomb shortly after your family arrived here when they were fixing up the guesthouse."

"It doesn't have a name..." I began to say.

He shook his head.

"Are there more graves? Maybe it's one of Samuel's ancestors..."

"No, they're buried in the old cemetery by the church."

I frowned as I looked at the inscription.

"Why do you think they didn't bury him there?"

Pedro shook his head as he packed the soil around one of the plants with his hands.

"They only denied Christian burial to a few..."

I looked at him.

"Suicides," I said.

"And murderers," he added. "But that didn't matter to his brother-in-law."

"Did Samuel have this made?" I said, starting to understand.

He nodded again, never stopping his work.

Lost in thought, I observed the delicate construction once again. I couldn't believe that Samuel had commissioned this in homage to an unknown dead person.

"That's the reason for so many flowers then?" I asked. "Because it's a tomb."

He shrugged.

I smiled, it was clear that he didn't agree with my brother-in-law's eccentricities.

"I suppose Samuel is attracted by the fact that he was an outlaw, an outcast... You know how he is."

"I will only say that if the church didn't want him there, there must be a reason. In my opinion, it would have been better to leave the grave as it was."

"And how was it?"

"There was a stone cross bearing the dates, right there, but they had to remove it to put up the gazebo," he pointed to the roof. "One day it's going to fall down from there and kill someone, and then the dead will curse us forever."

I looked at him, laughing, thinking he was joking, but he was deadly serious.

As I walked back to the house, I glanced at the gazebo and looked at the capital. Indeed, it was formed by a Gothic-style stone cross about eighty or ninety centimetres tall, which, placed up there, looked imposing.

I stopped and looked at it with concern, just as Pedro had said, if it fell on someone's head, it could kill them. As for the possibility of the dead person cursing the whole family, I had no doubt that could happen too.

On Sunday night, I was back home again, in my modern apartment filled with light and good heating.

I had spent three beautiful days, truly enjoying myself and enjoying my niece's company. That morning, she had taken me to the forest all by herself and showed me some of her hiding spots. The place was truly amazing, and the most incredible thing was that her parents let her freely explore the parks of the house with that dense forest bordering the property.

I must admit that I carried within me the fear that comes with living for years in a huge and dangerous city, where children don't walk alone on the streets even in their dreams, and where parents drive them everywhere, even as teenagers.

Samuel and Lucía would visit the forest with Adela almost every day, sometimes even in the rain. She knew the entire area perfectly and never strayed far from the gardens, but she was not yet four years old and her allowed independence sometimes worried me.

That week, I worked as usual, enjoying my patients. I felt grateful to be among those privileged ones who love their work. It had been years since I had stopped treating children with serious traumas, and now I focused on less complex cases. It had been a very stressful time in my life, and I certainly didn't want to go back to it.

I had also limited my consultations to three times a week, which gave me time for myself, to visit my family, and go out with my friends. In short, my life was almost perfect.

Almost.

I was packing everything in my briefcase when Marisa, my secretary, opened the door after a gentle knock.

"You're still here?" I asked, surprised.

"I was about to leave, and I almost forgot to give you this. It's the number of..." she looked at the paper before handing it to me. "Lucas Borghi. He called you twice and asked me to have you call him as soon as possible."

I reached out to take the note.

"Did he say what he needed?" I asked, noticing that my voice was trembling.

"No, nothing," she replied, oblivious to my agitation.

I left the post-it note on the desk, and she bid me farewell and left.

The name stood out in capital letters at the top of the small paper, and it seemed to enlarge and expand as I stared at it.

I sat down and tried to control my emotions.

Why now?

Years of forcing myself to forget, to suppress my feelings, years without even uttering his name or even thinking about him once...

A flash of the three of us laughing momentarily blinded me.

"Enough!" I said.

I stood up, grabbed my bag and cellphone.

'The Three Musketeers,' Lucas said, while Damian laughed. 'The Three Musketeers were actually four... We're missing one...'

I leaned over the desk to turn off the lamp.

'A girlfriend for Lucas!' I said, laughing. 'That's what we're missing!'

I rested my hands on the desk as tears welled up in my eyes.

"Enough!" I repeated.

'No!... Two foolish lovers are enough,' and while Lucas mocked, Damian took me in his arms and kissed me.

"Enough! Enough, please!"

I sighed and opened my eyes. A tear rolled slowly down and fell on the desk. It stopped still like a tiny magnifying glass on the dark wood. I couldn't resist anymore, his eyes looked at me through the haze of memories, and his laughter suddenly flooded the room.

IV

"How is it possible that you always arrive first?"

I looked at him as he reached out a hand to secure his next hand hold, and laughing, I sat on a rock in front of him. I was breathless and my heart was still racing. I took two deep breaths as he approached.

He pushed me to one side to share the rock.

"It's because I'm better trained than you," I replied.

"Hah! Sure!" he said.

I looked at him mischievously.

"Or maybe you're getting fat..." I added, trying to pinch his stomach.

He moved away, laughing.

"Getting fat? Getting fat?!" he asked, lifting his shirt.

He exposed his stomach for a minute, looking at me challengingly.

"Most men would kill to have these abs," he added.

I laughed as I stood up.

"You're too conceited. There's nothing worse than a man who thinks he's attractive."

"I am attractive," he clarified, raising an eyebrow.

I walked towards the edge of the cliff while laughing, looking down where the treetops seemed so distant.

"Be careful," he said, taking me by the waist.

We stood there embracing, our eyes drinking in the incredible landscape that stretched out majestically before us.

"I would love to come here every day, to watch the sunset from this mountain. It's wonderful!"

He let go of me and went to his backpack to fetch his camera.

"I have a thousand pictures taken from here, and they're all different. The colours change depending on the time, the season, the position of the sun, if there's a cloud..."

He turned towards me, looking at me through the lens.

"Just like you," he added.

I was tying my hair into a ponytail.

"Really? Do I also change with the seasons?"

"Of course."

"And when do I look best?" I asked, flirtatiously.

"In the summer."

"Why?"

"Because one can appreciate the colour of your skin," he said, lowering the camera and looking into my eyes.

I laughed.

"How typical..."

I turned around and walked back to our makeshift seat.

"Typical?"

"Men have an unparalleled talent for killing romance."

He tried to hold me in his arms, but I escaped.

"So, according to you, talking about the colour of your skin isn't romantic?" I shook my head.

"And if I mention your mole..."

"What mole? I don't have moles."

"You have one."

"No..."

"Yes."

"Where?"

"On your back."

I tried to look where he was pointing.

"That's not true."

"Yes, it's right here," he said, placing his finger at the base of my back, "blending into the edge of your pants."

Then he hugged me again. I didn't resist, and he took the opportunity to link his hands around my waist.

I moved closer to his chest.

"Damian..."

"What?"

"Do you love me?"

He leaned his head back and said, dramatically, "Love! What is a mere word compared to the feeling? How can one describe the most sublime of emotions with such a worn-out and dull term...?"

I hit his chest to make him stop.

"You're annoying! Look at what you do to avoid committing!"

"Commitment! How many truly understand what commitment means? Obligation and responsibility, or pleasure and devotion? Sacrifice or...?"

I stepped back, laughing.

"I can't stand you!"

"Alright, enough nonsense!" he said and took my hands. "I love you; I love you more than life and beyond."

I looked into his eyes; he wasn't smiling anymore.

"...and beyond death," he added.

He started to move closer to my mouth and pressed me against his body.

"So, you believe in the afterlife?" I asked.

He raised an eyebrow.

"I was being serious..." he said reproachfully.

"Answer me, do you believe in the afterlife?"

"Yes, don't you?"

I made a doubtful face.

"I would love to believe, but I really don't know."

"Well, it has been proven, many have witnessed that there is life after death."

I shook my head.

"Proven? I've only heard of people claiming to have come back, but it's not like they actually died..."

"If you're talking about someone who was dead and buried for months and then appeared to their family... Well, there are stories about that too. But I was referring to something else."

He looked at me for a moment.

"And now... can I do what I was going to do?" he said and brought his mouth closer to mine.

Later, when we could think of something other than ourselves, I was still in his arms when I said,

"I would like to believe that it doesn't all end here..."

He looked into my eyes for a moment.

"Let's make a pact," he said. "The first one to die will come back and tell the other if there's an afterlife or not."

I smiled.

"Agreed. Do you promise?"

He nodded.

"I promise.

I added, hesitating. "But what if you can't come back?"

"I assure you I'll find a way."

"And what if there's no afterlife?"

"I'll still come back to let you know, so you don't hold on to hope."

"And what if they don't let you come back?"

"Nothing will stop me from returning. I'll do whatever it takes to be by your side again."

And that day, I believed he was telling the truth.

"But you didn't come back, Damian. You were the first one to go. And you didn't come back."

V

Her piercing screams made their blood run cold and yet most of the onlookers found it impossible to avert their eyes. The flames grew around her, occasionally licking her skin and eliciting shrieks of agony.

The night was cold and the sky was clear. Tiny embers floated upwards into the vast blackness of the sky then randomly popped out of existence.

Finally, she fell silent, and her writhing ceased as if she had suddenly realised the futility of her fight for life. Her eyes fixed on the little boy who returned a look of disbelief and horror, then her head fell limply forward. Tongues of flame engulfed her, devouring her body and transforming it into nothing more than a mass of burning flesh, charred bone, and ash.

Then came the smell. An intense penetrating odour that not only assaulted their nostrils but also invaded their eyes, throats and minds.

Then came the silence, a deep, paralysing silence, almost as terrifying as the screams of some moments ago, fell over the onlookers like a blanket. The men and women of the village could not move or even look away from the smouldering husk.

The misplaced sound of laughter gradually began to rise, breaking the silence. The onlookers searched each other's faces for a logical explanation of this illogicality. Then as one, as if they sensed her presence before seeing her, they turned to see the source of this out-of-place mirth in their midst. Then, as if previously choreographed, they moved swiftly in one motion to form an almost perfect circle, with the laughing woman at the centre like an exclusion zone of fear.

The woman stood out among the villagers who invariably dressed in drab ragged garments. She, however, was dressed elegantly in a scarlet dress and cloak in stark contrast to her surroundings. The matching hood of her cloak was pulled up over her head, hiding her hair and obscuring her face.

As she started to stroll gracefully toward the bonfire the terrified villagers vacated her direction of travel; giving her a clear path to her destination.

She stopped, almost too close to the flame and threw back her cape, revealing a face of pale beauty and locks of fiery red.

Her eyes blazed in sympathy with the flames as she threw back her head to allow her red mane to fall into its natural position.

"How easy it was to kill her!" she said, looking at the still bubbling flesh. "How easy it was to catch and kill a witch!"

The people watched her in silence, their eyes widened with fear and fascination.

"Now you can sleep peacefully, your offspring will be safe."

She took two steps and scanned the crowd with her steel gaze. Then, turning her head towards the condemned, she reached her hand through the flames and traced a single finger over the smoking skull.

"Have you not wondered why she didn't use her spells here, in the fires? Or do you believe that these simple ropes were able to restrain such magnificent power?" she said, toying with the charred threads, and her laughter erupted once again, but this time murmurs of horror could be heard throughout the crowd.

Her red hair danced playfully with the breeze, as if it had a life of its own. Smoke rose and moved in sympathy swirling and enveloping the crowd.

No one moved or spoke; the crowd seemed to be under a form of mass hypnosis, clinging to each and every word. The terror emanating from the red woman was tangible and far from natural.

She left her questions hanging pungently in the air and the minds of the crowd as she walked away. The onlookers followed with their eyes until she reached the edge of the forest where she was met by two other equally majestic women. She joined them and then the three disappeared among the trees and into the darkness.

VI

On Saturday, I woke up early, with tired eyes and a weary soul. And I was afraid, panicked that everything would start all over again. It had taken me almost two years to overcome Damian's death. Two terrible years in which I couldn't even think straight. And now Lucas appeared out of nowhere, after all this time without a word. He disappeared, just when I needed him the most , leaving me alone, especially considering he was his best friend. What did he want now? We hadn't even spoken yet, and I already felt devastated...

When the phone started ringing, I jumped on the bed.

"Hello?"

"Hi. Jules! How are you?" I recognized Janet's voice and felt a little better.

"OK, I guess..."

"Why? What happened?"

"Nothing, I'm just tired," I lied.

"Really? Then I have the solution," she said enthusiastically.

I rolled my eyes and prepared myself for what was coming.

"Marilyn called," she said, "and she needs to see both of us today."

"Why?" I asked.

"I don't know, she didn't want to tell me. It's something she wants to share with us..."

"Does it have to be today? I'd prefer not to go out..."

"That's exactly why you have to come. I'll make reservations at Martino's for dinner together. Does 7 o'clock work for you?"

"No..." I started to say, but she ignored me.

"Alright, see you there at 7. Don't be late!"

Janet and Marilyn were my best friends. I had many other good friends whom I adored, but they were almost like sisters to me. We had met a year after Damian's death at the first Psychology Symposium I attended as a guest, while I was still a student. I felt insecure and completely out of my depth, but my psychologist and great friend and mentor named Juan, had asked me to accompany him. Of course, he didn't need me, but he knew that I needed it.

By chance -do coincidences exist?-, there was also a Paediatrics Congress taking place in the same city, and there were hundreds of doctors staying at our hotel. During dinner on the first night, Juan was mesmerised by a blonde woman with luscious hair who was laughing with her group of friends at a nearby table. It turned out they were actually a group of paediatricians, and the blonde woman was none other than Marilyn. The attraction was mutual and instantaneous. The next night, the two of us were sitting at the same table with all the paediatricians, and on the last day of the Congress, Juan and Marilyn left us in the middle of dinner.

One of the doctors turned out to be Janet, and I instantly felt comfortable with her. The friendship blossomed within a few months, and since the guys' romance ended in marriage, our bond grew stronger, and we became close friends.

Although they might not have known it, their friendship and love had healed my wounded heart. They had helped me forget and move on, and that's why the ties that bound me to these two women were unbreakable.

Even though they were well aware of everything I had been through, they couldn't accept that I was still alone and always found a new candidate to introduce me to, which often led to arguments. Every time we met, my single status would come up, just my single status, which wasn't fair since Janet was also single. I suppose that, unlike her, I gave an image of fragility that drove them to want to find someone to take care of me. A completely misguided image in my opinion, but one that I hadn't managed to dispel in all our years of friendship.

"Yesterday, a new doctor arrived at the hospital," Marilyn commented, as if in passing.

I noticed Janet looking at her inquisitively.

"Just imagine this guy, more than six feet of pure muscle..."

I kept my focus on my food.

"What's his name? How old is he?" Janet asked.

"Joaquín, and..." she paused, looking at us.

I looked up.

"He's single!" they both said at the same time, and of course, I couldn't help but laugh along with them.

We were still laughing when I noticed someone stopping beside me.

"Julia!"

I looked up, and I was so surprised that I didn't know what to say. He leaned in and kissed me on the cheek.

'Lucas.'

He straightened up and looked at me, still smiling. His blue eyes scrutinised my face, undoubtedly searching for traces of the girl from eight years ago. I was still furious with him, but I

41

couldn't look away. His eyes had me captivated. That was the only thing about him that hadn't changed, that and his voice. Everything else now belonged to a man with a strong jawline and fine wrinkles around his eyes. Then I saw the dimples, disappearing into the folds of his smile, and a warm feeling started to emerge, but I resisted by averting my gaze.

"What a coincidence to run into each other here!" he said amiably.

He looked at the girls, who were obviously looking at him with curiosity.

"I'm sorry," he said, "I didn't mean to interrupt."

I awkwardly made the introductions. They all smiled, and he turned to me.

"I called your office yesterday, I left a message..."

"Really?"

"Didn't your secretary tell you...?"

I noticed Marilyn's gaze on me.

"No," I replied, not adding anything else.

"Well, the thing is..." he said, feeling a bit uncomfortable, "I needed to talk to you. It's work-related, not personal," he added, as if justifying himself.

"I'll call you first thing on Monday," I said.

He smiled again.

"Perfect, we'll talk then," and he looked at me as if he didn't want to say goodbye just yet.

I lowered my gaze to my plate.

Then he took a step back and continued on his way.

I watched him as he walked away and joined a young woman who had stopped further ahead, waiting for him. He put his arm around her waist and guided her to the back of the room.

The girl looked at me, and I averted my gaze just as he turned around. Surely, he was explaining, 'Who's that, dear?' 'Her? Nobody, just a friend from my youth.'

"Who is he?" Janet asked, lowering her voice as if he could hear her.

"Lucas Borghi, a friend of Damian's..." I said, returning to what was left of my dinner.

Neither of them made any comments.

"He was actually Damian's best friend... and my best friend too."

A few seconds of silence.

"You never mentioned him..." Janet began.

"I'm sure I did. He was the one who helped me look for Damian when he disappeared, they were roommates."

"Has it been a long time since you last saw him?"

I nodded slowly.

"Almost eight years."

I looked up. Both of them were looking at me without knowing what to say.

Marilyn was the first to react.

"Darling, maybe it's good to see him again..."

"Good? Tell me, please, how could it be good? He disappeared after the funeral, didn't say goodbye, never wrote or called me. I didn't even know if he was alive or dead. He came back just to revive something I don't want to think about."

"If he was Damian's best friend, things couldn't have been easy for him either."

"I know," I said, "I can imagine. But I don't want to talk to him. I'm not interested in what he has to say."

"You should," Marilyn insisted.

"I won't go back there; I don't want to."

We continued eating in silence. But I had lost my appetite, so I put down my utensils on the plate.

"You know, Julia, you're the psychologist, but I think hiding from reality doesn't help overcome the pain."

"I've already overcome the pain, Marilyn. It took eight years of my life and months of therapy with your husband."

She lowered her head, and I sighed.

"I'm sorry," I said, taking her hand, "I'm sorry, girls, I don't want to talk about this. I don't want to ruin your evening."

43

They both smiled.

"Marilyn," said Janet, "you got us here because you were going to tell us something important."

A smile appeared on her face.

"Yes, and of course, this news deserves a toast," she said as she filled the glasses.

She raised hers, and we imitated her, expectant.

"Ohhhh, girls..." she said and then, almost shouting, she added, "I'm pregnant!!"

VII

The news of Marilyn's pregnancy had managed to brighten up the night and temporarily exorcised the ghosts of my past. She looked radiant, full of plans and with all the maternal instinct on the surface. We didn't know how she had managed to keep the secret during these past two weeks since she had received the results.

So, we toasted repeatedly -and understood why she had only had water with dinner- talked about baby names, maternity clothes, and prenatal classes.

Around 10 o'clock at night, we decided to say goodbye since the expectant mother had to start going to bed early. We left the restaurant together, and after hugging them, I headed to the car.

I reached the car shivering; that short journey had left me frozen. As soon as I closed the car door, it started raining, thankfully the deluge had the courtesy to wait until I was in shelter.

I started the car, turned on the windshield wipers, and just as I was about to press the accelerator, I heard a thump on the passenger side door.

The fright was such that I let go of all the pedals, and the car stalled abruptly. I looked towards the window, fearfully. A woman was pressing her hands against the glass, staring at me with terror in her eyes.

"Please," she said, anxiously glancing over her shoulder. "Please!" she repeated, pounding on the glass desperately.

Without further hesitation, I reached for the button to roll down the window, but then she moved away from the door and started to run. She briefly locked eyes with mine as she ran around the front of the car, then crossed the road and disappeared into a dark alley.

I let out a long breath after realising that I wasn't breathing. With my hands gripping the steering wheel, I looked to the left, searching for who or what had frightened her, but there was nothing and no one. Only the street, the drenched deserted street.

Several minutes passed before my heart rate normalised and I could start the car again. I looked at the time:10:22.

Without thinking too much, I turned the corner towards the highway; I didn't want to sleep alone in my apartment that night.

I arrived at Lucía and Samuel's house in 15 minutes. I suppose he saw me from the windows of his studio because as soon as I stopped, he opened the door.

Lucía, with Adela close behind her, came out to greet me despite the rain.

"What happened?" she said, hugging me. "Are you okay?"

I nodded, and as we entered the house, I recounted the strange incident that had happened just a few minutes ago.

"You should have called the police," she said.

"They wouldn't have come," Samuel said, handing me a cup of coffee. "They don't pay attention unless someone is dead."

Adela was playing with my cell phone, sitting on my lap. The fire was burning cheerfully in the living room fireplace where we were gathered; the smell of pine and coffee created a perfect sense of home and refuge.

I sighed and realised that I already felt calmer. I was protected there, surrounded by the people I loved the most in the world.

'I should come and live with them,' I thought.

"Did you have dinner?" Lucía asked.

"Yes, we had dinner downtown with the girls. All this happened after leaving the restaurant."

"Mom, I want more chocolate cake," Adela requested in her high-pitched voice.

"No," her mother responded.

"A little piece for Auntie and another for me. Do you want some, Julie?"

She was charming, she knew that's how she got everything she wanted.

"Too much chocolate will keep you from sleeping..." I began to say.

"Just a tiny piece," she insisted, showing me her fingers almost touching.

Samuel looked at her with a smile, while Lucía tried to keep a serious face.

"Speaking of sleeping..." Lucía started to say, "Kisses to Daddy, and let's go, Deli."

"No... Just a little longer..."

"I'll stay and sleep here, guys. I'm actually feeling much better now, but I got really scared. I don't want to go home alone."

"And I wouldn't let you go alone either " Lucía replied, getting up from the couch, "Let's make sure everything is fine in your room."

"Ma, the cake!" Adela complained, but Lucía ignored her and continued her way towards the stairs, with me following behind.

"Daddy... " She was going to try with her father, and I was sure that she would have succeeded with him.

We reached the room, I threw myself on the bed, and my sister sat on the small sofa.

As I undressed, I told her about Marilyn's pregnancy and the news of the week. Then, almost with astonishment, I remembered the encounter with Lucas.

"Lucas called my office yesterday."

"Which Lucas?"

"Lucas Borghi."

She frowned and looked at me.

"Did he return to the city? What did he want?"

I made a gesture of disbelief.

"A professional consultation, he told me today. I ran into him at the restaurant, can you believe it? What bad luck!"

"Why bad luck?"

"Why? Because I don't want to see him, obviously."

She stood up and started removing the cushions from the bed.

"Why do you blame him, Julia?"

"For leaving me, isn't that enough?"

She shook her head disapprovingly.

"He didn't abandon you, he had his personal grief to confront, he loved him too."

I didn't say anything. I didn't want to argue with her or rake the matter up further.

While I searched for clean underwear in the drawers and some pyjamas, she removed the quilt, preparing the bed for sleep.

I felt tenderness as she took care of me, always keeping that room ready: clean sheets, a made bed, my clothes in the closets, everything prepared in case I showed up unexpectedly like that night.

"Well, do you think you'll be okay? Shall I make you some hot milk? It wasn't a good idea to have coffee so late."

"No, it doesn't matter, tomorrow is Sunday, no need to wake up early. I'll stay up reading until I feel sleepy."

She headed towards the door.

"Come, let's have a piece of cake."

I smiled.

"No, I'm going to take a shower and go to bed. I'll taste it tomorrow. Did you make it?"

She shook her head.

"Samuel did, with Adela's help. She already ate more than a quarter of it by herself, she's addicted to chocolate, it's the only thing she truly loves. She barely had dinner tonight, that's why I'm not going to give her cake, she's being stubborn."

I laughed as she kissed me goodnight.

"Go give her a little kiss when she's in bed. Rest well, darling."

"You too," I said, "and thank you for having me."

"This is your home "she said, looking into my eyes, "don't forget that."

I filled the bathtub with hot water and added some bath salts to help me relax. I needed to relax! I needed to not think.

Lucía had turned on the bathroom heater, so I gladly got into the water. Looking around, I had to admit that the place was truly beautiful, with its tall windows and the porcelain bathtub in the middle of the spacious room. The walls were covered in small tiles in shades of blue and turquoise, matching the floor, and the golden faucets gave it a distinguished and noble air. The candle-like lighting also helped create a warm and elegant atmosphere.

I closed my eyes and for a few precious minutes, I tried to forget everything that had distressed me so much the night before. But it was impossible, images of Damian and Lucas kept coming to my mind. Most of them were happy memories from that time when we were inseparable, yet, perhaps because of that, they only brought sadness to me.

After telling Adela a story, I went to bed. I searched for the book I was reading on my mobile phone and prepared to read until I fell asleep. I was so comfortable and warm that after a few minutes, I started to doze off.

A sound, like a chair being dragged, forced my eyes open. I looked at the time, past 2 am.

I waited a few seconds, thinking that maybe it had been part of a dream, but instantly the sound repeated. The barely audible sound seemed to be coming from the room directly above mine, the library.

Indeed, in that room, there was a mahogany desk and a chair, and positioned near one of the windows there was an antique high-backed seat.

But nobody used that room, it was almost like a sanctuary with books from the 1800s to which Samuel had added his own collection. He would occasionally spend time there, but it was usually closed.

The ceiling creaked very softly, one, two, three times. Three steps, stopping above my head. Was Samuel in the library, or were they just house noises?

In response to my silent question, the steps returned to the window, and something slid softly. The armchair.

My heart raced as I sat up in bed.

I waited a few seconds and then, without thinking, I pushed aside the blankets and stood up. I walked down the hallway to Lucía's room, and the slightly open door allowed me to see the bed clearly; they were both there. Almost instinctively, I looked up.

The silence was absolute, as if the whole house were watching me, anticipating my movements.

At the end of the corridor, I could see the wide steps of the staircase ascending to the next floor. I climbed slowly, trying to listen intently and carefully placing my feet so the steps wouldn't creak. When I reached the third floor, I observed the darkness of the hallway and with my heart pounding rapidly, I walked until I reached Samuel's office. The door was open, and the drawn curtains welcomed the distant light from the park lampposts to illuminate the room with a faint yellowish hue.

I looked ahead to the next door; I knew it was the library, and the door was closed.

I stopped with my hand on the doorknob and pressed my ear to listen. As I lowered my gaze, I saw my bare feet and could observe a faint light emanating from under the door.

With a gasp, I took a step back, and the light went out.

Then, determined, I opened the door and saw a shadow moving away from the large desk. The high-backed armchair looked slightly crooked, as if someone had moved it when they got up.

Although I was terrified, I needed to know who was there, who had been sitting in that chair seconds before.

In a corner of the table, a candle emitted a thin trail of smoke. I approached and touched the small piece of burnt wick, which was still warm.

I heard a movement behind me and turned around, frightened.

"Who is it?" I murmured.

And I swear I heard a laugh, a deep and mocking laugh.

And unable to resist, the question escaped my lips almost involuntarily:

"Damian?"

Two steps made the wooden floor groan.

A shadow, enveloped in a strange halo of light, separated itself from the dark corner, and excitement completely overwhelmed me. There he was, after so many years, he had returned to fulfil his promise.

My eyes, clouded with tears, prevented me from seeing clearly; I could only distinguish the outline of his shoulders and his white hands approaching mine.

"Is it you?" I asked, sobbing.

But he didn't reach out to touch me; he moved away again into the shadows.

"Damian..." I pleaded.

And I heard, in the same mocking tone as seconds before:

"Damian is dead."

Trembling, I leaned on the desk, and then the door slammed shut. The temperature dropped spontaneously, and the light seemed to be sucked out of the room leaving it in a tomb like darkness.

At that point, any courage I had left disappeared; I ran towards the door and tried to open it. But it was impossible, it seemed to be sealed.

While I struggled desperately, I heard next to my ear:

"Look at me..."

It was barely a whisper, and the cold breath caressed my neck.

The blood froze in my veins, and I became completely paralyzed. Slowly, I turned my head to see a pair of eyes staring at me, eyes blacker than the surrounding darkness.

It was only then that I realised I was screaming. At that point I understood the term 'blind panic' as my hearing, my sight and even my thoughts were overloaded by an overwhelming urge to get away. Somehow the door opened and instinctively my legs took me through it.

I ran away, down the stairs, and as I turned on the last flight, I came face to face with Samuel, who was coming up towards me.

My cry of horror seemed to echo throughout the house.

"Julia! What's happening, my God?!"

"Samuel! There's something upstairs!" I cried, almost hysterical.

"What?!"

"There's something upstairs!!" I repeated. "In the library!"

"Don't shout, you'll wake the girls," he replied, lowering his voice.

He took hold of my arm and led me to my room.

He made me sit on the bed and closed the door.

"Can you calm down, please? You must have had a nightmare..."

I looked at him without understanding.

"It wasn't a nightmare! Aren't you going to do anything?"

"You've had a very stressful day, Julia..."

I stood up, indignant.

"Samuel, please, go and check, don't just stand there!"

He looked at me, hesitating.

"Fine, don't leave your room. I'll be back in a minute."

When he left, I turned on the bedside lamp and sat on the couch.

Instantly, I stood up and began pacing the room.

Samuel returned a few minutes later.

"And?"

"And what?"

"What did you see?"

"Nothing, a window opened in the library, that must have been what scared you. What were you doing up there?"

I looked at him.

"I heard footsteps..."

"It's the walls, it's an old house, full of noises."

"And voices," I said. "Someone spoke to me up there."

His gaze was unreadable.

"Go back to sleep, there's no one upstairs."

"Samuel, you have to believe me, there was someone, and they spoke to me."

He looked annoyed.

"Someone? Who? A ghost?"

I opened my mouth to respond, but I didn't know what to say.

"Go back to sleep, tomorrow you'll feel better."

VIII

It took me an eternity to fall asleep. First, I kept the light on for several hours; I just couldn't face the dark. The shadows seemed to have a life of their own and formed themselves into malevolent spectres the more I looked at them.

My ears were on alert, trying to perceive any sound coming from upstairs, but all was silent.

Then, as dawn broke, I was so scared that it wasn't until I saw the sunlight begin to peek through the pines that I could finally relax and sleep.

And I slept until past ten in the morning, so when I got up, the whole family was already enjoying their day off.

I didn't have a chance to be alone with Samuel to talk about the previous night's incident, although I didn't really know what I could say or ask him. He had left little room for discussing the event because, according to him, there wasn't even an event to discuss: nothing had happened... 'Just a window that had opened!?'

Of course, something happened! I was there, and beyond the shock of the moment, I was sure of what I had seen and heard.

I was also sure of what I had believed I had seen: Damian.

What stupid impulse had led me to utter his name?

And who had shattered my illusion by saying, 'Damian is dead'? A shiver ran through me as I remembered the fear I had felt in the presence of this apparition.

I returned home on Sunday night, and when I was already in bed, ready to sleep, I decided that the next day I would call Lucas and talk to him. I couldn't ignore everything that had happened or all the memories that had resurfaced.

So, on Monday, the first thing I did after getting my decaffeinated coffee with almond milk was to call him.

I expected to hear his secretary's voice, which would give me some more time, but it wasn't the case.

'Dr. Borghi's office,' it was his voice. 'How can I help you?'

I cleared my throat before answering.

"Lucas? It's Julia," and my voice sounded too high-pitched, with a crack at the end. Furious at feeling so nervous, I added, "Julia Vivanko..."

'Julia! Yes, I recognized your voice, but I transferred the call to the other phone, sorry. How are you?

"Very well, thank you. And you?"

'Marvellous,' he said, and I felt he was lying.

"I'm glad. Well, tell me what you need."

I heard a sigh.

'To be honest, it's the first time I have done something like this, but I really need a second opinion on one of my cases, and there aren't many people I trust.'

I hesitated for a moment. I was almost disappointed, hoping that it was all an excuse and that he actually wanted to talk to me, talk about Damian...

"Tell me a little about it. Then I will be able to tell you if I can help..."

'If there's anyone who can help me, it's you,' he said, and since I didn't know how to respond, I remained silent.

He waited a moment, then continued.

'I'm treating a six-year-old girl with PTSD. I can't make any progress. I started using hypnosis three sessions ago, but...'

"Hypnosis? At such a young age?"

He sighed again.

'I thought it was the only way to make her talk. She doesn't want to eat; they have to feed her. She doesn't speak, doesn't watch TV, doesn't play, doesn't interact with anyone.'

"Do they know what happened?"

'She disappeared from the house, was missing for two days, and her father found her in the garage, inside a box at the back of a closet. They don't know if she hid there on her own or if someone put her there, but since that day, it's as if she's in a catatonic state.'

I stood up and approached the window.

"What do the doctors say?"

'Since they had reported her disappearance, the police got involved and conducted a thorough examination. But they didn't find anything strange. She hadn't eaten for those two days and was somewhat dehydrated, but nothing more.'

I sighed now.

"And how can I help you? It's been over two years since I've treated children with such issues..."

'I know. I just wanted to show you the recordings of the hypnosis sessions and hear your thoughts. That's all.'

Although my natural curiosity and the possibility of helping that little girl were tipping the scales, I didn't want to commit just yet.

He sensed my hesitation.

'I'm just asking for a few hours of your time,' he said, and I don't know why his tone moved me. 'If you don't want to help me after seeing the recordings, I'll understand.'

I felt cornered. I couldn't refuse without appearing impolite, but I wasn't sure if I wanted to get involved in a case he was handling.

"Alright. I have a very busy week," I lied, "but I can reserve two hours on Thursday after my appointments."

'Perfect! Thank you, Julia. I really appreciate you agreeing.'

I didn't like his tone of humility, so I began to say goodbye.

"You don't have to thank me. I haven't done anything yet. See you on Thursday."

'At 7 o'clock? Do you know where I have my office now?'

"No, send me the address in a message, please," I said. "Goodbye."

I stayed there, looking out the window, the phone still pressed to my ear.

Perhaps he had acted wrongly, but I knew he was a good person and that he wasn't lying. What I didn't understand was why he had turned to me after so many years, when we both knew there were psychologists with more prestige and experience than me. He had said he only trusted a few, and apparently, I was on that short list.

I decided not to dwell on the matter any longer. I would go to his office and limit myself to doing what he was asking of me. If everything went well, our relationship would end very soon, and undoubtedly, that was best outcome for me.

The week passed without any surprises, and Thursday arrived. Around 7:00 in the evening, after a long day of work, I got into my car and headed to his office.

The offices were in a traditional building in the city centre. As I waited, I observed the room attentively: a large window on one wall gave me the impression of painting of the city against the evening sky, only to be given away by the movement of headlights on the highway. Several mustard-coloured leather armchairs combined deliciously with armchairs upholstered in ochre chequered patterns. In the centre, a low, large table was covered with carefully stacked books alongside fashion magazines.

A door to the left led to another small room where two small tables with matching chairs could be seen; some toys and children's books were scattered "carelessly" on the thick cream-coloured carpet, as if tempting the little patients and making the wait more bearable.

"You can come in now, doctor," said the secretary appearing through another door. "Lucas is available."

As I entered his office, I was amazed by the size of the room. It seemed as big as the waiting area.

The most peculiar thing was that it was almost empty, with only a huge mahogany desk facing the window and a couple of dark armchairs on the opposite wall. In the centre, there was nothing but the dense carpet and a low table. The side walls were covered with shelves made of the same reddish wood, filled to the ceiling with elegantly designed books.

"I'm sorry," he said as he approached to greet me, "I rarely run late for appointments, but today was a bit complicated."

I looked at him as he smiled. He looked tired, with gentle dark circles under his eyes.

"Don't apologise, I understand perfectly," I said, downplaying the matter.

He invited me to sit on one of the sofas and brought over an armchair.

As we talked, he placed a laptop on the coffee table and began searching for the files he wanted to show me.

"I know it must have seemed strange that I called you after such a long time without seeing each other," he said without looking at me.

"Yes, a little," I admitted.

He smiled and didn't add anything else. Apparently, he wasn't going to explain why he had reached out to me, and I didn't want to ask. Suddenly, I realised I didn't want to be there; I felt uncomfortable and tired.

"Here it is," he said after a few seconds. "This is the third session."

I sat up straight to get a better view.

The session had been recorded from the desk, showing the same sofa where I was seated, with a little girl lying down. Next to her, sitting and holding her hand, was a woman around forty years old, whom I imagined to be her mother.

"Despite her young age, she has responded very well to hypnosis. Look how she starts talking right away."

Indeed, the girl responded to Lucas' questions as if she were awake.

"But... you said she doesn't speak..."

"No, when she's awake, she doesn't even show signs of understanding what is said to her. She only speaks under hypnosis," he replied, looking me in the eyes.

I nodded and continued watching the scene.

"Amanda, I want you to go back to the day you hid in the box. Do you remember that day?"

"I don't want to."

"Why don't you want to?"

"I want to stay here, with mommy."

I saw the woman grimace in pain.

"Mommy will be with you, she is with you now. We are just going back to that day in your mind. Mommy will hold your hand. Can you feel her hand?"

The girl nodded, sighing.

"Squeeze mommy's hand, and let's go back to that day. Tell me what you were doing before going to the garage."

"I was playing."

"Where?"

"In the living room."

"Is there anyone else with you?"

"Aunt Lily."

"Where is Aunt Lily?"

"She's in the kitchen."

"Is there anyone else in the house?"

"Yes."

At that moment, the little girl started to move as if she wanted to get up from the sofa.

"Who? Dad?"

"No, Dad is working."

"Who is in the house, Amanda?"

"I don't know."

"Can you see them? Tell me who it is."

"No, I don't know."

Her voice sounded scared.

"Mom is with you, don't be afraid. Can you feel her hand? Squeeze her hand."

The girl started sobbing.

"Look at them and tell me who they are. What are they doing?"

"They are looking at me."

The sighs turned into sobs.

"They're looking at you? Who are they?"

"I don't know!"

"What are they doing? Are they approaching you?"

"I don't know! I don't want to! I don't want to!"

And here the little girl started writhing while continuing to scream, 'I don't want to, I don't want to!'

Lucas stopped the recording and looked at me.

I stayed silent for a few seconds, staring at the girl. Her mother had started approaching to take her in her arms.

"So, someone entered the house," I said.

"That's what it seems like."

"More than one person..."

Lucas nodded.

"The police found nothing, no fingerprints, no signs of a struggle, rape..."

"Nothing."

"Were there any strange events before?"

He shrugged.

"Her mother died a year ago, and until now, it seemed like she was getting over it..."

"Her mother died? Then who is she?"

"The aunt."

"Aunt Lily," I said, understanding. "When you hypnotise her, you talk about her mother..."

"She mentioned it the first time, she said something like 'I want mommy to come,' and Lily took her hand, and she calmed down..."

He stood up and went to place the laptop on the desk.

"What are you looking for with hypnosis?" I asked.

He made an indecipherable face.

"Something that will help bring her back."

I approached the desk and sat in the armchair; he leaned against the edge and looked at me.

"Maybe she doesn't need to remember. Perhaps it's better if she doesn't remember..." I said, and under his gaze, I lowered my eyes to my hands. "I know, it sounds strange, but..."

"It doesn't sound like the opinion of a psychologist," he said.

He was looking at me.

"I know, it's just that I believe that remembering isn't always the best thing."

"Yes, I understand what you mean. But in this case..."

"How do you know that remembering will bring her out of her state? Maybe it's better for her to forget... What guarantee do you have that she won't go further and further inside?"

We stayed silent, looking at each other for a moment.

"I don't know, but it's the only thing I can do."

"I'm not sure I completely agree with you."

"We were never completely in agreement," he said, and something in his eyes made me look away.

"Why did you ask me to come? What do you really want me to do?"

He turned around and sat facing away from the window.

Someone had closed the curtains, and the room was only illuminated by the lamp.

"Conduct a hypnosis session, just one. You have a lot of experience, more than I do..."

"No," I said. "If that's what you want, then you're wasting your time."

"You have had a lot of success before, I know, I heard that..."

I stood up.

"Yes, I achieved a measure of success with some autistic children, but this is completely different."

"You helped many children."

"And there were many others I couldn't help. I haven't worked with hypnosis for over two years. I'm sorry," I said, and went to the sofa to pick up my bag.

"I wouldn't ask you if I had other options. I knew you wouldn't want to do it, but I really need you, Julia."

"If you knew I wouldn't want to do it, you shouldn't have asked me," I said, as I approached the door. "I'm really sorry."

"I'm only asking you for one session..."

I sighed and looked at him, impatiently.

"Don't insist, please," I added, almost to myself. "I shouldn't have come..."

I heard a sigh behind me.

"No, I guess it wasn't a good idea. Obviously, everything has changed between us."

I turned around.

"Of course, everything has changed. What did you expect?"

"To find my friend again," he said.

"What friend? Are you referring to me?"

A reproachful expression appeared in his eyes.

"It wasn't my fault..."

"But was it mine?"

63

He approached as if to touch me, but I instinctively moved away.

"Do you think I blamed you for anything...?"

"No? Then why did you abandon me?"

He furrowed his brow, not fully understanding what I was saying.

"You left when I needed you the most, not a letter, not a call..."

He sighed, and I saw a glimmer of pain in his eyes.

"I needed to be alone, to suffer alone. I couldn't understand it either..."

I nodded and turned towards the door.

"I know. It was just very difficult to lose two of the people I loved the most, almost on the same day."

His eyes met mine.

He looked at me in silence for a few seconds. Then he opened his mouth, as if to say something, but closed it again.

"Goodnight," I said, and without looking at him again, I opened the door, and left.

On the way home, I realised that the anger was fading away and was being replaced by a familiar feeling of despondency.

'You helped many children,' Lucas had said, so sure of himself, giving undeserved credit to my distant work as a child therapist.

He didn't know. How could he know? I had taken great care to hide it well, but I had never been able to completely conceal the immense guilt and the heart-breaking memories.

I had helped many children, but the one I remember most, was the one I failed.

Andrew had arrived at my consultation accompanied by his father. He was already 14 years old, which should have been a valid reason not to accept him as a patient. But at that time in my life, I still believed I was capable of solving any problem, no matter how desperate the situation seemed. So that didn't intimidate me, nor did his story, his ghosts, or his vacant gaze.

I started seeing him twice a week. At first, he remained withdrawn in his own world, seemingly oblivious to everything I said. But one day, he lifted his gaze from his hands and fixed his eyes on mine.

"Why did you choose to become a psychologist?" he asked.

Without showing my surprise or joy at seeing him establish contact for the first time in almost two months, I responded, "To help people."

He held his gaze for a few seconds and then focused back on his hands.

"Do you think I can help you Andrew?"

"Do you think I need help?" he said.

"Maybe, or perhaps you just need to let out what's making you suffer. Maybe that will be enough," I replied.

He leaned his head back and sighed.

"I don't think you want me to do that," he said sadly.

I waited. Based on my experience, pressuring didn't help. I knew he was on the verge of starting to talk, and once he did, and I knew what was troubling him so much, then I could start helping him.

Just when I thought our conversation would end there, he began to speak and let everything out, as I had asked him to do.

It wasn't a very different story from others I had heard, although it still impressed me, especially because he recounted it with astonishing indifference.

When he finished, I asked him a couple of questions, to which he responded without looking at me.

When he left and I was alone, I understood that I still didn't know what he felt. I knew his story, but not his feelings; he hadn't spoken about that.

I needed to give him time. He had already taken the first step, which was talking about what had happened. I was sure it was the first step towards his recovery.

What a fool I was! How foolishly proud I was to think that I could do something for that boy with sad eyes!

The next morning, I received a call. It was from the police.

Andrew had jumped from the terrace of the building where he lived with his parents. That same night, just a few hours after speaking with me, he had gone up to the rooftop while his parents were sleeping and jumped to his death.

IX

The next day, I tried to immerse myself in my work routine to avoid thinking. I didn't want to think about Lucas, or Damian... or that new character I had met at Lucía's house library, who made a great effort to remind me that Damian was dead.

The three of them had appeared almost at the same time, as if they had conspired to disrupt the peace of my existence, disturbing my thoughts and unsettling my heart. One of the practices that had helped me the most during therapy after Damian's death was to "take one day at a time," and that's what I decided to do. "I just have to survive today, tomorrow I'll figure out what to do."

The days began to pass slowly, somewhat grey but bearable. On Monday, Lucía called me at the office.

"They awarded Samuel the prize for best fantasy novel from the British Fantasy Awards!" she shouted without even saying hello.

I jumped to my feet.

"What?! Really?"

"Yes! We are so excited! And surprised, of course. Not that he didn't deserve it, but..."

"I know. How wonderful, Lucía! I'm so happy for you guys!"

"We have to travel to the capital next Friday to receive it, will you come, right?"

"Of course," I said without thinking. "I wouldn't miss it for the world."

She began explaining all the details, and I started checking my schedule to see how busy I was the following weekend.

"I have appointments on Friday, but I can take the five o'clock flight. I would arrive around seven," I said.

"Yes, that's fine. We will travel in the morning so that the little one can rest. Otherwise, she will be unbearable at night."

I smiled.

"This is not just for Samuel, it's for you too."

"He says the same, but it's not true. It was all his own merit. He's the genius," she said proudly.

"Reserve a room for me," I reminded her.

"I already have," she replied, laughing. "Well, I'll let you go, Emilia is calling me. She's almost happier than I am! Goodbye, love you."

Emilia was the housekeeper, the wife of Pedro the gardener. They both lived in the guest house a few metres away from the main property. The house had been prepared when Samuel made all the renovations, so when Lucía hired the caretakers, the place suited them perfectly. Not only were they trustworthy, but they sometimes seemed like part of the family. Although Emilia was too bossy for my taste, Lucía got along very well with her, and they were good company whenever Samuel had to travel.

I hung up the call and stood thoughtfully by the window, the smile still clinging to my lips.

"How is it possible that the successes of the people we love make us happier than our own?" I thought.

With a joyful heart, I went to greet my next patient.

With the perspective of the award ceremony in mind, the days flew by. I had to buy a suitable party dress and fix my hair, rearrange my appointments for the following week so I wouldn't have to travel in a hurry... So, so many things to do!

On Thursday, Marilyn had invited me to dinner at her house. Supposedly, it would be a casual dinner with just the three of us, but when I arrived, I found out I wasn't the only guest.

From the moment I heard the laughter at the door, I wanted to turn around and go back, but I had already rung the bell, so I waited for someone to open it. Juan came out to greet me, smiling.

"Don't be mad," he whispered in my ear as he took my coat. "They came as a surprise."

I looked at him, raising an eyebrow. Of course, I didn't believe him. He always organised these trap dinners with some male guests.

"Who are they?"

"Marilyn's friends."

I didn't say anything and followed him to the living room. Everyone looked at me when I entered and smiled, greeting me. Juan introduced them: Nora and Robert, Tricia and Angel, and, of course, "the candidate": Joaquín, tall, dark, and handsome. The romantic cliché came to my mind so strongly that I decided to dislike him before he even started talking.

"Julia is a psychologist," Marilyn clarified, as if warning everyone.

"Do you work with Juan?" Joaquín asked, looking at me.

"No, I have my own practice."

"Already? How long since you finished your degree?"

I smirked, obviously, he was trying to compliment my youth, but I didn't believe him.

"Longer than it seems," I said. "I guess I'm surrounded by a pack of paediatricians or something, right?"

Everyone laughed.

"Well, no, I'm a teacher," Nora clarified. "I don't belong to the pack."

"Very funny," Marilyn said, getting up. "Let's go to the table. We were at a complicated medical meeting with Tricia and Robert, so after we finished, we decided to have dinner together to forget our troubles and fill our stomachs."

"So, you don't belong to the pack either?" I asked, looking at Angel.

"I do," he said, "but I wasn't at the meeting. Although I had the honour of being invited to dinner."

"Me too," Joaquín said, sitting next to me.

I suppose he expected to start a conversation, but Juan started talking, so I looked away and focused on him.

"Julia, tell us about Samuel's award, please. I found out yesterday, Marilyn told me."

I smiled.

"Yes, we're very excited. I still can't get used to having someone so famous in the family," I said, taking a sip of my drink.

"Samuel is a writer, surely you've heard of his trilogy 'The Three Ladies'..."

"Samuel Stone? Do you know him?" Tricia asked, astonished, looking at me.

"He's my brother-in-law."

"Oh, my goodness! I love his novels; I've read almost all of them. What award did he receive?"

We started talking about Samuel and the award, and then his works, and soon the conversation shifted to the realm of fantasy novels.

"I'm not a big fan of horror books or movies," Joaquín said. "But if they say he's so good, I'll have to read it."

"I think it's different, and that's what makes it so good," I clarified.

"I don't like horror books either, they scare me too much," Nora said, dipping her spoon into the ice cream glass, "even more than movies."

"I suppose it's because the imagination comes into play, which is more powerful than any of the senses."

"Exactly!" Marilyn chimed in. "And that's the advantage books have over movies."

"They say that every fantasy novel is based on something true and something fictional. Is that the case with 'The Three Ladies'?"

"I don't believe in witches, but if they fly, they fly..."

We all laughed.

"Before writing the trilogy, Samuel had written several books," I began to explain. "Always fantasy, but with different approaches. But about five or six years ago... Yes, five, before Adela was born," I said thoughtfully, "well, back then he found a compilation of legends from the area in the library of the house, and one of them was about three witches who were feared and persecuted, around 1700. Apparently, they were caught and killed near the house, in a place called, coincidentally, the Witches' Wasteland..." Everyone looked at me with curiosity. "They were drowned in the river that surrounded the woods, at the time it was believed that this was the only way to kill a witch."

"Not burned at the stake?" Nora asked.

I shook my head.

"I think burning at the stake was earlier. Anyway, there are those who believe they were never caught. But don't worry, Nora, it's just legends," I said, laughing.

The evening continued to entertain. We talked about various topics, and around ten o'clock, some began to say their goodbyes. I helped Marilyn clear the table while Juan and Joaquín had a drink in the living room.

"What do you think?" she asked, with a knowing smile.

"What do I think...?"

"Don't play dumb," she said, approaching me and lowering her voice. "Isn't he attractive and interesting?"

"Are you talking about Joaquín? Well, attractive... somewhat, interesting... not really."

She frowned.

"No one is good enough for you."

"And anyone is good enough for you."

"Do you know what he does? Did he tell you?"

I shook my head.

"He's a forensic psychologist. Interesting, isn't it?"

"Yes, definitely. Where do you know him from?"

"He works at the hospital; he was with us at the meeting tonight."

I looked up from the plate I was cleaning.

"Don't ask," she said without looking at me. "A very sad case. I hate it when those things happen to children."

I looked at her thoughtfully for a few seconds, but as she requested, I didn't ask any questions.

X

And Friday arrived. Incredibly, I had managed to organise everything. I had bought a nice party dress and had my suitcase ready at the office. My last appointment was scheduled for 3 p.m., and then I would head to the airport, with just enough time to catch the 5:10 p.m. flight.

I remember the time of the call perfectly because I looked at the clock on my mobile phone while answering: 9:32.

"Yes?"

"Miss Vivanko?"

"Yes, it's me. Who is this?"

"I'm Officer Kloster. Unfortunately, I must ask you to come to Central Hospital."

And before he could say anything else, I knew.

"I'm sorry," the policeman said slowly, "your family has been in an accident on the motorway just over an hour ago."

My heart stopped beating for a fraction of a second, and I had to catch my breath. It was as if a piece of life slipped away from me in that instant.

"Are they... Are they okay?" I pleaded.

"I'm very sorry. Your sister and brother-in-law have passed away," he clarified.

A sob emerged from my chest, rendering me speechless.

"Your niece is unharmed. She's at the hospital."

I began to sob, still holding the phone in my hand.

"Miss Vivanko, is there someone with you right now? Someone who can accompany you to the hospital?"

I left the phone on the table and took two steps towards the couch. I knelt on the floor and buried my head in the cushions to muffle my sobs.

"Miss Vivanko, can you hear me?... Miss Vivanko..."

Janet was by my side, hugging me.

Someone was speaking, seated on the other side of the desk, but I couldn't understand their words, as if they were speaking in a language unfamiliar to me. At times, I became aware of their presence and tried to pay attention to what they were saying, but no matter how hard I tried, I couldn't comprehend.

Suddenly, the door opened, and Marilyn entered, followed by Juan. She knelt beside me while he spoke with the man at the desk.

They made me stand up and led me to another room. Janet started rubbing my hands.

"My dear, you're freezing."

"I'll bring some coffee," Marilyn said, quickly leaving the room.

Juan pulled a chair up to the couch and sat in front of me.

"Julia, can you hear me?"

I nodded, looking at him.

"Do you understand what has happened?"

I looked at him and sighed.

"Of course I understand, Juan. Don't treat me like one of your patients."

He smiled and caressed my cheek.

"I'm sorry, my dear. I'm so sorry."

Marilyn came in with a tray of coffee cups. She offered one to me.

"No, thank you," I said.

"Something warm will do you good," she insisted. "Would you like tea or hot chocolate?"

"No, I'm fine."

She distributed the coffees, which everyone accepted gratefully.

"Do you want me to accompany you to see Adela?" Janet asked. "They've given her a sedative, but she'll wake up in a couple of hours."

I looked at her.

"Let her sleep," I said.

"Emilia and Pedro are with her," Juan explained.

I nodded.

"I want to see Lucía," I suddenly said.

Juan and Marilyn exchanged looks.

"I don't think it's a good idea now, maybe later."

I stood up.

"I want to see her now," and I headed towards the door.

Juan followed me and tried to stop me.

"Listen, Julia, you can't, you're not in a condition to see her..."

"I'm going to see my sister. Will you come with me? If not, I'll go alone."

Tears had started to fall again. They slid down my cheeks seemingly of their own volition, simply flowing one after another, forming a small river of sadness, a bright and deep groove on my face.

"Okay but let me talk to the doctors first."

I didn't remember the way to the morgue, although I had walked this way before.

The same path in the same hospital.

Years had passed, but things hadn't changed much in the old university hospital. But I just couldn't remember the way.

Juan walked beside me, attentive to my reaction. I noticed his gaze on me from time to time, and his arm was around my shoulders.

The hallways began to empty as we went. Naturally, it was a secluded room, away from people, a place everyone wished to forget and definitely didn't want to visit.

A double door with frosted glass and a small sign blocked the passage at the end of the corridor. It was the entrance to the world of the dead.

Juan slowed down and, removing his arm from my shoulders, took my hands, forcing me to look at him.

"You know as well as I do that this isn't a good idea," he said.

"I need to see her, I need..." I swallowed, searching for the right words. "If I don't see her lifeless body, I'll always be expecting her to walk through the door."

Juan looked into my eyes, and I could see a hint of confusion in his, but he said nothing.

"Okay, let's go," he said eventually and took a step towards the door.

"Wait for me here. I want to be alone with her."

"Are you sure? Julia..."

"I'll be fine. Don't worry."

I let go of his hands and turned my head, trying to make out something beyond the frosted glass.

"I'll be fine," I repeated.

I walked through the door. The hallway continued for about ten more metres. I took a few steps and saw the room on my left through wide glass windows.

It was large and cold. Too large and almost empty, except for a metal gurney in the centre.

A nurse appeared and asked for my name, then kindly invited me to sit on some plastic chairs with their backs to the windows.

In front of my eyes, the wall of the corridor stretched, smooth and grey, ending at the far end in a small window with the same frosted glass.

"You can approach now," the nurse said.

I stood up to follow him, but he pointed at the glass.

On the gurney, I could see a body covered by a white sheet. It seemed so small that my heart lifted with the thought they may have made a mistake, and that it wasn't Lucía's body.

"You can approach the window. I'll uncover the body so you can identify it."

"From here...?"

He nodded, smiling softly.

"It's better for you to see her from here. Don't worry, you'll have all the time you need."

And without saying anything else, he disappeared through the door leading to the room.

I saw him approach the gurney. Before uncovering the sheet, he glanced at me.

I nodded and held my breath.

I don't know what I expected to see, but the impression wasn't good. And not because the body was battered or difficult to recognize, no, there was something else. The wet hair fell from the gurney in tight strands; her lips, her face so pale as if formed from marble. They had only uncovered her to the chest, revealing her neck and part of her shoulders.

She was naked, of course, and her skin seemed hard and sallow. I knew that she was cold and that her blood no longer flowed in her veins. I know they had washed her to remove the bloodstains, closed her wounds, and showed me her face because it was still intact.

My little sister was dead and they had her there naked only covered with a sheet. Someone who didn't know her had bathed her, washed her hair, and placed her on that cold tray as if she were an object.

A feeling of anger began to fill my chest. How dare they touch her like that! She would have been furious if she had seen them treating her that way.

"Let's go, Julia," Juan said beside me.

I looked at him without understanding.

"We have to go," he said again.

"I don't want to leave her here."

Juan looked at me with moist eyes.

"I know, but you have to."

"She... Her hair is wet..."

Juan nodded as he hugged me.

"I know, darling, I know..."

"It's so cold... " I said, and I felt everything around me starting to crumble: the walls, the glass, and finally the ground beneath my feet.

And I began to fall into a well of emptiness, into an abyss of unending blackness.

XI

Adela slept embracing her pink blanket.

I was surprised that she had set aside her stuffed animals to go back to the old blanket, but it was logical. That blanket had accompanied her since she was a baby and had been a safe refuge for the past few years whenever she was separated from her mom. It was natural for her to return to it in moments like these.

But it still broke my heart to see her like this. She was the very image of helplessness: tiny, curled up in a corner of the cold hospital bed, holding onto that pink blanket, with dishevelled hair falling onto her pale cheeks.

A lump formed in my throat, and I wondered in horror if they had already told her. I looked at Emilia, who was watching her with a vacant gaze, and at Pedro, who was dozing off in a chair.

They loved Lucía and Samuel almost as if they were their own children. She seemed composed, a strong and determined woman, although I imagined she was actually shattered, just like me.

I took two steps towards the bed, and she saw me. She instantly stood up and came over to hug me. She caressed my back for a few minutes without saying anything.

"How is she?" I asked, sitting down on a chair next to her.

She made an indiscernible gesture.

"She has been sleeping since they brought them. They don't know how much she saw or how much she can remember, but they prefer to keep her sedated for a few hours."

"A few hours?" I asked.

She nodded.

"So I won't be able to take her home tonight?"

"I don't think so. But go get some sleep, we'll stay with her."

"Sleep?" I thought, "I don't want to sleep, I would..." but I didn't even dare say it in my thoughts.

"I think I'll stay here tonight."

Emilia looked at me and began to shake her head. I realised she was about to protest, but I guess something she saw in my eyes made her stop.

She smiled tenderly and caressed my hands.

"Well, then we'll go. Call us if you need anything."

I nodded and watched them leave.

Sitting in the chair next to the bed, I turned off the lamp and closed my eyes. My head hurt, and my neck felt stiff, muscles knotted with tension , my spine rigid. My eyes were hot and swollen from hours of crying.

Adela moved in the bed, as if she were dreaming. She muttered something unintelligible and turned over. The blanket fell to the floor, so I stood up and turned around to pick it up. I placed it carefully next to her hands and covered her again; something slipped to the floor, bouncing on the tiles with a plastic sound.

I bent down and looked under the bed, finally finding it. It was a small brightly coloured toy: red, yellow, and blue. I looked at the little car, astonished and horrified. It was part of Samuel's keychain, missing the metal chain with the ring and keys.

My eyes jumped to the girl. Where had she found it? How long had she been conscious during the accident? Had she seen her parents die?

With my hand over my mouth, I stifled the sobs, trying to calm myself. I sighed and silently moved the blankets, lying down next to her and, embracing her fragile little body, I fell asleep.

A day later, I was able to take her home. Pedro had brought some of her things: clothes, a few stuffed animals, and a few toys.

She didn't ask me any questions, except for the initial "Where is mommy?" when she first woke up.

It felt like the accident had also killed my knowledge and experience as a therapist,

I didn't even know how I would respond when she started asking real questions. My previous professional experience could not have prepared me for this. The words I would use in similar situations to other children did not seem appropriate to help Adela understand and overcome what she was going through. Now it became clear to me why one shouldn't be a therapist for one's own family; emotions get confused, fear of failure comes into the mix, and we become insecure and fragile.

I had transferred my patients to another trusted psychologist so that I could stay home with her. First, because we were still waiting for the funeral and all the administrative matters which preceded and followed, and secondly, I was in no condition to work, to think, or to help others. I could barely handle my own soul, and deep down, I knew that if I got up every morning, it was because of her, and for her. For Adela, I was capable of making any sacrifice.

However, Adela seemed happy. At three years old, she didn't have the capacity to comprehend the concept of death or separation. She might miss her parents, but the possibility of never seeing them again didn't cross her mind. After all, what does "never again" mean to a three-year-old child? She was fine, happy to be with me and to experience the adventure of sleeping at my house.

I watched her while she played, trying to imagine what Lucía would want me to do, what she would expect from me. When I realised that sadness was starting to creep in, I pushed those thoughts away from my mind. I couldn't confront that now.

Exactly one week after the accident was the funeral. Samuel's parents had taken care of everything, especially his father, a tough and cold man with an overwhelming air of efficiency. They had visited Adela a couple of times at my house, but understandably the girl hadn't approached them since she barely knew them. They lived far away, and their relationship with Samuel wasn't very good, so they had hardly visited each other since his birth.

But despite that, I felt sorry for Lila, Adela's grandmother, and her efforts to get closer to Adela. Of course, she loved the little girl and was devastated by the death of her son, and the unintentional rejections from the girl didn't help her feel any better. So instead of focusing on her granddaughter, they started dealing with other matters, which was a great relief for me.

On the day of the funeral, I woke up early, got dressed, and discreetly applied makeup to hide my dark circles. I left the little one in Emilia's care and, accompanied by Janet, Marilyn, and Juan, I headed with a heavy heart towards the venue.

It seemed like the whole city had come to pay their respects to my siblings. Lucía's friends, Samuel's friends and relatives, people who loved Samuel for his books, mostly people I didn't know. However, I received hugs and condolences from each and every one of them, an endless succession of faces and names impossible to remember.

The ceremony was long; I could barely pay attention to the words being spoken. I could only think of Adela and how much I wanted to be with her, both of us covered in a blanket, watching a cartoon.

When it was all over, I tried to escape without talking to anyone, but it was impossible. Once again, I had to listen to words of comfort and receive handshakes from so many people who cared about them. I felt inadequate receiving so many displays of affection, but there was nothing I could do but accept them.

Finally, as the crowd began to disperse, I started walking towards the exit with Marilyn by my side. In the back, a man was still sitting. I looked in his direction and stopped in my tracks, staring at him.

"I think he's here..." my friend began.

"...Lucas," I concluded.

He had his eyes fixed on mine. He stood up and took a few steps closer. His gaze was filled with anguish and pain, which impressed me, especially because I knew that he barely knew Lucía. That sadness was only for me.

I approached him, and once by his side, I rested my head on his chest. He wrapped his arms around me, resting his cheek on my hair, and I started crying with an uncontrollable anguish. I don't know how long we stayed like that, me crying and him holding me without saying a word, but when I managed to stop, after several sighs and sobs, we were alone in the back of the room.

"Let's go, I'll take you home," he said.

When we arrived, Adela was already asleep. Pedro and Emilia stayed a few more minutes, and after making sure I would be okay, they left calmly, knowing that Lucas would stay with us until we fell asleep.

"I don't need you to stay and take care of me," I said later while preparing coffee.

He looked at the time.

"It's only 10:00; I have nothing better to do."

I smiled without saying anything else. I felt good, almost happy to have him with me again. I knew that nothing could have comforted me more than him, his smile, and his hugs.

We started chatting as if we had never been apart, as if those eight years didn't exist. We talked, laughed, asked each other questions, and shared our lives. But despite how well we were, or maybe precisely because of it, neither of us mentioned Damian.

"When did you come back?" I blurted out, catching him off guard.

"Two years ago," he replied, averting his gaze.

"Two years?" But before I could accuse him of anything, he added, "Do you remember Dr Bold?"

"The Developmental Psychology professor, yes, more or less. I never really liked him."

He smiled.

"Me neither. However, funny thing, I came back because of him."

"Because of him?"

He nodded.

"Two years ago, he proposed that I come and assist him in his practice because he needed an assistant. He offered me a salary and, obviously, the opportunity to learn from him and treat his patients. I hesitated before deciding... I wasn't sure if I wanted to return.”

He fired me a quick glance before continuing his story.

"After a couple of months of working together, he confessed to me that he was dying and that he wanted someone to continue his work. That's when I truly felt moved and honoured. Until then, he had never shown any particular appreciation for me. He died five months later, fully conscious until his last day."

He paused as he took a sip of coffee.

"You can't complain; you were very lucky," I said.

"I know. In his will, he clearly stated that the practice was mine, that I could use these facilities for as long as I wanted, and that it would only become part of the family inheritance when I decided to give it up."

"Incredible," I said, sincerely amazed.

"Yes, it was the definitive step in my career. Although clearly, the merit is not mine."

I sat up on the couch and looked at him.

"The merit was in you becoming worthy of his trust."

"Perhaps," he said.

I placed my cup on the table.

"You were a rebel without a cause, I can't imagine what he could have seen in you," and I started laughing.

He joined me.

"We were..." he clarified.

"Not me! You guys..."

We looked at each other for a moment, smiling.

"I remember the first day we talked," he began, "you were wearing those worn-out jeans that were huge on you. It was impossible for anyone to know what your backside looked like."

"Who wanted to know what my backside looked like?"

"Men!" he said, laughing.

"Two days later, you showed up one afternoon with Damian, and I don't think we ever parted ways after that." I added.

Smiling, he looked at his hands.

"Always together," he said and looked up. "But you ended up with the better-looking one."

I shook my head.

"No, you were the better-looking one."

He looked at me, smiling.

"I remember that first afternoon as you walked me to my apartment," I continued. "Do you remember? It was raining."

He nodded.

"And I had that blue umbrella the girls had given me."

"You had it for years..."

"As we walked, every time I looked at you to talk, I couldn't help but think how your eyes were the same colour as my umbrella."

I laughed, embarrassed by such a confession.

"You were definitely the better-looking one..."

"Thanks, I always suspected..." he joked.

"But Damian knew how to win me over."

He nodded and looked at me.

"Why did you leave?" I blurted out.

He widened his eyes in a gesture of perplexity.

"I don't know..."

"You know why, tell me."

He sighed and settled into the chair.

"I should have stayed, I know, but..."

I waited.

"I couldn't bear to see you suffer like that."

XII

The phone rang very early on Monday morning. It was Lila, Samuel's mother.

"Good morning, Julia. How are you? How is the little girl?"

"Very well," I said, disguising a yawn.

"I received a letter from Samuel's lawyers. They want to meet with us to read the will."

"A will? Did Samuel leave a will?"

"It seems so. Did you receive anything?"

I stood up and went to the shelf by the entrance.

"I don't know, I haven't checked the mail... Wait, yes, I think this is it. Newman and Burtenshaw... They have scheduled me for Tuesday at 9 a.m. Are you also invited?"

She hesitated for a moment.

"No, ours is at 10. I suppose it will be separate then. Well, we'll see each other there. Do you want us to pick you up?"

"No, thank you, I'll go in my car."

And I ended the call wondering why Samuel and Lucía would have made a will.

"It's normal," Juan clarified that same night while we were having dinner at home. "Samuel was already earning a considerable income. His lawyers must have advised him to do it."

"Especially because of the royalties from his books. Writers, musicians, the profits from their creations continue for years, many years," Marilyn explained.

I put my fork down on my plate.

"Yes, I suppose you're right, but it's...," I sighed. "It's as if they knew something was going to happen."

"Don't think nonsense, it's fortunate that they did it, especially for Adela."

Yes, it was fortunate.

The girl would never have to worry about money. Not that she would become a millionaire, but she could live comfortably and pay for her studies. It was fortunate.

I arrived promptly for the appointment. I was nervous and had no idea what to expect. I had never been present at the reading of a will, and I knew very little about the subject.

They led me into the office of the notaries, which, as it seemed to me, was the main office.

The desk was empty, and the lawyers were comfortably seated in two black leather armchairs. They immediately stood up and came over to greet me.

After introducing themselves -Newman, the bald one, and Burtenshaw, the one with a beard- they began by offering their condolences and talking about how much they valued Samuel. Then I understood why they were personally handling this process. They were not just his lawyers; they were also his friends

88

from youth. Apparently, that's why Samuel had chosen them and trusted them completely.

"Julia, I know you must be wondering what role you play here today, and why you have been summoned to the reading of the will. Perhaps you can imagine, it has to do with Adela. Before we proceed with the reading and the formal and legal part, I must inform you that Samuel and Lucía designated you as the guardian of the child."

I swallowed hard and remained silent because I knew that if I tried to speak, I would burst into tears.

"Of course," Newman continued, "there is also the financial aspect, which, as Samuel stipulated, will be managed by this firm. Adela will receive a monthly allowance until she reaches the age of majority, which will be deposited directly into the bank account of your choice."

"We don't need money. She knew she didn't have to leave money, I don't understand..." I said.

The lawyer looked at me gravely.

"She didn't know she would die so soon. The will was made in the hope that it would never be read, at least not that provision. So the monetary allowance is part of what is usually stipulated. You had a good job, but she didn't know what could happen in the future, and the will was made with the future in mind," he concluded, looking at his partner.

Something in the look they exchanged made me wonder.

"When did they make the will?" I asked.

"Two years ago," they replied.

I looked at one and then the other.

"But the clause designating the legal guardian was added three months ago," Burtenshaw added.

I felt a knot of anguish tightening in my throat.

"You may think it's silly, but I believe mothers have a special perception for certain things. It was Lucía who insisted that we add this clause," the bald one gave him a reproachful look; it certainly wasn't the right time to make that comment.

They stood up, inviting me to follow them to another office.

"Anyway, you're not obliged to accept it. You can refuse, of course. In that case, Samuel's parents would become the guardians."

"Did she ask for that?" I asked.

They nodded.

"We have something you should read before we proceed with the will."

We had reached a small room. Newman continued walking, and the other invited me to enter.

"You can stay here, make yourself comfortable, and take your time. We'll let you know as soon as Lila and Andrew arrive."

He handed me a letter and gently closed the door.

I approached the sofa next to the window and sat down, keeping my eyes fixed on the envelope.

My name, carefully written, was the only thing standing out on the white paper. I recognized Lucía's handwriting and became mesmerised, staring at it.

I was afraid to open it and read what she had written three months ago. I tried to remember what we had done when we had been together at that time.

"When will you come to live with us?" Samuel had asked on that occasion. He or Lucía had asked that question many times before, but in retrospect, without me realising at the time, there was something different: a hidden fear in Lucía's heart, a premonition that time was pressing, or perhaps the panic that all parents must feel when they look at their children and see them so small and fragile.

I opened the letter and started reading, and the first sentence unleashed my tears.

"Little sis, don't be scared.

Unfortunately, I know that if you're reading this, it's because I'm no longer there with you, and you can't imagine how much it saddens me just to think about it. But I have to do it.

I want you to put the letter aside for a moment, close your eyes, and feel my embrace. I love you, little sister. I love you so much!"

I closed my eyes and tried to calm down, but the tears kept flowing.

"I can't do it," I thought, "I can't."

Then as if sent from afar a gentle breeze touched my face.

I held my breath as I felt the warmth surrounding my shoulders and the soft pressure against my chest. I didn't dare open my eyes because I didn't want her to leave me, and I knew that if I opened them, I would see that I was alone, and everything would disappear.

"I love you, Lucía," I whispered softly.

Then I searched for her face through a distorted veil of tears, foolishly hoping that she was really there, but it was hope unfulfilled. My loneliness became, if possible, deeper and darker.

"Now let me tell you that I have imagined this future many times. At first, it was hard until I realised that nothing could be better for Adela than to have you, and for you to have her.

That's why I ask you to live by her side and take care of her until she grows up and becomes a woman. I don't know how many years you'll have to do this alone, I hope they are very few. I hope that on the day we're gone, Adela will already be a teenager and can become a friend to you, and you can laugh with one another and console each other when needed.

But if not... Thank you for loving her and helping her grow!

I won't give you any advice; I know you will be perfect. How many can be fortunate enough to leave their daughter in the hands of a psychologist? I'm just going to ask you one thing: don't leave the house. It's the only truly important thing we can leave her, the place where she was born and lived with her parents. Please, move in here with her, learn to love this house, and try to make it your own. A piece of us will always be within these walls. I know you'll hate me for asking this, but someday you'll understand why I'm doing it.

I love you, remember that I'm leaving you my greatest treasure."

Perhaps nothing she could have asked of me would have surprised me more than this.

Living in that house, why?

I smiled, "You'll hate me for asking this," she knew me well.

The few plans I had made were centred around my house, the activities the city could provide for Adela, but now...

The door opened, and one of the lawyers stuck his head in.

"Is everything okay?"

I nodded.

"Are you okay with what she's asking?"

Of course, he had read the letter.

"Living in the house? Yes, I have no other choice," I said, smiling.

He entered and closed the door. He approached and sat next to me.

"I know this is the first time we meet, but my appreciation for you comes from the love I had for Samuel and Lucía. The day she gave me this letter, I could sense the pain she felt thinking about all this, but she asked me not to pressure you, to let you know that you could refuse. Nothing in the will or this letter is an obligation; it's just a request."

"I understand," I said.

"Not even living in the house, if you don't want to live there, the house will be taken care of by the caretakers. Samuel left a fund for the maintenance of the mansion, any necessary restorations, everything needed to ensure the house is in perfect condition when Adela inherits it at the age of 18. You don't need to decide all that now."

I smiled gratefully and stood up to follow him to his office, where Samuel's parents were already waiting.

The will was short, with very few clauses.

First, it talked about the properties, including the house, and mentioned the maintenance issue, clarifying that Emilia and

Pedro would continue to be the caretakers for as long as they wanted to remain in that position.

Then it addressed the royalties from Samuel's novels, which his daughter would continue to receive as the sole heir.

And finally, the legal guardianship of the child.

When Newman began to read this last clause, I saw out of the corner of my eye that Andrew settled on the couch. I don't know what his expression was upon hearing his son's wish, I don't know if he expected it or not, or if perhaps he hoped they would have that privilege, but he didn't say anything.

After signing, I went outside and saw, to my surprise, that Lila was waiting for me.

"I wanted to say goodbye; we're leaving tonight."

"But won't you come to see Adela?"

She shook her head, sadly.

"No, sweetheart. I'm sorry..."

"He's furious," I said.

"Yes, more than furious, but he'll get over it. Don't worry."

I received her hug, and before letting go, I said, "Don't abandon her, Lila, you are her grandparents."

She looked at me surprised.

"Of course I won't, I love that little girl more than my life. Even though he hasn't let me come to see her much, now he won't be able to stop me. I can't forgive him for keeping me away from my son. If only I had known..."

She couldn't continue; her voice broke.

I squeezed her hand affectionately.

"Then we're only saying goodbye for a few months; I hope you come back soon."

"I will," she said through tears, "I will."

XIII

"Bring the child," she barked without even a glance at the girl. The three watched the silent house from the forest treeline cloaked in shadow only mitigated by the cold luminosity of the winter moon.

The youngest of the three remained motionless but turned her eyes on the speaker noting how the cruelty in her steely eyes contrasted with her flawless skin and red hair that fell in perfect waves about her shoulders.

"Bring the child," she repeated, this time the command accompanied by a cold stare that spoke louder than her voice.

The girl looked at the house once again.

"Mother, perhaps this time we should..."

"I said, bring me the boy," her tone remained calm.

"No," came the retort. The girl winced internally as she realised the refusal sounded much more defiant than intended.

The red woman turned her eyes from the house and locked them on the young woman once more. The girl cast her eyes to the ground before beginning to speak.

"We don't have to do this, we can leave him here with his father, we can..."

"Please, explain your reasoning," she said, slightly condescendingly.

"I've seen them, they cry for them, they search desperately for them. They really love their children."

"And what does that matter? Those monsters that have persecuted our kind for centuries do not deserve our mercy. In this world those with power take what they want, it has always been this way and at this moment we are the ones with the power. They have dominion over the animals that they slay for food, do you see them cry for their sheep before they slaughter their lambs to consume them? You must understand that they are to us as cattle are to them."

"But they're not cattle, they're people..."

She approached again and caressed the girl's cheek.

"Don't let their appearance deceive you, they're nothing like us. Now go, bring the child."

The young girl lowered her head and walked towards the house.

They watched her walk away. Her black hair danced in the breeze as her slender figure glided silently over the dry leaves as if her feet didn't touch them, not even the slightest rustle could be heard.

"She's growing," said the blonde one, who had until now remained silent.

"Not enough, she's still too innocent."

"Do you think that's it?"

The redhead turned to look at her, inquisitive.

"I fear that the blood of her mother still runs in her veins..."

The movement was so quick that she barely had time to register her astonishment. In the blink of an eye the red woman's hand had closed around her throat like the grip of a vice.

"If you mention that woman again... it will be the last thing you ever say."

For only an instant the silver eyes flashed their displeasure and then she removed her hand and her voice returned to its previous dispassionate tone, "She has only one mother."

Both turned towards the young woman who approached with a little boy in her arms.

She looked at him once again before handing him to her mother.

The mother carefully took him and held him against her chest, almost affectionately. The little one sighed, still asleep, as the long, slender fingers brushed a curl from his forehead.

"His father?"

"He was asleep," the girl replied.

The three majestic, powerful women turned in unison and headed toward the heart of the forest parting the mists as they moved. Each strikingly different to the next; one red, one black and the other golden.

Moon and mist collaborated to provide the silhouetted forms of the three a halo of light around their perfect contours. Perhaps a trick of the moonlight lent them an air of supernatural beauty.

If anyone could have witnessed them in that moment, could never have imagined that such resplendent beauty could have hidden such dark hearts and that those clear pure eyes could be so indifferent to the pain and suffering of men. That those soft and delicate hands had taken so many innocent lives.

This deception was the most powerful weapon in their armoury: hypnotizing beauty hiding unparalleled wickedness, a charismatic smile hiding a blackened soul.

The younger one looked over her shoulder at the house one last time. A solitary light flickered in one of the third-floor windows. Her heart felt heavy when she imagined the father waking up to find his son's bed empty.

The thought elicited a glassy tear to form which gathered volume enough to fall. It traced a glistening path down her cheek to hang precariously from her chin. The tiny drop of condensed sorrow then fell onto her chest where hung a pendant of strange design, a tiny violet gem twinkling at its centre.

Pushing back another tear she grasped the pendant in her hand, as she had done many times before when she needed comfort, raised her head and continued to the dark forest.

XIV

We moved that same week. I couldn't keep Adela away from her home any longer; I felt guilty having her at my house. I had only packed a few of my things, leaving almost everything in my apartment, ready to go back at the first opportunity if necessary.

As we entered the mansion, the girl ran towards the kitchen and stood in front of the open door, looking inside.

"Mummy?"

I waited. I didn't want to repeat what I had already told her so many times. We had talked about how mommy and daddy wouldn't be in the house, but she, of course, didn't understand.

I approached and put my hand on her shoulder.

"Let's go see how Demetrio is doing," I asked, trying to show enthusiasm. "He has been alone for many days."

Demetrio was a blue stuffed dog, one of those rare specimens that manufacturers create with the sole purpose of confusing children's minds, but she adored him, and Pedro had forgotten to take him home.

She nodded and without saying a word, climbed the stairs. I could not help but notice her disappointment through the way she walked with head low and shoulders hunched.

As we left the kitchen, I glanced at the table where I had shared so much laughter and conversation with Lucía and Samuel. The rustic wood held so many memories of joy and hot coffee.

My senses activated and echoes of my life in the house flooded back. Footsteps on old floorboards, the tick-tock of the old wall clock, Lucía's infectious laughter ...

Suddenly, the pain of loss again overwhelmed me, drawing tears from my eyes. I wondered if it had been a good idea to leave the security of my apartment. It was going to be very difficult for us both to live there again.

I passed through the living room drawing memories from all around me. I was sure that Emilia had thoroughly cleaned the house and had stored all of Lucía´s personal belongings. However, she had forgotten something hugely important, something she probably could not have imagined meant so much to me; and could cause me so much pain. I approached and took a wooden figurine off the shelf, the one I had presented to Lucía when we found out that she was pregnant. It was an abstract, polished carving representing a father, mother, and baby, all holding hands. A gift that I had almost forgotten, even though I had seen it hundreds of times over these three years, but that morning it reminded me that Adela would never again see her parents again and they would never see their little girl become a woman, at that thought I could no longer hold back my tears.

The little girl peeked out from the first floor.

"Look where Demetrio is!" she exclaimed happily.

I wiped my tears and went to join her.

She had arranged all the stuffed animals on the carpet, in a corner, in front of the chalkboard, as if they were in school.

She sat on the floor among them and laughed happily.

"It looks like my class," she said. "Only the teacher is missing."

"You can be the teacher... Miss Adela," and she started laughing again.

I let her play and headed to the adjacent room; the one Emilia had prepared for me. According to her, it was more spacious than the bedroom I always used, and it was next to Adela's.

I looked at the bed, with a new bedspread and matching cushions, and without even crossing the threshold, I continued down the hallway.

I wasn't going to change rooms. Having decided, I returned to my old room and opened the door.

This was my room, the one Lucía had chosen for me, the one she always had prepared with clean sheets and one with my own clothes in the closet.

I sat on the bed and caressed the blankets, thinking about my sister.

"Here I am," I said with a smile. "I've brought your little girl home."

I was struck with an overwhelming feeling of helplessness and sighed, almost on the verge of tears. Again, I wondered how I was going to move forward without her.

However, in the following days, the weight began to lift.

Adela seemed happy to have me in her house, and she showed me all the secrets of the mansion. Like any old house, it had its quirks, things that only worked if you used them in a certain way, and others that were simply out of use. So, between her and Emilia, they helped me understand how to navigate my new home.

I missed some comforts; the house was still very damp and too dark. Not to mention that the cold seemed to seep into my bones on winter nights. Despite having heating in every room and fireplaces in every lounge, I could feel the dampness between the sheets when I went to bed.

Emilia insisted that I use the "hot water bottle," but that old contraption seemed dangerous to me. I imagined scalding myself from head to toe if the cap came off, so I preferred to endure the dampness and substitute the hot water bottle for a thick pair of socks and fleece pyjamas.

Adela behaved naturally; she seemed happy, and although she mentioned her parents from time to time, I worried that she didn't cry or miss her mother.

Even young children question the absence of their parents, but she hadn't asked me any more questions. After what I had told her at the hospital, it seemed like she had forgotten about it.

"Where is mommy?" she had asked me the day after the accident.

I had arrived early to take her home, I had put on makeup so she wouldn't see my dark circles, and I had come with a smile and a new stuffed toy.

I thought I was prepared to talk to her about what had happened, but her first question had dismantled my entire strategy.

"Do you remember the trip to the airport?" I asked, trying to keep my voice from trembling.

She nodded, looking me in the eyes.

"What do you remember?"

"I was playing with my tablet, and mommy was laughing, and daddy shouted..."

And I noticed that she held her breath.

"What happened next?" I needed to know how much she remembered, how much she had seen.

"I don't know, I fell asleep."

I sighed and tried to force a smile.

"My love, when you fell asleep, it was because you hit your head. Mommy and daddy also hit their heads because a car hit them."

She looked at me with her big brown eyes, seemingly so desolate that a lump formed in my throat, and I didn't think I could continue talking.

"Mommy and daddy have died, sweetheart."

She blinked once. That word, so terrible for me, meant nothing to her.

"Do you remember the little bird we found dead in the woods? He had fallen from his nest and mommy explained to you that he had died, that we should bury him and that he would never sing or fly again".

She nodded and turned her head looking for her blanket.

"When are they coming back?" She asked.

"They're not coming back, honey, they're dead."

"Where are they?"

I looked at her, and I felt as small as she did, trying to understand or accept everything that death implied. What could I say to her? I wasn't going to lie to her or use metaphors that she wouldn't understand, that would only confuse her even more.

I desperately wished to believe in the afterlife, like Damian did, and be able to say, "They are in a better place, they are waiting for you. When you die, you will be able to see them again." But I didn't dare because I had held onto that hope myself for many years, and now, after so much time and so many losses, I was no longer sure of anything.

"I don't know," I said, fearing the next question.

But it didn't come; she just stared at me, lost in thought. Then she took her blanket, put her thumb in her mouth, and curled up, turning her back to me.

I felt my heart break with pain. Perhaps if she had started crying, if she had hugged me seeking protection or if she had screamed saying that she wanted to see her parents, maybe it would have been easier. Her calm and resigned reaction after enduring such loss; for her to bear it alone and in isolation, broke my heart.

But now, almost a month later, I could see her happy again. She ate, played, slept like a little girl her age, and spoke of her parents in the present tense, which was normal. Every time she asked about her mum, I would repeat the same thing, and she seemed to accept it, but I knew that sooner or later, in some way, the terrible loss she had suffered would start to manifest.

"Simaco told me he doesn't like it when you take books from the library," she said one night after dinner.

We were both sharing the same couch, one at each end, covered by the same blanket. She was combing a nearly bald Barbie, and I was reading.

"Who?" I asked.

"Simaco," she said, focused on her task.

"Who is Simaco?"

"My friend."

"Oh, your friend..."

"An imaginary friend," I thought, "Perfect!"

"Does he always play with you?" I asked, setting aside my book.

"Sometimes. I like to talk with him. He talks weird," she said, smiling.

I smiled too as I looked at her.

"Why doesn't he want me to take books from the library?" I inquired, picking up the old copy of "The Count of Monte Cristo" I was reading.

"Because they are his, and he doesn't want you to take them."

I sat up straight in my seat.

"Alright, tomorrow I'll put back on the shelves the ones I've taken so that Simaco won't get mad. But tell him that this is my home too now, and I can use the books."

"I'll tell him tomorrow. He's sleeping now."

She continued grooming the doll, and I tried to read, but my thoughts drifted to that imaginary friend who had appeared just at the right moment to help and accompany her during this difficult stage of her life.

Once again, I marvelled at the complexity of the human psyche and especially the self-recovery power of young children.

A few weeks later, when the days started to get longer, the sun emerged from the eternal winter clouds, and spring timidly arrived, filling the trees and shrubs with new buds and tight blossoms that filled the air with exquisite fragrances.

Walks with Adela became almost daily, and without realising it, I began to enjoy my new life.

One afternoon, both of us emerged from the forest running. She always challenged me to catch her, and I almost always let her reach the destination first.

As I looked towards the house, I saw Emilia talking to a man on the driveway. Adela was the first to recognize him.

"Lucas!" she shouted and darted like a bullet, calling out to him as she ran.

Joyfully, I also hurried to reach them. It was the first time he visited us since we moved into the house, although he had been to my apartment several times.

The two of them hit it off almost instantly, as she was not shy at all, and he was truly charming with children.

I watched as he lifted her into the air while she laughed, and grateful, I blessed that man who took the time to alleviate the pain of a little girl.

We spent the afternoon together. Adela wanted to take him to the forest, so we strolled for almost an hour. Then, upon returning, we discovered that Emilia had prepared a delicious dinner, so we ate, chatted, and ended up enjoying dessert in the living room, in front of the fireplace.

The girl was tired, lying on the carpet in front of the fire, looking at some little books until she fell asleep.

"She looks good," Lucas said, nodding towards her.

I nodded.

"Yes, she hasn't shown anything yet."

"She's very young, maybe she never will."

I made a doubtful face.

105

"I hope so. But you know what? She has an imaginary friend."

"Really?" he said, smiling.

"Simaco."

"Simaco? Oh my, what a name! Does she play with him?"

"Never in front of me, but she tells me things she does with him. She says he speaks strangely... as if she spoke perfectly!"

We both laughed as we looked at her.

"And you? How are you?" He asked.

"Much better," I said honestly. "Although it's hard for me to admit it, this place has been really good for me. I'm more relaxed, at peace. I thought living surrounded by Lucía's things would make me suffer or miss her a lot, but the truth is that it makes me feel closer to her, and that's good for me."

Lucas looked at me.

"I'm glad," he said.

We fell into silence, accompanied only by the crackling of the fire. I observed him as he stared into the flames. He had changed. There was little left of the young man with whom we shared outings, climbs, and parties. He seemed to have grown, not only taller but more muscular. I wondered what he had been doing these years, besides finishing his studies. At that moment, he turned and met my gaze.

I smiled, and he asked, "What were you thinking about?"

"I was trying to guess how you ended up like this. I remember you as a skinny guy, and not a fan of the gym."

He laughed at my comment.

"Well, I wasn't that skinny, and I'm not that big now. About four years ago, I started practising vertical wall climbing."

"In the gym?"

"No," he said, making a disgusted gesture. "That's for amateurs."

I smiled.

"I haven't climbed again," I added.

He looked at me without saying anything, and I didn't want to continue. I didn't want to talk about Damian.

"Thursday is Adela's birthday. You will come, right?" I asked, abruptly changing the subject.

"Of course," he replied. "I'll be there."

That night, after putting the little one to bed and taking a shower, I went downstairs to watch a movie.

One of the things I missed was having a television set in the bedroom, but it was impossible because the connection was only on the ground floor and didn't reach the upper floors, so Lucía and Samuel had a single TV in one of the lounges.

The place was perfectly set up, with comfortable armchairs and a huge screen on one of the walls.

I wanted to watch one of my favourite movies, so I started searching until I found the right one: romantic, funny, and with a happy ending. No dramas or movies that showcased human miseries; I had enough of that in my own life.

I had prepared a plate with some cookies and a glass of milk. I settled into the armchair, reclining it a bit, and placed the plate on the small side table.

I was about to press the play button when I heard a loud noise that made me jump and scream involuntarily.

I ran up the stairs to Adela's room. The door was open, just as I had left it, and the little girl was sleeping peacefully. Using the light coming in from the hallway, I glanced around the room; everything seemed to be in order.

Suddenly, another thunderous noise above my head. I closed the door and took a few steps back.

I knew where the noise was coming from, but I didn't know what had caused it.

I looked toward the stairs and noticed my legs starting to tremble. I had only read of these types of reactions in a book, and I had always thought it was a good literary image to help the reader empathise with the protagonist. However, there I was, with the feeling of having lost control over my legs, which refused to move.

I stopped and leaned against the wall. After taking a deep breath, I placed my hand on my chest, trying to calm myself down.

I don't know where my courage came from. Perhaps it was logic and reason that led me to understand that my only option was to confront whatever was up there, and that if I didn't do it then no one else would.

Leaning on the handrail, I climbed the stairs. A sensation of cold and heaviness spread through my limbs, as if my blood had turned into lead.

I turned on the hallway light and walked to the library. There, I stopped and realised that now not only my legs and hands were trembling, but also my jaw, tense enough to make my teeth chatter.

The hinges of the door creaked for the longest time as I slowly pushed it open, to reveal a sight which made no sense, hundreds of books scattered all over the floor, as if they had all fallen from the shelves at once.

Even though I knew the room was empty I could sense that I was being watched by some malevolent presence. My eyes darted around the room searching all the darkened corners and alcoves for the eyes, those evil black eyes that held me in terror once before. Then without warning a wall of books to my left crashed to the ground eliciting a sharp scream from me.

Only one group of books remained in place, those between the two windows, right in front of me.

I looked closely at that part of the bookshelf, knowing they were going to fall, and they did. Just the one, closely followed by another, and another as if the fall of each book was the cause of the next. I was transfixed as they fell in perfect succession. The domino effect continued its pace until the supply of books was exhausted.

Dumbfounded, I stood in the doorway. My emotions ranged from terror to astonishment. I took an unsteady step backward using the opposite wall of the hallway for support. The open door in front of me revealed part of the desk and the high-backed armchair.

While my instinct screamed at me to run, for some reason, my feet stayed rooted to the floor unable to take me away from the horror. At that moment the armchair began to move, slowly at first, screeching as it scraped its wooden legs against the floorboards. Then a sudden increase of speed sent it crashing into the wall.

"Enough!" I shouted in a frenzy. "Leave this house!"

The door also began to move and slammed shut, silencing my words with a loud bang.

Then from my mix of emotion churning around inside of me, one emerged as dominant; indignation. Yes, I was indignant. This was my sister's house, and I would not allow anyone to take it away.

"I'm not afraid of you!" I added.

Perhaps this presence wasn't convinced by my anger because a few seconds later a mocking laughter echoed through the door.

A sharp scream came from downstairs, my anger was replaced by fear once again, but fear for Adela.

I rushed down the stairs as fast as my legs would allow me, and in an instant, I was by her side. She had sat on the bed and was crying.

"Don't be scared, little one, it's nothing," I said, embracing her. "Some books fell in the library, that's all."

The words were meant to comfort her as much as myself.

"I got scared," she said. "And I called you, and you didn't come".

"I know, my love, I'm sorry, I was upstairs."

"I told you Simaco didn't want his books touched," she added tearfully.

Hearing these words from the child sent a chill through my soul.

XV

The next day, I started organising the library with the help of Emilia and Pedro. As we entered, the two of them exchanged an indecipherable glance, and then they began gathering the books.

"I don't understand what happened," I said as I stacked piles of books on the table, trying to group the collections together. "They fell gradually, one shelf at a time. The strangest thing was that the bookshelves didn't come off the wall. Only the books fell."

Pedro gave me a sideways glance but remained silent. Emilia squatted near the window and approached the desk with a few books in her hands.

"You should arrange everything and close this room. It's dangerous for the girl and for you," she said.

I looked at her. "Of course, I'm not going to close it. Besides, I hardly ever come here, but this was one of Samuel's favourite places." Although he didn't spend much time here, he loved this place. He loved books, especially these books.

"Yes, but look what happened..."

I didn't respond. I wanted to find out what they knew, but I didn't dare ask directly.

Pedro sighed and looked at me. "It would be best, Miss Julia, to close this place."

I was astonished that Pedro was participating in the conversation; he was usually very quiet.

"Well, maybe we can secure the books in some way, put some kind of support so they don't fall again..."

"I don't think that's the problem."

I approached him. "What do you mean?"

"Miss, not everything that happens has an explanation, and sometimes it's better to leave them that way."

He averted his eyes from mine and crouched down to pick up more books.

"What are you talking about, Pedro?"

Since he didn't respond, I looked to his wife. "What's going on, Emilia? Is there something I should know?"

They exchanged a strange look.

"The house is very old, Julia, and it has its own things... Things that should be respected, or else this happens," she added, pointing at the floor covered in books.

"Are you saying that the house did this?" I asked. "Has something similar happened before?"

She shook her head. "Never, that's why I think you should close the library."

We spent almost the entire morning in the library, but neither of them wanted to talk about it anymore. From what little they had said, I deduced that no one had experienced anything like what I had. What had I done to provoke such anger from the resident of the library?

112

'Things that should be respected,' Emilia had said solemnly... There wasn't much I could do, and although it seemed ridiculous to admit that there was a ghost in the house, but, that was the reality. I had seen too much to believe otherwise.

In the following days, nothing strange happened. Although it was difficult for me to fall asleep that night, and I expected the same thing to happen again at any moment, our rest remained undisturbed.

We then focused on preparing Adela's birthday. I was determined to make it a special occasion for her, fun, and with many others to help her celebrate.

I invited my friends and some of Lucía's friends who had children Adela knew. We prepared the winter garden for the children to play in case it rained, and Pedro set up the pergola in the park with tables for the food.

There were balloons everywhere, and we had hidden gifts for the little guests in the gardens. Everything was ready, and Adela was tremendously excited about all the surprises. Suddenly, the house began to fill with people, and the music and chatter transformed the place into something completely different to the peaceful refuge where we lived.

The weather was wonderful, the sun was shining, and a cool breeze made the garden a perfect place to enjoy the party. The children were having fun, and the adults were chatting and laughing.

Around 7 o'clock in the evening, people started leaving. The children were already tired, and the mothers were eager to put them to bed after giving them a bath. So, there came a moment when only Marilyn and Juan, Janet, Lucas, Emilia, and I remained.

"Julia, should I take the little girl to bed?" Emilia said, standing up.

"Without giving her a bath?"

The girl had fallen asleep in Lucas' arms.

"I'll take her," Lucas said, getting up. "I don't think it will hurt if she doesn't bathe for one night."

They headed towards the house while I started to clear the plates.

Marilyn approached to help me. Her advanced pregnancy prevented her from walking naturally, which made me smile tenderly.

"Sit down and rest. I don't want that baby to come out prematurely," I said.

She smiled and disregarded me, starting to collect the glasses.

"So charming," she commented.

"I know," I replied, thinking she was talking about Adela.

"I mean Lucas."

I looked at her, and she was smiling.

"Oh, yes, him too," I said, and as she continued to look at me, I asked, "What?"

"Nothing, I'm just telling you again that this boy is charming."

Lucas was coming towards the table, so she didn't add anything more.

The night was truly beautiful, and it seemed like nobody wanted to leave. The conversation had become interesting, and Emilia had prepared coffee, so we stayed outside enjoying the fresh air.

I was watching Lucas as he spoke when I thought I saw something moving in one of the upstairs windows.

I looked up, thinking it might be Emilia closing the curtains in my room or Adela's room, but then I saw her walking down the path towards her house.

I looked again, and this time I clearly distinguished a figure in one of the third-floor windows.

Lucas was talking, but I stopped listening. I felt time stand still for a moment as I observed the man who seemed to be looking at me from the window. I stood up with my gaze fixed on his face and began to walk towards the house.

As I approached, his face became clearer, and I noticed that his eyes were indeed following my movements.

I passed through the front door, ran upstairs to the third floor, and without stopping in any of the rooms, went straight to the library.

I placed my hand on the doorknob and, realising what I was about to do, withdrew my hand and took a step back.

The memory of his sinister laughter made me shudder, and even though my friends were just a few metres away, waiting for me in the garden, my bravery evaporated into panic.

With trembling hands, I pressed my ear against the glossy dark wood and tried to listen for any sound coming from inside.

Something slid against the door from the inside. It felt like the gentle touch of his fingers, a caress. I realised that his hand was only a few centimetres away from my face, and I moved my head away, looking at the door in horror.

He knew I was there. He was playing with me.

I stood paralyzed, waiting, then I looked down and to my horror the doorknob slowly started to rotate. My hands clung to the handle, thinking that maybe I could prevent him from opening the door. I felt it starting to give way despite my efforts, until I could no longer retain my grip, and was forced to release it.

I fully expected the door to be flung open following my release but instead it slowly and dramatically creaked open until it rested on the wall

But the room was empty.

Turning on the lights and I paused at the threshold, not daring to enter.

There was a stack of books on the desk, and the curtains were open, two details that, I was sure, had changed since the day we had organised that place.

"Julia, what's wrong?"

It was Janet's voice, coming up the stairs.

"Nothing," I said, turning off the lights and stepping out into the hallway.

I looked once more into the dark room, and then closed the door.

Janet met me on the second floor.

"Where were you? What happened?" she said, looking at me alarmed.

"Nothing," I repeated, "I thought I saw a light up here..."

"And you got scared because of a light being on?" she said, following behind me.

"Scared? Why would I be scared?"

We reached the garden and I saw everyone looking at me anxiously.

"What happened? Are you okay?"

"Is Adela okay?"

"Nothing happened, just a light on the third floor..." Janet said, cutting off the interrogation.

I saw Marilyn raise an incredulous eyebrow, but before she could reply, I clarified:

"I'm terrified that it could start a fire, short circuits are common in old houses..."

Juan observed me with his typical scrutinising gaze, but he didn't make any comments.

I sat down and poured myself a drink, I noticed that my hand was trembling. I think Lucas noticed too because he took the bottle and finished pouring.

We started talking again, and I realised that everyone knew something was going on. On the other hand, obviously, none of them could even imagine what I had actually seen.

Marilyn and Juan left with Janet, around eleven. But Lucas stayed with me and helped me bring the dishes inside.

"Do you want me to make coffee?" I asked.

So, we stayed chatting in the living room until after midnight. I wasn't working yet, and it seemed like he wasn't in a hurry to leave.

116

In a moment of silence, when I looked up, I noticed that he was watching me.

I smiled, and he asked, "Are you okay?"

"Yes, of course!" I said. "Much better."

"What happened?"

"When?," I asked.

"When you ran towards the house," he clarified.

"Oh! Nothing, just what I said, a light on, I didn't want to forget to turn it off..."

"Come on, Julia, you can fool others but I know you well."

I lowered my gaze and smiled.

"It's a bit difficult... You'll think I'm crazier than I actually am."

He didn't answer and kept looking at me.

"I think... I think Damian's ghost is in this house."

I don't know what he expected to hear, but it was surely far from what I was telling him because his face changed dramatically from that confident and trusting look with which he invited me to tell him my secret, to complete confusion.

But he was a good professional and didn't express what he really thought.

"Why do you think that?" he asked.

"I've seen him. Twice."

He nodded, still looking at me. He was controlling his emotions, and now his face showed absolutely nothing.

"What makes you think it was him? Or that it was a ghost?"

I stood up and replied impatiently, "Come on, Lucas! I'm telling you something I wouldn't talk about with anyone, something I hadn't even dared to put into words until now, so please forget, for a second, your role as a psychologist," I turned and looked at him, "I need you to talk to me as a friend, and if you think I'm completely crazy, tell me. I think that myself, anyway," I added.

He approached me as I leaned on the fireplace.

"I'm sorry," he said and caressed my face. Then he adjusted a strand of hair falling on my forehead and stared into my eyes. "I'm sorry," he repeated and stepped away.

"What do you think?" I asked, sitting next to him. "Do you think it's possible? Do you believe that the spirits of the dead can come back and try to communicate with us?"

"Yes, I do," he said, and I saw that he wasn't lying. "I've always believed it. But you didn't answer my question. Why do you think it was him? Where was he? Did he speak to you?"

"Yes, but... I don't know if it was him, but I assure you there's someone up there," I looked up at the ceiling, "I saw him more than three months ago, before the accident, and I saw him again today."

"And does he look like Damian?"

"Yes... I don't know, maybe not. I haven't been able to see him clearly."

He leaned forward and took my hands in his.

"Are you afraid? Do you want me to stay here tonight?"

I looked at him, grateful.

"I would love that. Yes, I'm afraid. Not that he'll do something bad to me, or else I would run away from here right now, I would never risk Adela. But I'm afraid, and I don't know why."

He approached and held me close to his chest without saying anything.

"Alright, I'll stay the night," he said after a few seconds, pulling away. "You'll see that tomorrow you'll see everything more clearly and feel better."

A while later, we were laughing upstairs, preparing one of the guest rooms.

We had passed by the library, he had turned on the light and had been admiring the impressive collection of books gathered there. He had even sat in the high-backed armchair while we talked.

Then we left, turning off the lights and leaving the door open. Lucas' presence lent me confidence. Ghosts? Nonsense!

After making the bed, I searched for clean towels and checked that the bathroom on the third floor was in good condition.

Then he decided to accompany me to my room, and laughing, I allowed him to do so. It reminded me of our youth when he always behaved like a gentleman, taking care of me, despite Damian's teasing.

"Well, here I leave you, safe and sound," he said with a smile.

"Will you make it to your room safe and sound?"

"I hope so!" He lowered his voice and added, "I hope your ghost doesn't try to seek revenge."

"Revenge? What have you done to him?"

"He might be jealous."

Laughing, I looked at him, and what I saw in his eyes made me lower my head, confused.

I don't know if he sensed my confusion.

"Go to sleep, it's late," he said, winking, and walked away down the corridor.

XVI

I closed the door and approached the bed. Eight years had passed, and evidently, both of us had changed. We were no longer those friends, little more than teenagers, who believed they had their whole lives ahead of them. Tragedy had touched us, the truth of it confronting us in a way that was almost too cruel to bear.

When Damian disappeared, two days after my birthday, Lucas was the first to realise that something serious was happening. He came to my apartment very early, just as dawn was breaking, and when I opened the door and saw his face, I knew that something had happened to Damian.

"Is he here with you?" he asked.

I shook my head.

"He didn't come home last night," he said.

I closed the door and approached him.

"He must be at a friend's house..."

"What friend, Julia?"

We both knew that Damian didn't have any other friends, at least not someone as close as to spend the night at their house.

"Do you think something happened to him?"

He looked up and stared at me.

"His climbing boots are not there, nor his backpack with the ropes, and..."

"No," I said, "he would never leave without telling me."

All the fears intensified.

And we started looking for him: among his classmates, with his family, at the hospitals, until we finally turned to the police.

We held a vigil for five days and five nights of hope and despair.

I no longer remember the justifications that went through my mind trying to understand his departure and his silence, but never, not even once, did I imagine him dead. Injured, perhaps, but dead... never.

However, on the fifth day, a brief call from the police informed us that they had found his body.

I remember we were together in his apartment, and it was Lucas who answered the call. He repeated the message like a machine, without any emotion: "They found his body."

And I looked at him and stupidly asked, "Is he injured?"

He just looked at me and with a pained expression, repeated, "They found his body, he fell from Monte Negro."

And even though my heart wanted to continue denying it, my mind understood, and at that moment, my world completely fell apart.

It wasn't until after the funeral, when I was alone in my room, that the questions came, the ones that I hadn't been able to formulate until that moment: "Why did he go alone? What led him to commit the madness of undertaking that climb without a supporting partner? Was it an unfortunate fall or was it...?"

This last question haunted me, the doubt of knowing if he had decided to go alone because he wanted to end his life tormented me. And if that was the case... then why? How did I not realise that something was wrong, that something was troubling him? Why didn't he dare to talk to me, to tell me what was happening to him? Didn't he love me enough to stay with me?

Lucas disappeared a week after the funeral, and I was completely alone. Darkness enveloped me so deeply that I couldn't continue with my life. I abandoned everything, my studies, my friends...

The days turned into weeks, increasingly dark and empty. I stayed locked in my apartment for months until Lucía rescued me. She took me to live with her and accepted such a heavy burden and so early in her newly married life.

My attitude didn't change despite agreeing to live with them; I simply couldn't, no matter how much I wanted to show my gratitude and tried to get up and get out of bed every morning, I simply couldn't.

Until one day, as I left my room to go to the bathroom, I heard Lucía crying in her room.

Without thinking, I entered. She was sitting by the window, looking at something she had in her hands.

She looked at me, surprised.

"What's wrong?" I asked, squatting down beside her.

She shook her head.

"Nothing, I'm just a little tired."

"Tired? And that makes you cry?"

I watched as she closed her hands to hide the object from my view.

"It's been a long week," she said and stood up.

She walked to the closet and carefully placed what she was holding inside.

"Tell me what's wrong, Lucía. I haven't seen you cry in years, except maybe for a few soppy movies," I added, smiling.

She grimaced and lowered her head. Her shoulders trembled with another sob.

I approached to hug her, and that's when I saw what she was hiding in the drawer.

Carefully folded, I saw several pink garments: little shirts, socks, and even a tiny dress.

"Are you...?" I began to say.

"Not anymore," she replied, hugging me, and crying.

At that moment, I realised how selfish I had been, focusing all my thoughts on myself. Without caring about anything other than my pain, I had abandoned my sister.

That same week, I started therapy with the person who would become my best friend: Juan. He helped me understand that the only way to move forward was to stop tormenting myself with questions that had no answers. Only one thing was clear: Damian was gone and would never return.

No, he wouldn't even come back to tell me about the "beyond."

I sighed, amazed at how vivid these memories still were. I remembered insignificant details, I remembered feelings and sensations, and of course, I remembered the pain. And that was what I feared the most; I didn't think I could bear that pain once again.

I turned off the lamp and wrapped myself in the blankets; the night was cool. I closed my eyes and tried not to think about Damian anymore; I needed to sleep; it was almost two in the morning.

The house was silent, outside the wind was whistling softly, with a meandering melody that began to lull me to sleep.

That voice, so familiar to me, seemed to come from the depths of my consciousness:

"Julia..."

I opened my eyes and stared into the darkness.

Weak light of the park lampposts seeped in through the window to illuminate a narrow strip down the middle of the room leaving the rest in shadow.

The faint light, by contrast, made the shadows appear even darker.

I fixed my eyes on the corner where the small sofa was. A long and tormented sigh emanated from the dark corner making my skin crawl. I heard it despite the wind that howled at the window, despite my own accelerated breathing, it seemed to resonate in my ears.

"Why did you forget me, Julia? Why did you stop loving me?" his voice said.

My eyes, transfixed on the darkness, moistened as I sensed his sorrow.

"I didn't forget you; I could never forget you," I whispered.

I sensed the figure separate itself from the surrounding darkness and approach me. The figure engulfed in shadow stopped at the foot of my bed, waiting.

Though I couldn't see his face, I knew it was him. Damian was here, I didn't know why or how nor did I care.

I stood up and walked towards him, feeling the cold floorboards against my feet. I circled the bed, leaving the soft carpet behind.

He extended a hand; I could see its whiteness as it passed into the strip of light. I reached out and intertwined my fingers with his cold, bloodless ones and lifted eyes to his face. He moved forward slightly; enough that the light illuminated his face.

An involuntary scream escaped my mouth and snapped my mind into an awakened state. I sat on the bed and looked toward the sofa; it was in total darkness.

I became aware of footsteps on the stairs which made me turn toward the door in fear, when it opened, I screamed once more. The light turned on, blinding me for a second or two.

"Julia! What happened?"

I looked at Lucas as he entered and sat beside me. It took me a second to remember that he was sleeping upstairs.

"I'm sorry," I said, getting out of bed. "I had a horrible nightmare."

"Where are you going...?"

I walked down the hallway to Adela's room, checked that she was asleep, and then returned to my room.

Lucas was waiting for me at the door; he hadn't followed me but was there.

I smiled at him, grateful to have him close tonight.

"What did you dream about?" he asked, sitting on the bed while I covered myself up to the chin.

I looked at him. Should I tell him? What would he think?

"I dreamt about Damian," I responded, observing his reaction.

But he waited for me to continue.

"His face was disfigured, just like when we saw him at the morgue. I thought that image had been erased from my mind, but it seems it hasn't," and I lowered my gaze.

Without thinking, I approached him and clung to his neck. He held me tightly against his chest, and I hid my tears on his shoulder. The contact was warm, and the gentle perfume he emitted seemed to calm me.

Sighing, I pulled away, but he continued holding me, so our faces were very close.

"Will you be able to fall back asleep, or do you prefer to chat for a while?" he asked, his eyes fixed on mine.

"No, I'll be fine. Go to sleep."

"Are you sure?"

"Absolutely."

Then his eyes lowered to my lips. I felt a strange tremor in my stomach, and I sensed the muscles in his chest tense as he held me closer to his body.

His eyes didn't stray from my lips. His lips parted as if to speak, but instead, he started bringing his mouth closer to mine.

A scream forced us apart, startled.

"Adela," I said, recognizing her cry.

He let go of me, and I stood up. Without looking at him, I hurriedly walked back to the girl's room. She was sleeping, probably dreaming or, like me, having a nightmare.

I carefully covered her and left the room.

Lucas was by my door again.

"I'm sorry," I said.

He raised an eyebrow in question.

"For waking you up..." I clarified.

"It's nothing. Try to sleep."

"I will."

He turned and began walking towards the stairs.

I watched him go, after hearing my scream, he had only put on his pants, and his bare torso displayed defined muscles, just as I had suspected.

"Lucas..."

He turned around.

"I'm glad you're here."

"Me too," he said.

It wasn't easy to fall back asleep.

What I had felt when he hugged me, and then when we were about to kiss, left me bewildered and somewhat worried.

I had never imagined feeling something like that for Lucas. He was my best friend, Damian's best friend. I had never had any other kind of feelings for him, but of course, Damian was between us before.

The next morning, everything returned to normal. We had breakfast together, chatting and laughing, with no traces of the romance from the previous night.

I told myself it was my imagination, that he was just trying to comfort me, and I tried to push those ridiculous ideas out of my head. My denial helped; I wasn't ready to deal with romantic problems at this moment of my life.

Calm reigned on the third floor. No strange noises, no footsteps, no voices. The occupant of the library seemed to have vanished.

That night, we went to bed early. We had spent the whole day organising the house and the gardens, so I was exhausted.

The phone started ringing at midnight, or so I thought, although it was only 10 o'clock.

Surprised that Janet was calling me at that hour, I quickly answered the call.

"Are you asleep?"

"Sort of," I said, rubbing my eyes.

"I'm at the hospital with Juan," I jumped out of bed.

"What happened?" I asked, alarmed.

"I think Marilyn lost the baby. They're going to do an ultrasound now, but..."

I put the call on speaker and while Janet explained what had happened, I started getting dressed.

Then I called Emilia and asked her to come and stay with Adela, and although the poor woman only took a few minutes, it felt like an eternity to me. I ran to the car and drove at a speed not recommended on the forest road.

Although the night was clear, with a bright moon lighting the road, darkness still lurked among the trees.

I quickly wiped away my tears and tried to focus on the road.

I couldn't imagine the pain Juan and Marilyn were feeling at that moment. So many shattered hopes! Their baby was dead, their son, who already had a name, their little Mateo.

Why did death claim those lives? How did the Reaper choose its victims? Why take my siblings and leave behind an abandoned little girl? Why take a baby and leave these devastated parents?

Death surrounded me.

Wherever I went, I always had to face it, as if it were mocking me. It appeared every time I started to feel happy, as if it fed on my joy and the happiness of those I loved.

The first person I saw upon arriving at the hospital was Juan; he was talking to a doctor at the reception desk.

I approached and took hold of his arm, trying not to interrupt their conversation.

The doctor looked at me.

"She's my sister," he said, surprising me.

The man nodded and continued speaking.

"The hardest part will be the delivery; she will have to do all the work."

I understood what he was saying, and my heart sank.

"Isn't a caesarean an option?" Juan asked.

"I don't want to take that risk."

Juan nodded and looked at me.

"That's fine, let's go to her," he said, and we started walking down one of the corridors.

With my head resting on his shoulder, I held onto his arm.

"How is she?" I asked.

He made a face, closing his eyes.

"She'll be fine, she's strong."

Upon entering the room, I saw Janet sitting on the bed. Marilyn lay on several pillows with her eyes closed. I thought she was sleeping, but she opened them and looked at me.

She seemed serene; her eyes weren't red, yet her natural beauty had faded, and she looked pale, with wrinkles I had never seen before, as if worn out.

The bulky eight-month-pregnant belly was discreetly covered by blankets, but that didn't stop all of us from involuntarily focusing our gaze on it.

I approached her; Janet made room for me, and I took her hand in mine.

I didn't know what to say, and even if I had wanted to, I couldn't speak. A lump in my throat prevented any sound from coming out.

All I could do was look into her eyes and cry with her.

"He's gone," she whispered.

The next morning was the delivery, and two days later, we accompanied them to the cemetery where they tearfully said goodbye to their little boy, leaving the tiny coffin covered in dirt and sorrow.

But despite the suffering, even though perhaps for them it was impossible to conceive of a life without that child, despite all that, life continued.

One day, she was able to get out of bed, and one day, he was able to forget the pain for ten straight minutes while attending to a patient, and life went on. Because that's what happens when someone dies, the world stops turning, for an instant, and then moves on.

XVII

With the passage of time, I began to feel more comfortable in the house, and I realised that I no longer saw it as a dark and gloomy place. I was growing fond of it and had started to appreciate its virtues. Living in that secluded place had its charm, without a doubt. I found a peace that was hard to find in the city, and life there with my little one was starting to seem perfect.

Almost five months had passed since we moved, and the good weather, so ephemeral in those latitudes, was beginning to fade. The days were getting shorter and colder, and the nights darker.

I had decided to go back to work since some of my patients still wanted to continue their sessions with me, and many others were waiting for my return. So, I enrolled Adela in a school near my office for her morning classes. I adjusted my schedule to only have patients until noon, and everything was perfectly arranged: when she finished school, I would pick her up, and we would return home together.

Our lives had settled into a routine, and by the time the next winter arrived, a year after the deaths of Lucía and Samuel, peace and happiness had returned to my life.

Lucas still visited us; we used to see each other almost every week. Although everything was fine between us, something had changed. It was a subtle change, as if part of the camaraderie that existed before had disappeared. Sometimes I would sense a little awkwardness from him, as if he didn't feel at ease in my presence. That saddened me; I truly missed that camaraderie and trust. But despite that, he remained my best friend, and now that Lucía was gone, he was the person I trusted the most in the world.

We started going out again with Marilyn and Janet. After what we had been through together, we were closer than ever, and our outings became an important part of my life. I loved chatting and laughing with them, and since I was fortunate to have Emilia and Pedro to take care of Adela, we maintained our tradition of having dinner together once a month. However, I always slept at home. Although Emilia assured me more than once that I could stay at my apartment in the city, to avoid driving late at night, I never wanted to. It wasn't because I felt guilty leaving my little one in their care, as I knew they would take better care of her than me. It was simply that I needed to be close to her, in what was now decidedly my home.

One of those nights, on the way back from dinner at Janet's house, something happened that I could say was the first in a series of events that showed me to what extent humans are unaware of their surroundings.

The night was dark, and winter was already encroaching. As usual, a thick fog covered the road. The highway was practically empty, and as I turned onto the narrow path that led to the mansion, I noticed that the fog was closing in even more, so I

132

slowed down. The road snaked dangerously through the trees of the forest, but I knew it perfectly well, and even though the fog didn't allow me to see more than a few metres ahead, I drove with confidence.

I rounded one of the curves, and as I turned left, I saw a woman standing by the roadside. She seemed to be waiting for something or someone. When I saw her, I was a little startled, but I didn't slow down. As I looked in the rearview mirror, I saw her coming out of the woods and stopping on the road. She turned towards the car, and our gazes met for a split second through the mirror. That brief moment was enough to send chills down my spine as I saw her eyes shining under the hood of her coat. I looked away to focus on the road and make sure I didn't crash into the trees, and before taking the next curve, I glanced at the mirror again. Surrounded by swirling fog that obscured my vision, I managed to make out not one, but three women standing in the middle of the road. Then the trees once again hid them from my sight.

A strange cold seemed to seep into the car accompanied by a wave of terror which engulfed my senses. Despite the poor visibility, I accelerated to reach the safety of my home as quickly as possible.

I didn't bother parking the car in the garage but left it abandoned in front of the house and hurriedly got out. The door was open, as always. I entered and locked it with a double turn of the key and latch.

Emilia was waiting-up for me, awake. She didn't like sleeping outside her house, no matter what time I came home. After greeting me and talking for a few minutes, she took her eternal knitting and headed towards the little house just a few metres away from ours.

When she heard me enter, she spoke from the kitchen.

"I'm here," she said. "Do you want a warm tea?"

I was looking out of the windows toward the trees trying to make sense of real or imagined shapes in the shadows.

133

I took off my coat and went to the kitchen.

"Yes, thank you," I said and sat down in front of her.

She looked up from her work and asked, surprised, "But child, what's the matter with you? You look like you've seen the devil."

I told her what had happened. It certainly wasn't the devil I had seen, but those women didn't seem like angels either.

"I don't know if I should call the police or..."

"The police?" she asked.

"Who else?"

"Why would you call them? What can they do? Being on the road at night is not a crime."

"No, but do you think it's normal for them to be wandering in the woods at this hour?"

She shook her head disapprovingly.

"Nothing is normal these days. They were probably up to no good, but the police won't pay attention to you."

She seemed very calm, unlike me, who was seriously alarmed.

"I'm scared," I said, looking at her. "I don't know if it's my imagination or if there's something sinister about all this."

She put down her knitting and got up from her chair.

"Don't worry, I'll call Pedro and tell him I'm staying here with you tonight."

While making the call, I looked at her tenderly. She was a small, thin woman who could do little to defend us, but her character made her seem so strong and determined that I felt safe by her side.

When I woke up the next day, Emilia was already preparing breakfast. Pedro was also sitting at the kitchen table.

"Hello, Pedro," I greeted. "I'm sorry for depriving you of your wife's company last night. I'm a fool, I know."

He made a gesture to downplay it.

I smiled gratefully.

He got up from the table and leaned against the counter, holding the cup in his hands.

"It's just that all this ghost stuff has me spooked," and when I realised what I had said, I looked up. They were staring at me wearing matching frowns.

"What ghost?" Emilia asked cautiously.

"The ghost they say appears in the forest," I responded casually, trying to correct my mistake. "In this area, there are more than ten ghosts that appear from time to time, did you know?"

Pedro just looked at me over his cup, but it was Emilia who showed her surprise.

"And may I know where you got such nonsense from?"

I started laughing at her expression.

"I've heard that this town holds the Guiness World Record for the highest number of ghosts per square metre."

She made a face before continuing to spread butter on a toast. She handed it to me while responding.

"Well, I've heard of some, but ten? That seems like an exaggeration."

"Have you ever seen any?"

"Not me," she said, looking at Pedro.

"And you, Pedro?"

"Yes," he said. "But it was a long time ago."

I sat up straight in my chair and asked with curiosity, "Where? Here, in the house?"

He shook his head.

"In the church, in the cemetery."

The village church was an old 17th-century building that, as was customary, had a group of graves in the park. Of course, it had been hundreds of years since anyone was buried there.

"Tell me," I said, interested.

"What do you want me to tell you?" he asked, somewhat shyly.

"I don't know, What was it like? Where did you see it?"

He walked over to the sink and started washing his cup.

"I don't remember anymore. It was over fifty years ago."

"But you do remember," Emilia interjected. And since he didn't seem willing to talk about it, she began the story.

"He must have been around twelve, right, Pedro? At that time, kids did silly things like spending the night in the cemetery to show their bravery. Silly things, as I say, but now they do a lot worse."

She paused and got up to put the butter back in the fridge.

"He had snuck out of his house and met his cousins and a friend at the cemetery gate. Lucio, who died last year, right, Pedro?" He nodded. "They waited, but since nothing happened, they fell asleep."

As Emilia paused, I looked at Pedro, our eyes met, and he raised his eyebrows with a resigned expression.

"Then he woke up, because of a noise or something, right, Pedro?"

"Because of the sound of a door," he clarified.

"A door? In the cemetery?"

"Ah, now I remember. Someone was coming out of the chapel. A woman."

And Emilia looked at me, trying to inject some drama into her story.

"The ghost of a woman or just a woman?"

"The woman in red," Emilia explained.

I waited for clarification.

"Didn't you say you read about ten ghosts in your book? Didn't the woman in red appear?"

"I don't know," I confessed. "I didn't finish reading the whole article..."

She looked at me with annoyance.

"Well, she's the only true ghost, seen by someone I trust. The others are pure inventions."

"What happened next, Pedro?" I asked, looking at him.

"Nothing, she walked among the graves and left."

I sighed, disappointed.

"And how do you know it was a ghost? It could have been a woman just walking around..."

"What would a woman dressed like that be doing at that hour in the cemetery?" Emilia interrupted me.

And Pedro started to speak.

"You can think whatever you want, but I know what I saw."

"No, Pedro, I believe you, it's just that..."

"I'm telling you, Miss Julia, that I always cursed the idea of going there, it wasn't a good thing. But we were foolish kids. What's done is done."

I looked at him for a moment; he seemed embarrassed to show his feelings, and I was amazed to see that what he wanted to hide was the fear he had felt.

"What was she like?"

"Why are you asking?"

"I don't know, curiosity... Was she very terrifying?"

He shook his head and looked away towards the window.

"On the contrary... I have never seen a more beautiful woman."

The day passed calmly.

The dawn had brought with it a cold rain which continued that way until evening. Adela insisted on going to play in the forest, but I convinced her otherwise by organising games inside the house. I improvised a treasure hunt that kept her entertained for almost an hour, and then we read stories, watched movies, and finally baked a chocolate cake together.

Emilia and Pedro left for their house before it got dark, after making sure we would be fine that night.

"Remember, the telephone rings in my room, so even if we're already in bed, if you need anything, call me," she said when saying goodbye.

Of course, they didn't use mobile phones, besides, the coverage there was very poor. I attributed it to the dense forest surrounding the house. It felt like we were in a pit surrounded by hills with tall, dark pine trees.

During the day, I had occasionally thought about those women again, but little by little, fear had given way to reason, and I realised that it was stupid to be afraid. They were probably just some teenagers in costumes or maybe not even in costumes. They could easily be a group of girls fooling around in the forest that night. I smiled at the thought of how happy they would be if they knew they had managed to scare me.

After putting Adela to bed, I decided to watch a movie since it was still early. My mobile phone rang just as I was about to turn on the TV.

"Hello, are you busy?"

It was Lucas, and I was glad to hear him.

"No, I was looking for something to watch..."

"Do you want me to recommend a good movie?" he asked.

I smiled.

"Okay, tell me."

"Open the door and I'll show it to you," he said, so I jumped out of my seat and went to the front door.

Maybe my reception was too enthusiastic; I hugged him, hanging onto his neck, but I didn't care. It was only when I received his embrace that I realised how lonely I had been feeling.

He didn't seem surprised by my displays of affection; he held me in his arms for a moment and then planted a loud kiss on my cheek.

"I missed you so much," I said, taking his hand and dragging him into the living room. "It's been ages since you last visited."

"Really?" he asked, laughing.

He sat next to me in one of the armchairs in front of the TV and grabbed the plate with my cake, starting to devour it.

"It's so delicious!"

"Didn't you have dinner?"

"Yes, but it was early. Do you have more?"

So, he accompanied me to the kitchen, and while we chatted, I served him a big slice.

Then we watched a movie, not the one he wanted, but another one, and we laughed and continued chatting until he looked at his watch and stood up.

"I have to go, it's really late."

"Tomorrow is Sunday, you don't have anything to do."

"And how do you know? I have a thousand things to do."

"Why don't you stay the night so you can see Adela tomorrow?"

He looked at me with a mischievous smile.

"Why are you using Adela as an excuse?" he said.

"Excuse? You know what? Go back to your house, we don't need you here," I said, pushing him towards the door.

When we reached the entrance, he turned and looked at me, still laughing.

"Do you want me to stay?"

"I would love that," I confessed.

"Did something happen?"

I shook my head, with little conviction.

"Tell me," he said. We sat in front of the fireplace; the fire was burning cosily creating the mood for the sharing thoughts and guarded secrets.

"Actually, nothing remarkable has happened, on the contrary, things are getting better all the time. But... I don't know how to explain it without sounding dramatic."

I stopped talking and looked at him. He was waiting, observing me with that gaze that had always made me feel understood, loved, and needed.

"I feel lonely. It's as simple as that, terribly lonely. Despite having Adela, despite sharing my life with someone now, despite being two... I feel desperately lonely," I added with a grimace, "And I don't like it."

"Maybe it's the house, the place is very lonely, maybe it depresses you a bit..."

139

"I don't think it's that. But never mind, it's silly."

He moved closer to me and put his arm around my shoulders.

"You're not alone. You have me."

"I know," I said without looking at him.

"And a bunch of people who love you," he added.

I nodded.

Then he placed his fingers under my chin and forced me to look at him.

"Do you believe me?" he asked.

I couldn't answer; his gaze was so intense, so blue, that I was paralyzed.

I closed my eyes when his lips brushed mine. Just a slight touch, I could feel his warm breath on my mouth.

He slid a hand down my neck to the nape and placed another soft kiss on the corner of my lips. I remained with my eyes closed, waiting. Slowly, as if holding something extremely delicate, he took my face in his hands and pressed his lips against mine. He slightly parted his lips, caressing my mouth, inviting me to follow suit. I was conflicted; part of me felt that this should not be happening with my best friend but part of me didn't want it to stop.

I timidly kissed his lower lip and felt a shuddering sigh make him tremble. He ran his hands down my back and pulled me closer, pressing my body into his, his mouth ravaged mine with ardour.

For a few minutes, I lost awareness of time and space; lost in the intensity of the moment. But then he, like a true gentleman, stepped away from me, sighing. He held my face for a moment between his hands, and planting one last delicious and tender kiss, he said:

"Thanks for the cake."

And looking at me in such a way that I thought would melt me completely, then he stood, and left.

XVIII

I must admit that it was quite difficult for me to fall asleep that night. Besides the surprise of understanding what I was feeling for Lucas, I was consumed by anxiety about what would happen next.

I also worried that he had left without saying anything more than "Thanks for the cake." Although I wasn't the most romantic person, I would have liked to hear something sweet after that incredible kiss. Or was it perhaps that it hadn't meant anything to him? I knew how much relationships had changed in recent years, and how now friends behaved like lovers and lovers like friends, but I wasn't like that. And as far as I was aware, Lucas wasn't either.

The worst thing was not even receiving a phone call the following week. It really started to irritate me and made me think that to him, the kiss had been just a kiss, perhaps given out of pity for seeing me so sad, perhaps out of desire to have me so close, but just a kiss. As I turned it around in my mind my feeling of disappointment gave way to fury.

Proud as I was, I swore to myself that I wouldn't be the one to mention what had happened between us, so I didn't call him and, with considerable effort, I tried to focus on other things to avoid even thinking about him.

The following week passed without any news. One night, after dinner, we stayed in the living room enjoying the warmth of the fire. While I was completing some reports for my patients on the computer, Adela was playing in front of the fire, and without realising it, the hours passed. When I looked at the clock, it was eleven o'clock at night. I closed the laptop quickly.

"Time to sleep, baby," I said, standing up.

But she wasn't on the rug where I had seen her minutes before.

"Adela! Where are you? It's time to sleep. You won't be able to get up tomorrow."

The absolute silence of the house unnerved me.

"Deli!" I called again as I went to the kitchen.

The ground floor was deserted. I tried to remain calm and went upstairs. "She probably fell asleep playing in her room," I thought.

The top floor was wrapped in darkness, and the little girl was nowhere to be found. I kept searching on the third floor, and before checking the last rooms, I realised I was getting hysterical.

I rushed downstairs and called Emilia. A few minutes later, they both joined me in my feverish search of the house.

We checked every room, every corner, even the closets, as I knew that sometimes children tend to hide there and fall asleep. We couldn't find her; and were forced to admit that she was nowhere to be found in the mansion.

Desperate, I called Lucas, and then the girls. By one in the morning, we were all busy searching throughout the house. Lucas and Juan searched the parks with flashlights, although I couldn't believe that she would have ventured out into the gardens at night, but we had to exhaust every possibility.

"You should call the police," Janet suggested, "it's been almost four hours."

I looked at her without responding and realised that I didn't want to do it because that call would mean accepting that she had disappeared.

But I did it, and I felt worse when I heard the officer say that we had to wait twelve hours before they could start a formal search, although he suggested that I call relatives and friends to search on our own.

Enraged, I hung up the phone.

I started to fill with anguish and helplessness, understanding that there wasn't much else I could do.

When dawn broke, we spread our search into the forest, although I didn't believe it was possible for her to be there. But by then, I felt so desperate that anything was better than sitting and waiting.

When twelve hours had passed, two uniformed officers showed up at the house. They asked me a thousand questions as if I were the prime suspect in Adela's disappearance.

Although everyone was visibly annoyed by the interrogation, no one dared to say anything until Lucas replied in a tone that surprised even me: "I think that's enough, officer. Julia has recently suffered a terrible loss; she doesn't deserve to be treated this way. I suggest you start doing something useful, we are losing time."

The policeman looked stunned. His wrinkles became more pronounced, and he squinted his eyes, annoyed. Obviously, he wasn't used to being talked to like that, but Lucas's authoritative tone left no room for further discussion.

"It is essential to know the details before devising a search plan, sir," he said dryly.

"Perfect. Please explain to us what the plan will be," Lucas said.

The man cleared his throat. "A volunteer group is usually assembled on these occasions, in addition to the police and firefighters. We could sweep the area in a few hours, especially the forest and the area beyond the river."

I sighed. "I don't think she went that far," I said. "She's only four years old."

"Children can walk long distances, and the worst part is that they usually do it in a straight line, moving further away each time," the man explained.

I looked at Lucas; he furrowed his brow. "Alright," he said. "Organise everything immediately, please."

And so, the search began that same afternoon. The search party was quite large, about thirty in total, including some of our friends who came to help when they heard the news.

Taking advantage of the few remaining daylight hours, we went out to explore the forest, dressed warmly and wearing wellington boots.

I led the way, showing them places we used to visit with Adela. When we reached the end of one of the paths, the fire chief approached us.

"We should venture further into the forest. She knows this place; she would have known how to come back. Most likely, she has wandered too far and got lost in the dense vegetation," he said.

"She's only four years old," I said, tears filling my eyes.

The man squeezed my arm and took the first step towards the thicket.

The uneven terrain slowed our progress, so after nearly two hours, we had covered only a few hundred metres.

Suddenly, a whistle sounded, and we all stopped to listen.

Two, three more whistles. Someone had found something.

Instead of rushing towards the source of the sound, I remained frozen in place. Feelings and thoughts conspired to keep me from moving forward both physically and mentally in fear of discovering the unthinkable.

Had they found her? Was it her? Was she okay? Or was she...?

Suddenly, I took control of my limbs, and I began to run, stumbling and slipping until I saw the small group gathered around a thick ivy-covered trunk.

Juan was talking to one of the police officers. He turned and saw me. Something in my face made him quickly approach me.

"It's just a doll," he said, showing me the object.

It was a stuffed sheep that had once been white.

"Does it belong to your niece?" a firefighter asked.

I shook my head and squatted down to avoid falling. My head was spinning, and I felt like I couldn't breathe.

Lucas approached, with Victoria, another one of my friends.

"Come, sweetheart, I'll take you home," she said. "There are many people helping, you should rest."

"I'm fine," I said, standing up again. "It was just a dizzy spell."

"You should go with her," Lucas said.

"We can take care of things," added Holmes, the officer in charge. "We'll let you know if we find anything."

I sighed and looked at them. Although their intentions were good, they weren't helping me.

"If it were your daughter, would you go home, officer?" I asked.

He looked at me with a stern face and shook his head.

"Let's continue, then," he said, addressing Juan. Taking the little stuffed animal, he added, "I'll keep this. Given the time it has been in the rain and handled by everyone, I don't think it will be of much use to us."

Juan frowned but didn't respond.

It was the kind of stuffed animal that babies use when they go to sleep, soft and delicate, the kind mothers place next to their pillows.

As the policeman had said, it was dirty, as if it had been lying in the rain for months. However, it wasn't an old toy; you could even see the brand label peeking out from under one of its paws.

Holmes put it in an evidence bag and tucked it into his pocket.

Like a zombie, I followed them as we ventured deeper into the heart of the forest. I looked without seeing and listened without hearing. My body was there, but my soul was searching for Adela's soul to comfort her. My little girl was alone, how scared she must feel! Night was approaching, and I didn't believe I could last another minute without her.

Finally, darkness prevented us from continuing. Although there was still a little light, not enough of it filtered down through the trees to ground level. They gave the signal, and everyone began to retreat.

Even though the searchers walked in groups, no one spoke. Sadness hung over each of the volunteers like a black cloud, and the helplessness and frustration strangled all conversation.

With a heavy heart, I said goodbye to my friends and returned to the house. I asked the guys to go and rest since they had been with me since morning. Janet and Marilyn protested; they wanted to stay and sleep at the house, but I didn't allow it.

Lucas was the last to leave.

"I'm going to take a shower and come back," he said.

I shook my head.

"No, I want you to rest. I'll be fine. I'll take a bath and then go to sleep."

He put his hand on my shoulder.

"I don't want to leave you alone," he began.

I smiled, taking his hand in mine.

"I'll be fine. Thank you for everything you've done. It has been... " I swallowed hard to hold back tears. "It has been a great comfort to have you with me."

After he left, I prepared a hot bath. I tried to relax and push away the distressing thoughts that kept recurring in my mind.

"How many hours after a disappearance does the risk of finding the victim dead begin?" "Don't think that! She's not dead!"

"How long can a four-year-old girl survive outdoors in the middle of winter?" "Enough!"

Before going to bed, I made myself a cup of camomile tea. I needed to sleep, and I knew I wouldn't get any rest not in that state.

I drank it too quickly, turned off the light, and closed my eyes.

The tears that I had repressed all day could no longer be contained, and I poured all my sorrow into the pillow.

I knew that if anything happened to her, I would simply go mad.

As if her life depended on my hopes, I forced myself to imagine her alive, playing in the house, telling me a story, laughing with her dolls.

The exhaustion and tension I had endured were such that I fell asleep almost without even noticing.

I woke up to the sound of noises that I couldn't identify at first. Then I recognized footsteps in the library.

I realised that being alone made me feel more scared than ever. Before, Adela's presence had given me courage in the face of danger, but now...

The footsteps had stopped right above my head, next to the bookshelf on the right.

And then...

"Julia."

I covered my mouth to stifle a scream. I knew I wasn't ready to go upstairs, but for some inexplicable reason I knew I had to.

When I got out of bed, the cold penetrated my bones. I grabbed the sweater I had left on the armchair and opened the door.

I turned on the light and walked to the stairs, quickly ascending, and stopping at the entrance.

Only then did I realise my recklessness. What was I doing there? What power did this thing exert over me that compelled me to enter its domain while I still trembled with fear?

With shaking hands, I opened the door to the library and turned on the light.

The room was empty and silent. I looked around and approached the bookshelf on the right. In one of the corners, something red in colour caught my attention. As I leaned closer, I realised it was one of Adela's hair bands.

As I picked it up I noticed one of the books slightly sticking out. I looked at the title: "The Canterville Ghost" by Oscar Wilde, and instinctively I pushed it to the back of the shelf.

A dry sound, as if a piece of wood was breaking, resonated inside the wall, and slowly the entire bookshelf began to move, revealing a narrow passage.

I took a step back in surprise, then peered into the passage. It was in complete darkness, so I picked up the lamp from the desk and turned it on.

Cobwebs covered the upper corners of the passage, but the central part looked clear. So, it was true, the house had secret passages, and perhaps it was also true that Lucía had explored them with Adela many times. A glimmer of hope made my breath quicken.

I walked a few metres, tilting the lamp to avoid being blinded.

"Adela," my voice trembled, "Deli, are you there?"

The rustic stone walls seemed to move in sync with my steps in the lamplight as I walked along the corridor. The lamp's light only illuminated a few metres ahead, and shadows closed in behind me as I went.

The initial fear had given way to an agonising anxiety. In my mind, almost like a chant, I repeated the same words over and over, "Please, please."

The passage took an unexpected left, before continuing I looked back, searching for the panel through which I had entered. Through the darkness a faint light could be seen far away.

I heard a moan, so soft and distant that I was unsure if it was real or imagined.

"Adela!" I repeated.

And then I heard it clearly this time:

"Julie..."

I advanced with large strides, moving the lamp from side to side.

"Where are you, my love?"

"Julie," I heard it again.

I lifted the lantern, and about five metres away, I could make out a small figure.

Leaving the lamp on the floor, I ran towards her and knelt down.

My heart stopped. In the passage, the wood had given way, forming a hole where my little girl was wedged. She hadn't fallen, but she couldn't move either. I hugged her and let her cry in my arms for a few minutes, while I reached in to touch her legs and see if she was hurt.

Fortunately, the lower boards were intact, so she was almost sitting in the middle of the hole. I grabbed her by the waist and pulled slowly to get her out of the gap.

I stood up with her in my arms.

"Oh, thank heavens, you're okay! You are, aren't you?"

And as I held her against my chest, I started walking toward the exit. When we reached the library, I sat her on my lap and inspected her little legs.

"How did you get in there, my darling? Are you okay? Does anything hurt?"

She shook her head.

"I'm hungry," she said.

I smiled, tears filling my eyes.

"Of course, baby! You haven't eaten since yesterday!"

"I told Simaco that I was hungry, but he didn't have any food."

I looked at her, not understanding.

"Was Simaco with you?"

She nodded.

"The whole time?"

"No, when I fell, I called you, but since you didn't come, he did."

I hugged her, and she rested her head on my chest.

"I'm glad he kept you company," I said with a sigh, "I couldn't hear you."

She moved away and looked into my eyes.

"I know," she said in her high-pitched voice, "that's why he went to find you."

XIX

After giving her a warm bath, I laid her down in my bed. I called Lucas Immediately and told him that I had found Adela.

"Please," I said after answering all his questions, "call the guys and let them know. I want to put her to bed, she looks exhausted."

"I will, don't worry. I'll come by tomorrow."

"Yes, come, she'll be thrilled to see you."

"And what about you?"

I took a moment to respond.

"Me too."

Now it was his turn to take a few seconds before continuing.

"See you tomorrow then. I'll bring dinner."

I didn't want to dwell on him. He had been by my side the past few days, taking care of me and offering his help as the great friend he was. For now, I couldn't think of him in any other way...

I prepared some milk and cookies for both of us and we went to bed. Adela was watching cartoons on the tablet, so I took the opportunity to call the police. I needed to inform them that I had found the little girl.

While waiting for someone to answer my call, I checked the time. It was almost four in the morning, but surely someone would be on duty at the police station.

After what felt like an eternity, someone finally answered. I explained that I had found the girl and that, since it was no longer necessary to continue searching in the woods, they should contact the group of volunteers who had kindly accompanied us the day before.

I noticed that the officer seemed reluctant to end the conversation.

"So, Miss Vivanko, you're saying the girl was hidden... in a corridor?" he asked incredulously.

"No, in a secret passage. The wooden floor broke, and she got trapped there, and even though she was calling for help, we couldn't hear her," I replied, looking at Adela with sadness, thinking about the terrible moments she had spent there all alone.

"A secret passage," he said slowly, as if writing it down. "Like in the movies?"

I sensed his tone was somewhere between ironic and amazed.

"Exactly like that."

There was a pause.

"And how did you realise she was there?"

I hesitated for a moment before answering, searching for the most believable way to explain what had happened.

"I couldn't sleep, so I went to the library and noticed that a book was out of place. When I moved it, the passage opened."

"Ah, I see," he said, as if registering everything I was telling him. "If you want, I can call tomorrow and explain everything better. It's very late now, and I'm exhausted."

"Okay, don't worry. If they need to ask you anything else, they'll get in touch with you. Good night," he replied quickly and hung up the call.

I laid back on the pillows and pulled Adela close to me, hugging her. I kissed her little head while once again expressing my gratitude for having her with me.

Although my eyes were closing, she seemed wide awake and not very interested in sleeping.

"Julie," she asked, looking at me with that face that was impossible to refuse, "can I sleep with you?"

I smiled and continued to give her more kisses.

Of course, I let her stay in my bed, and after a couple more episodes, she finally fell asleep.

I was awakened by knocks on the door. Startled, I sat up in bed and checked the time. It was only eight in the morning, Emilia would still be at her house, and she had a key, so I wondered who was trying to break down the door.

I covered Adela carefully and looked out the window. Although it was still dark, I could see two cars at the entrance: a black sedan and a police car.

Angrily, I looked for something to put on over my pyjamas and went downstairs. Before turning on the light, I could clearly see the face of a man peering through the glass panels flanking the door.

Upon opening the door, I found Officer Holmes, who greeted me with his usual friendliness, and as I looked at the other man, he introduced him.

"This is Inspector Sarabi, in charge of the investigation."

I looked at him indifferently and quickly decided not to like him.

"What investigation?" I asked.

"May we come in?" he said, looking me in the eyes.

I hesitated, but realising I couldn't refuse, I stepped aside.

They followed me into the living room and sat on one of the sofas. I settled into an armchair and hid my bare feet by folding my legs onto the seat.

"What investigation, Inspector?" I repeated, trying not to show my annoyance.

"A child has been missing for several months now, and some of the clues have led me to this forest," he said.

I nodded.

"And how can I help you?"

"I would like to see the girl and also the place where you say you found her."

"Why? I don't understand what Adela has to do with your investigation."

He held my gaze but didn't respond. He reclined in his seat and glanced around the room.

"Nice house," he said. "I understand it belonged to your sister."

"It used to," I said, "she passed away."

Not even a hint of surprise.

"It's yours then."

"No, it's part of Adela's inheritance."

His scrutinising gaze made me uncomfortable.

I looked at Holmes, who observed me in silence. Although the old policeman had shared my anguish for a few hours, it became clear to me that he distrusted me but tried to hide it. The inspector, however, with his James Bond smile, looked at me as if I were a serial killer.

"Unfortunately, Adela is sleeping, and I'm not going to accompany you to see the passageway now. You should have called, and we could have organised this visit better," I stood up. "I'm sorry you came in vain."

Sarabi looked up at me without getting up.

He nodded, feigning surprise.

"Very well," he said, standing up. "Should I bring a court order then?"

154

I looked at Holmes.

"What does this mean? Why do I have to endure this intrusion in my house?"

And I added, imitating his threatening tone.

"Should I call my lawyers then?"

He returned my defiant gaze, his eternal smile curving his lips.

"Perhaps you should," he said.

They both headed towards the door as I gave him a deadly look.

"We'll be in touch," he added before leaving.

The next day, we spent the day receiving friends, and everyone brought gifts for Adela. Although she didn't quite understand what it was all about, being a good sport, she joined in the celebrations and enjoyed the presents.

Around nine o'clock at night, Lucas arrived. She ran into his arms, laughing. It was incredible how much they loved each other and the close bond they had built in just a few months.

We talked for almost an hour and had Chinese food that he had brought. Then, while the little girl played by our side, he wanted to know about the passageway.

"Did you know the house had secret passages? I didn't think those things really existed."

"Me neither," I said, "but I assure you it's there, and obviously Deli had already visited it before. I haven't asked her about what happened that night yet," I added, lowering my voice, "but it seems to me that she and Lucía had explored those corridors together."

He raised his eyebrows in surprise and looked at the girl.

"Do you think she went in there looking for her mother?"

I looked at him sadly. It was an idea I had considered.

"Is it the only passageway?" he asked, changing the subject.

"I don't know, I suppose I'll have to look for the house's blueprints, but it was built in the 1800s..."

I looked at him with a sceptical expression.

"If you really want to find out, I can talk to Jason, do you remember him? He's an architect. I guess with a look at the house, he could tell you if there are more passageways."

"Do you think so?"

We kept talking for a few more minutes, and then he accompanied me to put Adela to bed. She insisted that he tell her a story, and Lucas agreed.

I went downstairs to prepare coffee, and as I waited at the kitchen table, I tried to sort out my feelings for him, which now seemed more confusing and intense than before.

I didn't hear him approach; he simply appeared in the kitchen doorway, startling me.

He smiled and sat across from me.

"What a stubborn little girl, she reminds me of someone..." he began.

I looked at him, raising an eyebrow.

"I can't think who you could be referring to."

He laughed heartily.

He looked at me, and his blue eyes lingered on mine a little longer than I would have liked.

"I'm glad everything is fine," he said, taking my hands. "I'm glad you can smile again."

"Me too."

"And I'm glad to be here, to have come back."

My heart started beating faster, and his warm hands caressed my fingers for a few seconds before letting go.

"It's late, I have to go."

He hesitated for a moment, looking at me as if he wanted to say something else.

Then he stood up and started walking towards the exit. I accompanied him to his car. I felt stupid standing there, not saying anything, I couldn't let the opportunity to speak honestly slip away.

"Why did you kiss me, Lucas?" I asked. He fixed his eyes on mine, and I could sense his confusion. But he always had control of the situation.

"Why do you think?"

I smiled mockingly.

"Oh, have we started the therapy session now?"

He looked at me without responding.

"Are you afraid to tell the truth?" I insisted.

He lowered his gaze to his hands and sighed.

"Yes, maybe that's it."

My heart sank at that moment, I realised how certain I had been about his feelings. I truly believed that he felt something for me; I had placed my hopes on that, and the reason was that I was starting to fall in love too. But it seemed like I had been wrong.

"Alright," I said, genuinely saddened. "You don't have to say anything; maybe it's better this way."

He put his hands in his pants pockets and shrugged slightly.

"That kiss was a mistake, I'm sorry. It shouldn't have happened, and..." he averted his gaze before continuing, "...let's forget it. We have something too beautiful, Julia. I don't want to lose you."

I tried not to show how disappointed I felt.

"Alright, forgotten," I said and smiled. I approached him and kissed his cheek. "Call me tomorrow."

Then I turned and entered the house. I closed the door and leaned against the cold wood. I waited, hoping to hear him leave, but it took several minutes for the car to start. When I finally heard the faint rumble of the engine leaving the park, only then did I allow the tears that flooded my eyes to fall.

Before going to bed, I went to check if Adela was well covered. I opened the door gently and was surprised to find the bed empty. Nervously, I went to my room. "Please, let her be asleep in my bed," I pleaded. But she wasn't.

I started to search the house, looking for her. I checked every room on the ground floor and the upper floor. Then I headed to the library. The lamp was on, but Adela was nowhere to be seen. I quickly went to the corner to open the panel and enter the passage, but at that moment, I heard a noise behind me, a soft scratching on the wooden floor. A shiver ran through me as I turned.

A small hand suddenly appeared from under the desk. I jumped back in alarm, until I noticed the familiar pink blanket she was holding.

"Adela!! What are you doing here?" I exclaimed.

She crawled out on all fours and sat at my feet on the carpet.

"I'm playing," she replied.

"Playing? Weren't you sleeping?"

She shook her head, looking at me intently.

"I couldn't sleep, so I went to your room, but you weren't there..."

I sat down in the armchair in front of the desk.

"I went to say goodbye to Lucas. What were you playing?" I asked.

"I was playing with Simaco."

I settled down and sat her on my lap. Since she didn't seem ready to sleep, I could take the opportunity to find out some things.

"Tell me about Simaco. I want to get to know him better," I said.

She looked at me and smiled.

"I don't think he wants to."

"Why? We can be friends."

She looked at me hesitantly as she adjusted her little blanket on her legs.

"You have known him for a while?" I asked

She nodded enthusiastically.

"Yes, he's daddy's friend."

Perplexed by such a response, I took my time to ask the next question.

"Does he come often to see daddy?" I finally inquired.

"No," she said, nodding her head again, "he lives here."

"Here...? In the house?"

She looked at me and smiled, then lowered her voice and said, "Here, in the library."

She had started playing with my hair, so she straightened it to one side of my head.

"So he lives here," I said, trying to maintain a normal tone. "And does he often play with you?"

"No, he doesn't play. I play while he does other things..."

Curiosity was killing me.

"What things?"

"He likes to read, that's why he lives in the library," she replied with that childlike logic.

"Ah, I see. Is he here now?"

"No, he left."

"Oh, what a pity. I wanted to meet him. Can you ask him to come back so we can chat?"

"He's not going to come back."

"Why?"

"He left when he heard you coming up the stairs."

"Oh..." was all I could say. I waited a few minutes to see if she added anything more.

"Did daddy tell you his name?" I asked, following her habit of talking about her father in the present.

"No, he told me. He... he... introduced himself," she finally blurted out, proud to have remembered the word.

She got off my lap and went to the centre of the room. Then, putting one arm behind her back, she bent forward, making a funny bow.

"He did this and said, 'Miss, my name is Simaco...'" and something else that I don't remember. That's how you introduce yourself."

I looked at her in astonishment. I couldn't believe she was making all that up.

"What is he like?" I asked.

159

"I don't know..."

"I mean, what does he look like?"

"Do you want to see a picture?"

A picture! How could she have a picture of an imaginary friend?

"Do you have a picture?" I said, surprised.

She nodded, smiling, and ran back to the centre of the room. Then she looked at me and pointed a tiny finger at the wall behind me.

I turned around and saw the painting hanging between the two bookshelves. I had seen it before, but I had never paid much attention to it.

Slowly, I stood up and walked backward, looking at the painting.

"Is he... Is he Simaco?" I asked, pointing at the artwork.

"Yes," she simply said.

The man portrayed appeared to be around thirty years old. His face, with pronounced cheekbones and a straight nose, although not beautiful, had something attractive that I couldn't define. A thin moustache framed his upper lip, and a beard covered his chin, giving him a slightly sinister look. His eyes were perhaps the most striking feature of his face: dark and hidden beneath thick eyebrows, they seemed to penetrate everything.

He was sitting, with crossed legs, in a high-backed armchair by the window. To my surprise, I realised it was the same armchair that was right there. I approached the painting to observe the details better. Indeed, it seemed that he had been depicted in that very room.

A small metal plaque embedded in the frame of the painting, right in the centre at the bottom, caught my attention: Sir Michael Stone, October 1834.

I lifted my gaze and fixed my eyes on his.

Fascinated, I read the name again: Sir Michael Stone... Sir Michael... Sir Michael...

Si Maco...

Simaco...

XX

Adela's revelation had left me more than disturbed, with countless unanswered questions: Simaco was Sir Michael Stone. Years ago, Samuel had told me about the man in the painting.

It was obvious that Adela hadn't invented this name and Simaco was her childish attempt to pronounce it. So, was Sir Michael my ghost then?

Was he the one who had awakened me to tell me where Adela was? I knew for certain that without his help, I would never have found her. The girl would have died of hunger and thirst trapped in that hole.

Now I could say that I had confirmation of his presence. Undoubtedly, he had been inhabiting the house for many years, and perhaps even Lucía knew about his existence but had never dared to confess it because of my fearful attitude when I was in her house. She knew that I didn't like to walk through the corridors at night, that the house scared me, and maybe that's why she had never revealed it to me.

Adela had said that Sir Michael visited Samuel, that they were friends. Now I understood why he had downplayed my encounter with the ghost that night.

However, for some reason that I still didn't fully understand, I didn't like him as much as apparently the rest of my family did. He seemed to enjoy tormenting me.

The next day, after putting Adela to bed, I returned to the library. I hoped not to run into him. My intention was to search for information to find out who I was dealing with because the idea of sharing the house with a spectre did not please me at all.

I reached the third floor and turned on the lights in the hallway, then walked decisively towards the library and opened the door. I also turned on those lights and took a look from the threshold, to make sure he wasn't there.

Leaving the door wide open, I entered.

The first thing I did was search the crowded shelves for any notebooks, records, personal diaries, anything that belonged to that era or to him, anywhere I could gather information.

But there was nothing of the sort, only books, an extensive and expensive collection, but nothing else.

Without turning off the lights, I headed to Samuel's study, hoping to find something among his notes.

I didn't know if Samuel kept a diary, and I had never entered his study until now. When he was alive, that was his private place where he spent most of his day, and on his laptop, which he always kept on the desk, he stored all the information about his books, from the preliminary research he conducted before starting to write each novel to the various drafts, cover proofs, and everything related to his works.

But accessing his laptop was impossible. I knew I would never discover the password, and I didn't even want to try.

But perhaps he took notes in an old-fashioned notebook.

With this in mind, I started going through the desk drawers. I found several notebooks, but after taking a glance, I realised they were mainly notes about his books, random ideas, ideas for other works, a little bit of everything, but nothing that mentioned Sir Michael Stone.

Annoyed, I sat in the swivel chair and set it gently in motion and scanned the room as it rotated.

The room was much smaller than the library and had only two tall bookshelves. Samuel kept a collection of suspense novels and another one of horror there, both by one of his favourite authors. I could also see other books, mostly contemporary authors, more or less famous. And, of course, his collection of his own novels, some of them repeated with different covers from numerous editions.

I stood up and approached the bookshelf and took the first book he had written, which, curiously, despite him always saying it was his best, hadn't had that many sales. It was a copy of the first edition, probably one that the publisher had sent him as soon as it was published. I looked at the spine and read the title: "The Man Without a Face." Just as I was about to put it back on the shelf, I saw something at the bottom of the vacant slot. Removing a couple more books, I turned on the flashlight on my mobile phone and illuminated the object. To my surprise, it was a small lever. "Another passage?" I thought. I pressed it, and the bookshelf moved slightly. With both hands, I pulled on it, and before my eyes, a small room, barely one square metre in size, appeared, with some boxes stacked inside. They were filled with folders, old essays, and notes that seemed to be from the time when he attended university. Underneath everything, there was a wooden trunk, it was tightly squeezed into that confined space. I removed the boxes and knelt on the floor, trying to lift the heavy lid of the trunk. After two failed attempts, I realised that a rusty padlock was keeping the lid closed.

Frustrated, I sighed. Where could he have kept the key?

Knowing that it was a question without an answer, I decided not to waste any more time. I went downstairs and went to the kitchen. Emilia had a box with some basic tools that Pedro had prepared for small repairs around the house. I searched the toolbox and returned to the study armed with a hammer.

Without a trace of guilt I closed my eyes and swung the hammer. Either I was very strong, or the lock was very old because it shot off, causing the lid to bounce against the back wall.

The papers stirred as if that trunk had been closed for centuries and the air was entering it for the first time.

I took what seemed to be important documents and, upon reading, discovered that they were birth, marriage, and death certificates. They were not arranged by date, but they belonged to Samuel's ancestors, with the surnames Stone and Warrington appearing on almost all of them.

Suddenly, I recognized one of the names: Michael Oliver Stone. Was it him?

I kept reading: "Born in Coomsby, Cumberland, on May 17, 1805. His parents were Edward Stone and Epiphany Hope Lowell..."

Yes, it was him.

With a strange feeling, I placed the paper next to the others.

There was the man, not the ghost. The one who had once lived in this house, where he had laughed, loved, and cried. The one who had brought happiness to Epiphany and probably many others.

I was about to close the trunk when I saw what looked like a newspaper, just as yellowed as everything else there. It was folded, so I took it and tried to carefully open it to avoid tearing the pages.

It was indeed a copy of the London Chronicle from Friday, November 27, 1835. On the front page, a drawing occupied almost a quarter of the page; it was a man hanging from a ceiling beam with a twisted neck and bulging eyes. Below, standing out in bold print, it read: *"The macabre murderer of Cumberland found hanged."*

Filled with astonishment, I began to read:

"Last Sunday, the murderer, Sir Michael Stone, was found dead in his own mansion."

An anguished moan accompanied my exclamation, and tears filled my eyes without me understanding why.

"A dramatic story that shows that evil dwells not only in the hearts of the indecent brutes of our city but also in the hearts of privileged nobles of the prosperous lands of the north."

"Surrounding the village of Coomsby in the county of Cumbria is one of the most terrifying forests in Great Britain. This place is famous for hosting numerous ghosts, among which Sir Michael Stone's will undoubtedly join. He killed his own four-year-old son before hanging himself from a beam in his own library."

Instinctively, I glanced around, and even though the lights were on, I reached out and also turned on the lamp on the desk.

"The Stones have lived in the region for centuries, being one of the most powerful and respected dynasties in northern England.

But the death of Lady Stone forever changed the fate of this aristocratic family. The servants and tenants claim that the count became a different person after his wife's death, becoming reclusive and distrusting even his own employees.

Just a few days after her death, the nobleman's frenzied screams startled the housekeeper, claiming that someone had stolen his child during the night. Indeed, the little one had disappeared, and despite searching for over two days, they couldn't find him.

When the authorities of the village tried to approach to help in the search, Sir Stone prevented them, driving away the servants and all the neighbours with shouts and insults, and locked himself inside the house.

The old servant claims to have heard him exclaim, amidst cries of pain, that the witches had taken his child, but she suspects that the man, in his madness, had killed him.

This version of events quickly spread through the village, and finally, the outraged villagers decided to enter and capture the murderer, seeking justice with their own hands.

When they reached the doors of the house, demanding that Sir Michael present himself and account for his actions, he didn't respond. They eventually managed to enter, but the mansion appeared to be empty.

They searched in every room until finally, on the upper floor, they found the man hanging from a rope from the ceiling of the library. He had taken his own life days before, and although the body was beginning to decompose, it wasn't that which horrified the men of the village, but the tears still streaming from his eyes."

My own tears prevented me from seeing clearly, but as I wiped them away the room lights flickered and went out, leaving me in darkness.

I quickly stood up and trembling, I turned on my phone to cast a welcome but inadequate light around the room.

Without taking my eyes off the shadows, I folded the newspaper and held it in my other hand as I headed toward the hallway. The lights were still on out there, so I peered down the hall and saw that the library was also illuminated, just as I had left it minutes before.

I tried to reason, "It's just a burned-out bulb." Something normal that happens in any house.

As I walked towards the library all four lights flickered in unison then extinguished.

I stopped, trying to control the panic rising in my chest, and instinctively moved toward the only surviving light. I entered the library and closed the door. I moved over to the desk and turned on that lamp also, as insurance.

Every corner of the room was illuminated, but my fear stubbornly refused to leave.

My eyes, fixed on the door. Yet again I wiped my panic induced tears from my eyes.

Then a voice uttered my name.

"Julia," and all the lights went out.

I screamed as I pressed myself against the wall, searching for him in the darkness.

The sound of my erratic breathing was all I could hear against the backdrop of silence, until a deep, mocking laughter emanated from the direction of the high-backed chair by the window.

"What are you looking for?"

I covered my mouth with my hand, trying to stifle my sobs.

I was unsure if my mind was playing tricks in the dark or if I could see those eyes, his eyes. Burning with dark malevolence, sapping my strength, dissolving my courage.

I tried to control my breathing, but it was impossible. I couldn't even move.

"What do you want to know? Ask me, and I will tell you," he added.

I walked with my back against the wall and tried to open the door. It was locked.

"Who are you?" the question finally escaping my dry mouth..

"You know who I am."

"No, I don't know."

He laughed, with his deep, mocking laughter. Barely a grave murmur that seemed to lurk in the corners of the room.

"But you know who I'm not. I'm not Damian..." and he laughed again.

"Of course, you're not Damian," I whispered," he would never do this to me."

He didn't respond, even though he was not visible to me, I could feel his eyes surveilling my every move.

"What do you want?" My voice was a desperate plea.

I noticed some motion within the shadows, then to my absolute horror, I saw him take a few steps out of the shadows to approach me.

My mouth opened in a scream that never emerged, but stayed trapped inside. My eyes, wide open, looked at him in disbelief.

"This is my house," he said.

He took another step until only a hand's breadth stood between us.

"I haven't decided yet if I'll let you stay, so don't bother me again."

A shiver ran down my spine. His dark eyes were so close that I could perfectly perceive the depth of his gaze.

In awe, I realised that his appearance was as natural as mine.

I couldn't quite imagine what I expected a ghost to look like, but certainly he didn't seem like one: he wasn't translucent, nor did he appear ethereal or floating. He stood firmly on his feet, walking solidly on the ground, and his skin looked dense and real though perhaps somewhat pale. The ghost seemed as tangible as me.

"Did you kill your son...?" I blurted out, surprising myself.

His eyes hesitated, he frowned, and his eyebrows furrowed in anger.

Instinctively, I took a step back and collided with the chair. Trapped there, I watched as his face changed, acquiring an almost transparent texture. It was only a fraction of a second, but in that fleeting moment, I could distinguish the bones of his face and the empty sockets of his eyes.

"Go away," he said.

I decided not to argue and slid behind the desk slowly making my way back to the door. I moved carefully hugging the wall as if attempting to evade a sleeping cobra. To my great relief I found it open and quickly took refuge in the corridor. I looked back at him but he had disappeared.

I reached my room trembling.

I sat on the bed, and in the safety of my room, I burst into tears. My whole body shook with sobs, and I couldn't control the trembling. Finally, little by little, I began to calm down, breathing deeply, trying to regain my composure.

Not only was there a ghost in the house, not only had he spoken to me and terrified me, but he had also threatened to expel me.

As I remembered his malicious laughter, I shuddered again. Yes, without a doubt, he was capable of that and much more.

However, Adela considered him her friend, and so did Samuel.

With trembling hands, I opened the old newspaper again.

I reviewed the last paragraphs and continued:

"The sight had such an impact on the men of the village that they didn't dare touch him. They left him hanging there and, horrified, abandoned the house.

It wasn't until days later that one of the magistrates from the neighbouring town was commissioned to bury the body and search for the child.

Assisted by some locals, he searched the mansion down to its foundations but found nothing. Nevertheless, the investigations are still ongoing."

I tucked myself under the covers and read the news again from beginning to end.

Despite Simaco's unfriendly treatment towards me and despite feeling genuine terror in his presence, I realised that I couldn't believe he had killed his son. I couldn't explain why, but I felt that he hadn't been a bad person when he was alive, let alone a murderer.

Now I understood to whom the remains resting beneath the gazebo in our garden belonged, and I also understood why Samuel had wanted to honour them in that way. Sir Stone had not been a murderer to him either.

I stayed awake for a couple of hours, listening for any noise in the library. The visitor seemed to have vanished, or perhaps he was comfortably seated in his armchair, reading or lost in thought.

And for the first time since I had met him, I wondered what ghosts did during the night besides bothering the living. Did they sleep? No, obviously they didn't... Did they think? Remember? Suffer?

And for the first time, my heart went out to him.

XXI

At night, the forest loses all its beauty. The lush beech trees, intensely green in the daylight, with hundreds of saplings at their feet, reaching up to seize the elusive rays of the sun, transform into twisted bony hands that scratch and harm. The thick, rugged roots turn into cunning snakes that coil and suffocate the unwary, and the moon appears to populate the path with treacherous shadows that only seek to deceive and confuse the imprudent wanderer.

For that reason, no wise man dares to wander there once the sun sets. But these were not men; they were women of cruel intent. They reigned over the night, darkness their domain, and the forest their empire.

The middle of the three, the golden haired one, walked one step ahead of the others marking the way.

She stopped, and the other two followed suit. Directing their gaze toward the house she pointed to: a majestic mansion surrounded by a well-kept garden that merged into the forest.

"Here?" asked the redhead with a hoarse voice.

"Her mother died over a year ago, sister."

The other nodded.

"Then it's time."

They were surprised by the audible sigh of the youngest, which almost sounded like a sob.

A light turned on in one of the rooms on the third floor, and all three turned their heads as if drawn by a magnet.

"It's him," said the blonde.

"I know."

"What do you plan to do?"

"Wait," the one being questioned replied.

"And the woman?"

The blonde smiled.

"She's asleep."

The youngest stepped forward, looking at the house.

"But he's not," she said, "he knows what we're going to do." The sisters exchanged glances. "He hates us, and he won't allow it," the girl added in a sombre tone.

The woman in red turned to her, and for a moment it seemed that the entire forest had conspired to express her anger. A cloud momentarily passed the moon and poured its gloom upon them, a sudden rush of wind whipped the leaves from the trees and the birds took flight in fear.

Then a sudden silence spread upon the forest like a cold blanket over the dry leaves, and all was quiet once again.

"No one can stop it," her eyes seemed ablaze and as red as her attire, "especially not him."

She took two steps and furiously pushed aside a branch that had become entangled in her cloak.

"He's an insignificant being, he has no power over us."

Her voice had become a deep rumble that seemed to shake the earth.

"What concerns me is the woman..."

The blonde raised an eyebrow, and a disdainful smile appeared on her lips.

"She? What could she do? She's not the girl's mother," she retorted, her eyes fixed on the house.

"No, but she loves that girl as if she were her own."

Neither of the other two replied.

However, the brunette turned her eyes toward the house and fixed her gaze on the illuminated window.

She knew the man was watching them, she knew he recognized them, and that his thirst for revenge was the only thing that kept him there.

The other two had turned their backs on the mansion and were walking toward the heart of the forest, so only she saw the movement of the curtains and the slender figure standing behind the glass.

He too, was waiting for the opportune moment.

But he had all the time in the world, while they did not.

XXII

For almost a week, I didn't dare to go back to the library and tried to keep Adela away as well. I wanted Simaco to remain calm, and although I couldn't resign myself to having him installed in the house, I needed time to figure out what to do.

I realised that, although he still scared me, much of the terror that previously clouded my actions had diminished after seeing him. He wasn't a monster; he was just a man... A dead one, yes, but a man, nonetheless.

The annoying Inspector Sarabi had called me twice, insisting on seeing Adela and exploring the passages of the house. I agreed to take the girl to his office for an informal visit, just so she could meet him, but I made it clear that he couldn't ask her any questions about what had happened. He accepted, so one morning when I had to take her to the city for a dental check-up, we stopped by to see him.

The police station where his office was located had nothing to do with the one in Coomsby; it was a large, modern three-story building surrounded by wide flowerbeds with pine trees and flowers. Quite beautiful, to be honest.

As soon as I gave my name, a very young officer escorted us to Sarabi's office. When we entered, he stood up and approached Adela with a big smile.

"Welcome," he said. "Would you like to have some hot chocolate while we chat?"

He looked at me, and the girl let out a loud "Yes" that left me with no choice but to smile.

We sat down, and he picked up the phone to order the hot chocolate.

"A coffee?" he asked, looking at me.

"No, thank you."

Adela watched him from her chair, swinging her little legs.

"Do you know who I am?" the inspector asked her.

"A police officer," the girl replied, "but police officers wear blue clothes."

He smiled again, and I was surprised to see how his face transformed when he removed that smug smile that I had come to hate; he even seemed almost attractive.

"That's true, but some police officers don't wear uniforms. And do you know what police officers do?"

She shook her head, but just then the door opened, and the same officer from before came in with a tray, which he placed on the desk.

Sarabi took a cup and brought it closer to Adela, leaving the other one in front of him. I helped Adela settle near her cup while he commented.

"Police officers take care of people; we're here to protect you and your..." He hesitated for a moment and looked at me. "...your aunt."

The little girl was focused on the hot chocolate and paid little attention to him.

He then shifted his attention to me.

"Will you allow me to visit the passages?" he asked.

I made a gesture with my head, indicating Adela; I didn't want to talk about it in front of her.

"Call me, and we'll arrange an appointment. Why are you so interested in that?" I asked.

"Your house borders the forest."

"Yes, I know."

"And perhaps it has many of these 'special places,'" he added, glancing at the girl out of the corner of his eye.

"And?"

"Maybe one can enter or exit directly into the forest through one of them..."

I looked at him horrified.

"What are you trying to say?"

He raised his hand as if to calm me.

"I'll explain it to you when I come to your house."

However, his comment had left me extremely disturbed because it could have been true. And I was especially concerned that there could be a direct entrance from the forest to my house.

"Adela, do you really like playing in the forest?"

The girl nodded as she drank.

"Do you always go alone?"

"She never goes alone," I clarified, "she's four years old."

The little girl looked at him, finally got off the chair, and approached one of the shelves that was full of books. Something had caught her attention.

"Have you ever seen anyone in the forest?"

Annoyed, I stood up.

"I think that's enough, call me and I'll see if I can help you."

Adela had approached the desk again.

"I once saw Simaco, but he didn't see me."

My eyes widened in astonishment, but I tried to hide it.

"Who is Simaco?" Sarabi quickly asked.

"My friend," she replied.

"An imaginary friend," I whispered.

"Really?" he said, and before he could ask anything else, I gently pushed Adela towards the door.

"Come on, Deli, we have to go home."

And with the inspector's suspicious gaze, I dragged the girl out of the office.

Although I expected him to call me the next day, he didn't.

And as I was trying to restore normalcy and routine back into our lives, I soon forgot about him.

Adela went back to school, and I went back to work. I started to relax and felt encouraged to go out again because I needed it.

So, one Friday, after settling my little girl in the film room with a bowl of popcorn, I said goodbye to Emilia and left.

The country road was empty as always, despite the approaching weekend. I drove quickly, only slowing down in the tight curves, as the darkness of the forest seemed to envelop me. The fog did its part too, entangling itself in the lower bushes and among the thick trunks, forming a thick blanket on the right and left.

Something crossed the road, perhaps a small animal seeking shelter, which forced me to brake. Then other small shapes darted across the road in front of my car at high speed. I looked curiously at what appeared to be squirrels followed by hedgehogs or something similar, and instinctively turned my gaze to the right, from where the animals came.

A flock of crows, owls, and who knows what else flew over my head, emitting a deafening cacophony of screeches.

It took me only a second to react. I shifted into first gear and spun around, accelerating to return home without looking back. If there was something in the forest, and I was sure there was, I wasn't about to leave my child alone.

I entered the house and, after locking the door, approached the window. Everything seemed calm, and I could even say that the night had a certain beauty with the fog spreading over the grass and gently edging its way between the trees.

Emilia appeared from the kitchen.

"Julia? Is that you?"

"Yes, it's me," I replied, moving away from the window. "Is Adela still awake?"

"I left her watching a movie five minutes ago. What's wrong?"

I didn't want to scare her; it wouldn't be a good idea to tell her what had happened.

"My stomach hurts a little, I don't know if it's nerves or something I ate."

I grimaced.

"It's because you're under stress," she replied.

She followed me into the living room. Adela was sprawled out on the sofa, peacefully asleep.

Both Emilia and I looked at her. Emilia had a smile of tenderness, while I felt worried. The elderly woman turned to me.

She knew me well and could tell something was wrong.

"Are you okay?"

"I was just worried about her. I think I'd rather stay here. I'll let Marilyn know," I said.

She sighed.

"The girl will be fine. Stop worrying and have fun."

I looked at her hesitantly.

"You can ask Pedro to come and keep you company. I don't like you being alone."

"He's here with me. We're playing cards," I smiled.

I sat next to Adela for a while, watching her sleep. Then I picked up my phone and called the police. I informed them about what I had seen in the forest, and I was surprised to hear their response.

"Don't worry, miss. Apparently, a group of teenagers has been causing trouble in the area for the past few weeks. Several neighbours have complained about them causing a disturbance in the vicinity of the forest."

"But the animals seemed to be fleeing from something. Are you sure that it was just kids?"

"Yes, yes, we have confirmed that. They won't bother anyone anymore."

With a few more words, the conversation ended. Although I didn't feel completely at ease, I had to admit there was a possibility they were right. I tried to convince myself that the feeling I had was just exaggerated worry. After Emilia insisted that I return to the city, I kissed the little girl and left.

Marilyn and Juan had invited several friends over. Normally, I didn't like that, but this time I realised that some social interaction would help me take my mind off the tensions. In addition to Joaquín, whom I had seen several times at Juan's house, and Tricia and Angel, Marilyn's paediatrician friends, and Janet, I was surprised to find Lucas there.

I suppose he noticed my surprise because he justified himself by saying, "Juan invited me," as if he had to explain himself.

I didn't want explanations, nor did I have the right to ask for them, but the truth was that his presence felt intrusive, even if it sounded ridiculous.

As I sat down, the conversation resumed after my arrival.

"I don't understand how a child can disappear like that, without a trace," Janet said, looking at me.

"It's a very big city, there are many dangers."

"But the little one didn't leave the house, right, Lucas?"

He shook his head while sipping his drink.

"She hadn't gone out for months," he said curtly.

I observed them, trying to understand what they were talking about.

Marilyn, guessing my thoughts, asked, "Do you know about the missing girl, Julia?"

"No. Here, in the city?"

"In this very neighbourhood," clarified Juan, refilling the glasses.

"Did you know her?" I asked.

"No," Marilyn replied. "Those poor parents."

I noticed the pain that talking about it caused her.

"She only has her father, her mother died over two years ago, from what I've read."

"How terrible!" I said, remembering the desperation we all went through with Adela. "What happened? They say she disappeared from the house. Was she kidnapped?"

"It's not known, she disappeared during the night."

We all fell silent, and a sense of emptiness filled the room.

"She was Lucas' patient," Janet explained, looking at me.

Lucas turned his head towards me.

"Amanda."

I looked at him without understanding, and then I remembered the little girl lying on the couch during a hypnosis session in his office.

"Amanda?!" I exclaimed anxiously. "Has she disappeared?"

He nodded.

"Julia saw one of the videos from a hypnosis session, it was over a year ago," he explained to the others.

I continued to stare at him, dumbfounded. I couldn't believe it.

"Perhaps she's hiding again..." I ventured.

"No, they've searched the house. This time she has really disappeared," he said.

"She talked about several people who had entered the house. Does the police know about that?" I asked.

"Yes, but they haven't found any fingerprints or any evidence that someone actually entered. Exactly the same as the previous time."

"Just like the boy who was found in the woods," Marilyn said thoughtfully.

We all looked at her in silence. She raised her gaze and upon seeing so many eyes fixed on her face, she said uncomfortably, "I'm sorry, it's not a good subject..."

"It's true," Joaquín replied. "The boy from the Medical Board. He appeared without a scratch after over a month of being missing."

"Is he alive?" I ventured hopefully.

Marilyn looked at me with sad eyes and shook her head.

Joaquín, perhaps conscious that he shouldn't have shared that information, added as if his comment could give us hope, "He died without suffering, it seemed like his heart just stopped beating, as if he had fallen asleep..."

Juan stood up and clapped his hands, trying to break the sombre moment.

"Well, let's go to the table. Dinner is ready," he said, with enthusiasm.

Soon, laughter and lively conversation returned, but I was lost in deep thoughts. Perhaps having experienced something similar up close made me remember those dark moments once again.

Even before dessert, I wanted to go home. I stayed a little longer out of respect for my friends, but as soon as I saw the opportunity, I apologised to Marilyn and began saying my goodbyes.

She walked me to the door.

"Are you okay? Did it bother you to see Joaquín?"

"Joaquín? Why would that bother me?"

She smiled as she helped me put on my coat.

"Lucas, then?"

I furrowed my brow.

"You're crazier than ever," I replied, kissing her on the cheek. "I'm just tired, that's all."

She made a face and was about to reply when both of us turned as we heard someone approaching.

It was Lucas, putting on his jacket.

"You're leaving too?" Marilyn asked, somewhat bewildered.

"I'm going to accompany Julia," he said.

"I have my car."

"I know," he said. "I'll follow behind."

I started to protest.

"I don't care what you say, I'm going to follow you all the way to your house."

And without looking at me, he kissed Marilyn and went out onto the street.

She looked at me smiling.

"I don't think you have a choice."

I got into my car and saw that Lucas was already in his with the headlights on.

Despite it seeming like madness, I felt grateful for his company. Suddenly, the idea of crossing the woods alone in the middle of the night filled me with unease.

When I arrived home, I parked, and since he didn't get out, I approached his car.

"Do you want to come in for a coffee?" I offered.

"No, thanks, I'm dead tired," he nodded.

"Alright. Thank you, thank you so much for accompanying me."

He smiled.

"Kiss Adela for me. I'll wait until you go inside."

I touched his hand and headed towards the house.

All the lights were off, except for the one at the entrance that Emilia left on for me, and the one in the kitchen where she and Pedro would be having tea.

However, a soft glow could be seen through the windows of the library. A candle, perhaps? My eyes searched the shadows for him, and finally, there he was, hidden behind the curtains. I thought he was looking at me, but when Lucas's car started moving, I saw that his gaze followed the car's trajectory. Then he lowered his head towards where I was, I observed him for a moment before entering the house.

After saying goodbye to the caretakers and taking a bath, I went to bed with a book, but instantly I realised that it wasn't what I needed. I felt nervous, anxious, and frustrated.

Lucas's indifferent attitude was partly the reason for my unease; things were not right between us. Yes, he had accompanied me home, but he hadn't wanted to come inside, and he never acted like that. Fatigue had been an excuse, and I knew it.

However, seeing Simaco at the window helped me calm down. Knowing that he was in the house somehow reassured me, knowing that Adela was not in danger, an unequivocal sense of security that he would not allow anything bad to happen to her.

I made a cup of chamomile tea with honey and returned to my room. I drank the tea slowly, sitting on the windowsill with the lights off.

The night was clear, a round, yellow moon illuminated the park, and the fog spread here and there with careless brushstrokes.

The last street lamps were located right at the edge of the woods, delineating the park. Their yellow lights barely penetrated the dark wall of trees.

Once again, I wondered why Samuel hadn't put up a fence around the park. I knew the woods belonged to the property, but I didn't understand why he hadn't installed a gate or a fence to protect the house gardens. It was something I should do myself soon; I didn't like the idea of anyone being able to reach the house from the woods.

Swayed by my own thoughts, I was surprised to see a figure emerging from the trees and stopping just a few steps inside the park. It was a woman, wearing a long dark cloak that covered her head and body.

The cup fell from my hands, spilling the remaining tea, and I stood paralyzed, watching that slender silhouette motionless as she observed the house. I took an uncertain step, hiding behind the curtains, and she instantly turned her head toward the window.

I felt my heart pounding wildly and slipped through the shadows to grab my mobile phone, nervously searching for the emergency number.

I returned to the window, and what I saw almost made me scream in terror.

On the edge of the woods, there were now three women.

With trembling hands, I pressed the call button as I stared at them in astonishment.

And then, as if in a choreographed dance, the three pushed back the hoods of their cloaks, revealing long hair, and all three, as if moved by invisible threads, turned their heads toward my window.

The wind stirred their cloaks, and the fog swirled at their feet, and then, slowly, they began to walk toward the house.

A stifled sob escaped my mouth, and for the first time in my life, fear completely paralyzed me. I couldn't move, I couldn't think. The only thing I could do was to watch them as they advanced step by step. And the most terrible thing was that deep inside, I knew there was nothing I could do to stop them.

Then the door opened, and someone passed by me like a whirlwind and closed the curtains, while firmly pushing me away from the window.

Taking two steps back, I looked at the intruder in confusion. For a few seconds, I thought it was Lucas, but then I noticed his carefully trimmed beard and the thin moustache.

"Sir Michael..." I whispered as the room began to rotate about me and I fell heavily onto the bed.

XXIII

I woke up late that morning to the laughter of Adela who was playing in the park. When I woke up I felt my body numb and frozen. I reached for the blankets, and realised that I had slept on them all night. I covered my body precariously with the pillow and closed my eyes again.

My head felt heavy and it hurt terribly, but I could remember everything that had happened the night before, at least everything up to the moment of my blackout.

Because that was what had happened, I had actually passed out and luckily for me I had fallen on the bed.

However, I knew that what I had seen had not been my imagination, Sir Michael had entered my room.

I opened my eyes when I remembered his hands pulling me away from the window...

How was it possible? Was he not dead? How could he have touched me?

I closed my eyes again, exhausted, and turned on my side. Then the memory of the three women looking up at me through the window, not only opened my eyes but made me sit upright on the bed.

Who were they? What would they want?

I stood up and walked to the window. I looked for Adela with my gaze, finally I saw her sitting on the ground next to Pedro who was pulling weeds from a flowerbed. Her red cap moved as she spoke and her little hands looked like restless crimson birds, fluttering around the gardener like a butterfly.

As I watched the girl run from here to there I tried to collect my thoughts. I felt confused as to what to feel towards Sir Michael, until now he had only shown me his dark side, scaring me, using all his powers to make sure that I kept myself in my place; away from the library and from him, however the previous night...

I sighed as I massaged my tired eyes. The night before he had entered my room, I did not know why or how, but he had come to keep me away from danger.

Adela screamed, startling me.

I put on a sweater over my pyjamas and headed for the stairs.

He was undoubtedly a very particular and contradictory man: he had a special bond with a four-year-old girl which decidedly did not extend to me. Although he had left his shelter to protect me, and that showed me that he knew something that I didn't.

I quickly went downstairs and out into the garden.

Adela jumped among the flowers, ignoring Pedro's protests. When she saw me, she came running over. I took her in my arms and she let me shower her with kisses for a few seconds.

"What are you doing out so early?" I asked as she pulled my hand to lead me to the park. "I can't walk on the grass!" I'm barefoot! I said laughing.

"Come" she insisted, " I want to show you something".

She stepped away and I watched her walk into the gazebo. Within a few minutes she came rushing back, I crouched down to see what she had in her hands. At first I thought she had a toy, but to my surprise I saw that it was a golden brooch.

I took it in my hands and looked at it curiously. I had never seen it before, and I knew for sure that it had not belonged to Lucía.

"Where did you find it? "I asked.

"Over there," she said, pointing to the gazebo. "It was on the bench. Can I keep it?"

The little brooch was plain, just a smooth rim and a name engraved in the centre.

"We can take it for safekeeping," I said thoughtfully, "it's very valuable and someone must have lost it."

The girl looked at me for a second.

"Who?" she asked.

"I don't know," I answered.

She, ignoring my pensive look, returned to her game.

I looked at the clasp once more, it was small, the type of clasp that was used in the old days to hang pacifiers from babies' clothes. The chiselled name did not belong to any of our ancestors and was totally unknown to me: Joseph. However, I felt something very deep, as if there was somehow a connection with that little boy.

Adela rushed past me like a bullet, snapping me out of my reverie, went into the house, and I, putting the brooch in my pocket, followed her up the stairs.

When I caught up with her on the second floor, she dodged me again, continuing her run to the top floor.

"Where are you going?"

"To see Simaco," she said, and she disappeared around the turn of the steps.

I followed her slowly, I wasn't sure I wanted to go there, although Adela's company gave me courage, I knew that he would contain his fury in front of her.

Entering the old drawing room, I was surprised to see the curtains open and daylight flooding the room.

I walked over to the armchair and ran my hand over the space that a seated man was supposed to occupy, verifying that he wasn't there.

"Aren't you going to call him?" I asked Adela.

She shook her head as she took the case with her coloured pencils out of the desk drawer, and climbed into the chair.

"If he doesn't come it's because he's busy," she said solemnly, and began to draw.

"Busy?" I thought as I paced the room, "How busy can a ghost be?"

"Tell him that... that I'd like to talk to him," I asked the girl in a whisper.

She looked up from her drawing and looked at me.

"Maybe he's not coming because you're here. Why don't you go downstairs to have a cup of tea with Emilia?" and I felt like I was the little girl. Then she added, going back to her drawings: "He doesn't like visitors".

"I'm not a visitor, I live here," I replied, slightly offended.

I went to the high-backed armchair and sat down, resting my hands on the armrests.

"I'll wait for him, I have nothing to do." Then approaching the bookcase I chose a book and began to read.

It lasted an hour, but Adela had abandoned me after fifteen minutes.

Finally, already annoyed and in a foul mood, I left the library slamming the door.

Obviously he wasn't willing to have any kind of relationship with me, except of course using his adorable personality to terrify me.

But I wasn't going to leave things like that, somehow I had to steel myself and talk to him. And the sooner I did it, the better.

I got dressed and, after making sure that Adela was in Emilia's care, I got into my car.

I drove to town and walked the streets looking for the police office. The one I had been to when Adela had disappeared, it was just an office in the Town Hall building... Which was not really an autonomous Town Hall, but a dependency of the nearby city.

As I entered I was greeted by the grumpy face of the officer who had been in my house with Holmes when Adela disappeared.

"Good morning," she said, looking at me blankly, "how can I help you?"

I approached the counter.

"I want to file a complaint".

"Again?" She asked slightly mockingly.

"Someone broke into my property last night, and I need you to investigate, please," I said, ignoring her annoyed face.

"Do you want to make your statement now?" She asked, looking at me over the top of her round glasses.

I nodded.

She held her gaze for a moment and sighed before she rounded the counter.

"Join me, please".

She ushered me into a small office and invited me to sit down.

"An officer will be here in a few minutes".

The officer appeared about twenty minutes later, as I was about to get up and leave. He sat across from me, desk in between, and started typing on a computer while he asked me questions.

After the first rigorous questions, such as name, address, profession, etc., he began with the real interrogation.

He would ask, almost expressionless in his voice, and I would answer, imitating his monotony:

"What time did you see the intruder?"

"About twelve at night. He was not an intruder, there were three.

"Three?"

I nodded.

"Could you describe them?"

"There were three women, they looked young, they wore dark cloaks, all three dressed alike".

A quick glance as he typed with two fingers on the keyboard.

"Did you see their faces?"

"No, it was very dark".

"Then how do you know they were young?"

"They seemed young, they had long hair, and from the way they walked...

Now it was he who nodded.

"What did they do besides go into the park?" Did they break something?

"No...

"Did they go into the house?"

"No.

"Did they force any doors or windows?"

I shook my head.

"But you say that your property was invaded..."

"They entered the parks of the house, it is a private property".

The man sighed.

"Ma'am, I don't know if you understand that if they haven't forced a door or window, if they haven't broken anything, there's no reason to believe that those women had bad intentions".

"Bad intentions? Of course they had bad intentions! Why would they go into the park, if not?

"What else did they do?" You say they walked to the door, and then?

I looked at him a little embarrassed.

"I don't know... I... fainted."

He raised an inquisitive eyebrow.

"Did you pass out?"

"Yeah, I guess it was fear..."

"Why didn't you call the police immediately?"

I don't know, I tried but...

He kept writing for a few more seconds.

"I suppose they are the same young people from past days gone by, several neighbours have complained about disturbances in the woods, and bottles were found in the cemetery..."

"They told me the same thing yesterday when I called."

He looked up and watched me for a few seconds while he kept typing.

"Okay, I'll give you a copy to read and sign, wait here please."

A moment later he returned with some sheets that he handed me. I read, signed and he gave me a copy. Then he gave a quick salute and turned to walk away.

A little confused, I took a few steps towards him, following him into the hallway.

"Excuse me. When do you think they will start investigating?" He looked at me expressionlessly. "Maybe you can go tomorrow?" I added

"Investigate?"

"Yes, they will look for those women, right?"

"I don't know, I'm just in charge of taking the statements. In any case, I wouldn't worry."

And since it seemed that he was going to continue on his way, I insisted.

"You mean that no one is going to go to my house to look for prints, or do something?"

I saw him looking at the woman behind the counter.

"Surely someone will stop by your house very soon, don't worry," he said again. And with a grimace that wanted to resemble a smile, he finally said goodbye, vanishing in a hurry.

I stood looking at the place where he had been. I then looked at the woman, she immediately lowered her eyes and seemed to be concentrating on her work, so in utter frustration, I left the office, knowing that I had wasted over forty minutes of my time.

I came home furious, and between snorts, I told Emilia everything.

She let me speak with virtually no comment, then said lowering her voice:

"What do you think they were looking for?"

She meant the three women, of course, but I didn't know what to say. Because I really didn't know what they wanted, but the memory of the three of them walking towards the house with the mist at their feet gave me a chill.

"I don't know... what do you think?

She raised her shoulders in a quick gesture.

"I think you shouldn't worry, maybe it's what the police say and it's just about unruly teenagers.

"They didn't really look like teenagers..."

She looked at me for a moment, then looked down.

"Emilia, what do you think?"

"You will say that I am a crazy old woman...

"Tell me," I insisted.

"Maybe they're...ghosts."

I looked at her frowning.

"Ghosts?"

"Well, you asked me..."

And she stood up walking away towards the cupboard.

"But... what do they want?"

"Scare people, that's what ghosts do."

I shook my head.

"What are you missing?" You said that the town was full of ghosts," she added, standing up and putting water on to heat.

"I know, but..."

We look at each other for a second.

Suddenly what Emilia was saying didn't sound so crazy, and, even though it seemed illogical, that reasoning made me feel less afraid of them.

Perhaps in part it was because I knew a ghost, a real ghost, with whom I had talked and argued and fought. A ghost that looked very little like the ones in the books or the movies, that had not only scared me more than once, but had also taken me in her arms to get me out of danger.

"Ghosts..." I said, almost to myself "I hadn't thought of that, maybe you're right.

The cell phone started ringing and I jumped.

"Miss Vivanko?"

"Yes, it's me.

"This is Inspector Sarabi speaking" and since I didn't answer he added, "Do you remember me?"

I sighed.

"Impossible to forget, Inspector," I said sarcastically, "How can I help?"

"Could I stop by your house to walk through the corridors?"

"What an annoying and obsessive man!" I thought. But I realised that since he wouldn't stop insisting, the best thing was to let him come and end everything once and for all.

"Give me a second," I said and covered the phone's microphone.

"Emilia, could you take Adela to your house for a while? The inspector wants to come and see the passage, and I don't want her to see us going in there."

Emilia agreed, so an hour later, I was climbing up to the library with Sarabi to show him the place.

"Who else lives here?" he asked as we walked along the long corridor on the third floor.

"Just Adela and me."

"Does anyone else have access to the house? Caretakers? Gardeners?"

I stopped in front of the library door and turned to look at him.

"I would like to know why you are so interested in the house. What do you expect to find here?" I crossed my arms and raised an eyebrow. "Or do you suspect me?"

Once again, he gave me that smug smile.

"Of course, I suspect you. Everything that happened with your niece was very strange, and besides, a child was found dead in the forest just a few hundred metres from your house. Do you remember the doll they found when they were looking for your niece? It happened to belong to him. And, as if that weren't enough, it turns out that this house may have passages that directly communicate with the forest, so what would you think if you were me?"

I stared at him, unable to believe what I was hearing.

"What do you mean? Are you crazy?"

"No, miss, I'm not crazy, I'm just investigating. That's my job," he looked away and pointed at the door. "Is the passage here?"

I rested my hand on the doorknob while we were talking. I looked at him and withdrew my hand, saying:

"I think it's best if you leave, Inspector. Perhaps you should bring a search warrant next time you come to my house."

"Miss..."

"Please," I said, pointing to the staircase, "I want you to leave."

I saw him purse his lips, and without saying anything more, he began to descend.

When he reached the exit, he turned around.

"You've misunderstood me. I don't think it would be in your best interest to take that attitude."

"And it wouldn't be in your best interest either," I said, opening the door. "Good afternoon."

With clenched jaws, he looked at me one last time and left.

The last thing I needed, after everything we had been through, was to be accused of murder. Was that man crazy?

A child had died, could it be the same child they had talked about at Marilyn's house, the child from the medical board?

I realised that man had managed to unsettle me with his accusations and comments, especially knowing that those women or ghosts were lurking near the house, and that perhaps the house had some access from the forest.

I tried to push those thoughts aside and enjoy some special time with Adela, but it was very difficult for me.

We played in the garden and cooked together. As the evening fell, we played a board game, and after giving her a good bath, I put her to bed. I stayed in my room reading until past midnight. Attentive to any sound from the upper floor, I was surprised not to hear anything at all.

A horrifying thought came to my mind: "What if those women had harmed him?"

I dismissed the idea immediately with a shake of my head. "He's dead, what could they possibly do to him?" But I was surprised to find myself concerned about his well-being. After all, he had tried to defend me, and if he had suffered any harm because of it, the blame was mine.

I left the room quietly and, after confirming that Adela was sleeping in her bed, I went up to the third floor. The door to the library was closed, so I gently lowered the handle and entered. The old oil lamp was lit and rested on the desk, illuminating the room with a warm yellow light.

So, that lamp wasn't just a decoration as I had thought, an old object that Samuel kept as part of the house's antique furniture. Someone was using it, and I wondered who would fill it with oil.

In the elegant armchair, facing away from the windows, sat Sir Michael with a book in his hands. His legs were crossed, and he held the book with one hand while resting his chin on the other.

My first reaction was terror. I remained paralyzed, staring at him. He looked up and locked his eyes with mine. To my surprise, he didn't seem surprised or angry. It was as if he had been expecting me.

He observed me for a moment without moving, then once again lowered his gaze toward the book .

"What do you want?" he said in his icy voice.

"I came this morning to talk to you," I stammered from the doorway.

He looked at me again without saying anything. Then, with mild annoyance, he closed his book and stood up. He walked to the right wall and placed the book on the shelf.

"I know," he finally said.

"I thought..." I couldn't finish the sentence.

He sat back down and looked at me once more, resting his elbows on the armrests and intertwining his fingers.

"The daylight is not for me. I don't usually come here in the mornings," he said.

It was hard for me to concentrate on what he was saying. I couldn't stop looking at his hands, long and slender; his slender body, his deliberate and confident walk. It was difficult to remember that he was dead. For a moment, I even doubted it.

"What are you?" I surprised myself by asking such a stupid question.

A faint smile barely curved his lips.

"I am a dead man. I prefer the night."

I walked slowly towards the desk, never taking my eyes off him, and sat on the chair behind it.

His black eyes didn't waver from me; they were fixed on mine, observing me with coldness.

"Who were those women?" I dared to ask at last.

"I don't know," he said.

"You don't know?"

He slowly shook his head.

"Why did you come to my room last night, then?"

"Because your screams made me fear for Adela."

"But you moved me away from the window..."

"What do you want to know?" He interrupted me.

His question and the tone of annoyance made me fear another outburst of anger.

"I want to know if Adela and I are in danger."

His eyes were inscrutable, but I perceived an unfamiliar fear in his expression that bewildered me. He lowered his gaze to his hands.

"No, they won't enter the house."

"Last night, they seemed very determined to do so..." I said, remembering with a shiver the fear that had paralyzed me.

"I said they won't," he repeated, emphasising each syllable.

I looked at him from my corner and began to speak.

"This is my house, and I must protect Adela."

"This is not your house."

His eyes bore into me. He stood up and approached me, lowering his voice.

"This is not your house."

Unable to look away from his eyes, I stood up and pressed myself against the wall.

"You're right, it's my sister's house. I only live here, but I won't allow anyone else to disturb our peace."

For a moment, his face seemed to show a hint of tenderness, then he looked away and went to the bookshelf. With agonising slowness, he began to rearrange the books that protruded to perfect uniformity on the shelf.

"What peace are you talking about? Do you want me to believe that you are at peace?" He turned to look at me.

I shook my head, looking into his eyes.

"No, I am not at peace. And you? Why are you still here?"

"I am here for the same reason as you: out of obligation," he replied, leaving me perplexed.

"I'm not here out of obligation. I chose to come to this house..."

A deep sound came from his throat, something akin to a bitter laugh. Ignoring my comment, he added:

"You don't need to deceive yourself, Julia. You hate this house, you should leave..."

"You are the one in the wrong place..."

He raised an eyebrow with feigned surprise.

"Where do you think I should be?"

"Where people go when they die... In heaven," I added.

Looking at me sarcastically, he replied:

"So, you believe in heaven..."

I opened my mouth to respond, but then a memory came to me with such vividness that it startled me.

I could almost see Damian standing in front of me, with his beautiful smile and his beautiful eyes looking at me with tenderness: "Nothing will stop me from coming back. I will do whatever it takes to be by your side again."

No, I didn't believe in heaven. I didn't believe there was another life where we could see our loved ones, an "afterlife."

Yet, here he was, someone from that afterlife. A dead man who looked at me with contempt and spoke to me with irony.

"Why did you stay?" I asked.

"I don't know," he said.

Something compelled me to stay silent, perhaps the barely perceptible sigh that accompanied his words, or the sense of defeat emanating from his bowed head.

He looked at me again.

"Go to sleep, it's late."

Turning his back to me, he returned to his armchair and, as if he had already forgotten my presence, began to read.

I didn't want to insist; I decided to give him the privacy he asked for.

I left, closing the door softly, and obediently went to bed.

XXIV

The next morning, I called Lucas. Despite our relationship not being in the best condition, he was still my friend, and at that moment in my life, he was the only person I could talk to about a troubling issue.

Over the phone, I hadn't given him many details, I just told him that I preferred him to come in the evening when Adela would be sleeping.

He arrived around nine, we greeted each other and talked about trivial matters for a few minutes, and it almost seemed like everything was fine between us.

Finally, in a moment of silence, he placed his cup on the table and asked, looking into my eyes, "What's troubling you? I know you're not okay, but I didn't want to press you with questions..."

"I know... Thank you for being patient," I said.

"It's not patience, it's..." he left the sentence unfinished. Our eyes met, and for a moment, I could almost walk into his heart, but then he looked away, closing the door on me.

"We're friends," he concluded.

"I know, that's why I'm talking to you," I hid my legs under my body on the seat and added, "the girls are also my friends... and Juan, but... I don't know if I can talk to them, it's a delicate topic."

He leaned forward, resting his elbows on his knees.

"Well, you know I'm not easily shocked, so go ahead."

I sighed.

"Do you remember when I told you that I believed Damian's ghost was living in the house?" he nodded. "Well, I know now that it's not Damian, I'm sure of that."

"Are you saying there's no ghost in the house?" he asked.

"No, I'm saying that he's not Damian."

Lucas nodded, waiting.

"His name is Sir Michael Stone, he's Samuel's ancestor."

Lucas nodded again, looking at me. I scrutinised his eyes, trying to discover what he was thinking.

"Simaco," I said, and waited.

He raised his eyebrows.

"Yes... What about it?"

"Simaco. Do you remember Adela's imaginary friend, Simaco?"

He furrowed his brow in confusion.

"Sir Michael is Simaco."

He leaned back on the sofa, widening his eyes.

"The ghost is Adela's imaginary friend?"

I nodded.

"She talks to it?"

"Yes, she adores him."

"Have you seen it?"

"Yes."

He observed me closely, and although he tried to hide his feelings, he couldn't. I knew him very well.

"You don't believe me," I said.

"No, it's not that."

"Then what is it? What does that look mean, Lucas?"

He sighed and looked away.

When he started speaking, I realised he was choosing his words carefully.

"I want you to try to see this objectively. Look at it from the outside, at least try."

I nodded.

"Both of you have suffered tremendous loss, the pain you've been through is indescribable. You know that in such cases, it's not uncommon to cling to..."

"...a substitute figure? But this isn't the case, Lucas. Why would we cling to a ghost? What you're saying is ridiculous."

He looked at me, raising his eyebrows.

"What I'm saying is ridiculous?"

I stood up.

"Fine, let's leave it here. Forget what I said."

He stood up from the sofa and approached me.

"It's not a matter of forgetting. You have to try to do something, what's happening is not good for you or Adela."

"Do you think everything I've told you is my imagination? Or do you think I'm going crazy?"

He didn't answer, and perhaps that was the answer.

"I thought you knew me, Lucas," I complained sadly.

"It's this house. You must leave, go back to the city..."

"No, this is our home."

He grabbed me by the shoulders.

"Julia, if there really is a ghost here... Why stay? It's madness..."

I pulled away from his hands.

"I'm not afraid if that's what you mean."

At that moment, I felt more alone than ever, and as I looked at him, it seemed like an abyss opened between us, a rift that broke the ground and kept widening, separating us until we were so far apart that we could barely see each other.

"Go home," I said from my distant end, "it's very late."

The next morning, I received a call from Jason, Lucas' architect friend. Apparently, Lucas had contacted him a few weeks ago to come and review the house plans. Despite being angry with him, I still felt grateful for what he had done.

We agreed to meet the next day, and when I saw him, I immediately remembered him. He hadn't changed much in these eight years.

"Superb construction," was his first comment.

Fascinated by almost everything he saw, I had to help him focus on what I wanted to know.

"Can you find out if there are more passages and if any of them have an exit to the forest or something like that?"

We were in the library, slowly walking through the corridor as he observed every detail.

Later, even though I would have preferred not to stay chatting there, he sat down in the armchair and took a paper that Adela had left on the desk and started drawing.

"Usually, passages connect two rooms. They were usually used as shortcuts, sometimes by the servants and sometimes by the lords," he looked at me, smiling, "to visit a lady's room."

I nodded.

"This one in particular," he said, pointing to the entrance behind the bookshelf, "connects the library with the last room on this floor, which was probably the bedroom of one of the owners of the house."

He was making a small plan as he spoke.

"As you can see, the passage is built along the walls that face the corridor. You can tell where there is one because they are usually wooden walls, partitions."

"Then we should check if there are any on the ground floor. Is it possible that they have an exit to the forest?"

"If they built a passage on the ground floor, it was for the sole purpose of creating an escape route in case of an attack. So, yes, it probably has an exit to the forest."

I felt overwhelmed with anguish.

"But there is a good chance it will be sealed," he said, seeing my expression, "let's go downstairs and find out."

I followed him to the living room, and he started running his hands along the walls, tapping lightly from time to time.

In the living room where the home theatre was set up, he went straight to the fireplace. It was located between two thick columns, slightly protruding outward, semicircular and they seemed to be made of stone.

He touched them, and raising his head towards the ceiling, he said:

"Look at the ceiling."

When I looked up, I saw nothing, but then following the direction of his hand, I noticed some gentle circular marks where the paint was a bit worn out.

"This column moves, there's a passage here. The column is made of wood, not stone."

He began to carefully examine the fireplace and the shelves above it. Suddenly, he touched something that caused the column to move forward, revealing a dark and dusty corridor.

As I approached, I saw that it was completely covered in cobwebs and dust. He extended his hand, pushing aside the delicate threads, and turned back.

"Do you want to come?" he said, inviting me to follow him.

He turned on the flashlight on his mobile phone, and we started walking.

"It seems like we're going down," I said after a few minutes.

"It's likely a tunnel," he responded. "The exit won't be in the house walls, but much farther, in a well-hidden place."

We walked for about five minutes, constantly brushing away the cobwebs that freely extended along the walls and ceiling of the passageway. Spiders of all sizes imaginable quickly fled in our presence, along with some small animals, the species of which I didn't bother to analyse.

Finally, the corridor began to ascend again, and Jason illuminated what seemed to be an iron door, covered in dry leaves and branches.

"There it is," he said.

As we approached, I saw that it was closed. He pulled with force, but then I noticed a padlock with a chain.

"It's locked," I commented, relieved.

"I imagine you don't have the key, do you?" he asked, smiling.

"Well, no."

I approached and tried to remove some of the dirt.

"I'd like to know where we are," and I tried to peek my head through the small gap between the bars.

"Listen," Jason said, putting a finger to his lips. "Is there a river near the house?"

Indeed, it sounded like the sound of water running in a stream.

"There's a small one in the woods. I haven't explored much around there, but I imagine it could be that."

I looked outside again. The darkness of the night made it impossible to guess where we were. Suddenly, I spotted a glow among the trees, about a hundred meters ahead, as if someone had lit a bonfire.

"Look," I said, pointing outside. "Do you see that?"

Jason leaned over, but the light had disappeared.

"I don't see anything," he said.

"It looked like a bonfire or a torch."

"In the woods?" he asked. "I don't think so. It could be the light from a car that made its way through the trees."

"Yeah, maybe," I replied.

I didn't want to insist, but I was almost sure it wasn't a car, and as I turned to follow Jason back to the safety of the living room in my house, I felt happy and grateful for that padlock that protected the iron gate.

Days passed, and nothing came to disturb our peace.

I didn't know if Emilia was right and those women were ghosts or not, but I realised I had nothing to fear. They couldn't harm us, not with Simaco in the house taking care of us.

So gradually, the matter was almost forgotten for me.

Christmas was approaching, and Adela, excited, helped me decorate the house. Lucía kept countless decorations in one of the closets in the guest rooms, but I decided to buy some new ones anyway, and together with Emilia, we adorned every corner so that the joyful spirit of the season could also brighten our hearts.

I had decided to celebrate Christmas with my best friends; it would also be a way to remember Samuel and Lucía. It had been over a year since my sister had passed away, and although the pain had diminished, not a day went by without me missing her.

Since the house was far from the city, I could accommodate our guests for one night, so we cleaned and aired out the rooms on the third floor.

It had been a while since I had been to the library; I had decided to leave Simaco alone, and it seemed like he had decided the same. Perhaps that was the right way to coexist, respecting our spaces.

However, the night before the celebration, I gathered the courage to go talk to him. Knowing that I wouldn't be able to find him during the day, I waited until late at night and made my way to the library. The door was open, but the room seemed empty. I looked for the switch to turn on the light, but then I heard his voice.

"I prefer to be in the dark, please," he said from his corner.

"Alright," I replied without moving from the door. "I'll only be here for a few minutes, I need to tell you something."

He didn't speak or move, so I continued.

"Tomorrow, some friends will come to celebrate Christmas, and we'll stay up late, so some of them will stay overnight."

I waited for him to process my words. As he remained silent, I asked, "Are you there?"

I heard a sigh.

"I'm here."

I didn't know how he had gotten there, but he was beside me, almost close enough to touch. I turned my head, sensing an unfamiliar scent, a strangely pleasant mix of wood, earth, and forest...

I closed my eyes and breathed softly. I felt him move, as if he had come even closer, and something brushed against my cheek.

Surprised, I took a step back and searched for him with my gaze.

He was there, where I had supposed. He looked at me, although the glow coming through the window illuminated his back, leaving his face in shadows.

"Did you touch me?" I asked.

He shook his head.

"Yes," I said. "You touched me. Just like the other night when you pulled me away from the window. How is that possible? You don't have a body, you're..."

I didn't know what to say; I didn't even know what he was: a spirit, what some people call a soul?

"Don't let your guests come here," he said, as if he hadn't heard me. "That would put me in a very bad mood," and he turned his back to me, approaching the window.

His face looked very pale in the moonlight, and his eyes were very dark.

"Did Samuel visit you? Was he... your friend?"

"We used to talk from time to time."

"And Lucía...?" A tightness gripped my chest.

He shook his head.

"No, she never came here."

210

Hesitantly, I asked the question I had asked myself so many times since I had met him.

"Have you seen them? Do you know how they are?"

He turned around, and once again, his face was shrouded in shadows.

"They're not here."

"I know, but..."

"They're gone, Julia."

My eyes began to burn, and I felt such intense frustration that tears started to fall.

"How do you know that? You don't even know if heaven exists. You know nothing. Maybe they're here, taking care of their little one, maybe she stayed close to her daughter too."

Sobs prevented me from speaking, my whole body seemed to tremble with crying.

"She's gone. Adela has you."

"And me? I'm alone, I... I miss her so much..."

He approached a little closer, his fingers rested on my cheek and slowly wiped away my tears, a gentle touch as if it were a warm breath on my face.

Then he stepped back and disappeared into the shadows.

"Michael..."

"You're not alone, I'm here."

And those words, spoken from the darkness by a ghost with a deep voice, comforted me more than anything I had heard since Lucía's death.

When Adela jumped on me, it felt as if I had just fallen asleep, but when I looked at the clock, I realised it was almost nine in the morning.

I wrapped her in the blankets to convince her to sleep a little longer, but it was impossible.

As soon as she could, she ran down the stairs to inspect the presents.

"You can't open them yet!" I shouted from upstairs.

Then, resigned to failure, I went downstairs as well. Emilia greeted me with a cup of hot chocolate, and I went to sit with her and Pedro in the kitchen.

"Are you going to open the presents now?"

"I wanted her to have breakfast first..."

"Let her open just one."

He got up and went to a corner.

"Look, this one isn't on the tree."

He smiled knowingly.

"Is it your gift? You can't stop spoiling her!"

"It was actually Pedro's idea, so don't blame me..."

As if she had heard the conversation, Adela appeared in the kitchen doorway.

"What's that?" she asked.

"It's for you," I said, "a gift from Emilia and Pedro."

She ran to Emilia, who was holding the box, and climbed onto her lap.

"I knew there was something else," she said.

"Something else?! Shameless! You have like twenty gifts, all for you."

She didn't listen to me, she had gotten on her knees on the chair to open the box.

Pedro approached to help her.

"Be careful!" he said.

I smiled tenderly as I saw how he transformed when he spoke to the girl. Especially for them, who had not had children and would never have grandchildren, Adela was undoubtedly someone very special.

The little girl's shout abruptly pulled me out of my thoughts.

"A puppy! Look, Julie, a puppy!" she exclaimed, showing me the small furry bundle she was holding in her arms.

"A puppy!" I said, looking at the little animal with resignation. "Just what we needed!"

But as I saw Adela's joy, I realised that maybe it was exactly what she needed.

As Emilia had said, all the other gifts became completely insignificant. And although she opened them later, they were left abandoned near the wrapping paper as she ran after her new friend.

When it started to get dark, we got dressed and went down to greet our guests.

I had ordered the food and drinks, so all I had to do was enjoy the evening with my friends and have a pleasant night.

Everyone came early, except for Lucas, who arrived when we were already having dinner. He seemed somewhat distant, focusing all his attention on Adela.

Marilyn had noticed his strange behaviour and my discomfort, and after dessert, she approached me.

"What's wrong with Lucas? Are you okay?"

I sighed.

"The truth is, no," I said.

"What happened?" she asked.

I looked at her without knowing what to say, but Juan's arrival saved me from having to invent a lie.

At midnight, I decided it was time to put Adela to bed. I had allowed her to stay with us late to prevent her from waking up too early in the morning. My intention was to get some more sleep.

She said her goodbyes to everyone present, and with tears in her eyes, she went upstairs.

"Come on, don't be stubborn, Deli. It's midnight! Midnight! You've never stayed up so late before."

"I want to stay until everyone goes to sleep," she protested.

"We're almost going to bed," I replied.

She shook her head.

"Liar. You're lying."

I finished putting her pyjamas on, and she crawled into bed.

I was already hugging Demetrio when she sat up again and started pushing the blankets away.

"Where are you going? To the toilet again?" I asked impatiently.

"I have to wish Simaco a Merry Christmas," she said and started running towards the stairs.

"No! Adela, come here!"

Of course, she ignored my order and ran up to the third floor. She hadn't turned on the lights, so when I arrived, she was in the dark library. She had stopped in the middle of the room, looking so small in the huge space.

When my eyes adjusted to the dim light, I saw him squatting next to her.

"...you could come, just this once," Adela said.

"No, you'll come tomorrow to show me your gifts," his voice sounded strangely warm.

Suddenly, the girl hugged him, surprising me almost as much as him. He stood still, unsure of what to do.

Adela let him go and said, "Merry Christmas," and as if justifying her outburst, she added, looking at me, "Is it still Christmas?"

I nodded, he looked at me and stood up.

"Merry Christmas, Julia," he said with a gentle smile.

"Merry Christmas, Michael," I replied.

Adela walked past me and without waiting for me, she went down the stairs.

"Is your party going well?" I asked.

"Yes, everything has been perfect. Too noisy for you?" I asked.

He didn't respond, maintained his half-smile, and looked towards the hallway.

"Adela also likes parties," he said.

I smiled.

"She reminds me of my sister Laura."

I shivered when I heard that. But somehow, Michael's blood ran through Adela's veins, so it wasn't that surprising.

"The noise will end soon," I said to distract him from his sad thoughts. "Just a little more..."

He nodded.

As I looked at his resigned face, I felt guilty.

"I'm sorry for invading your sanctuary. But don't worry, no one will come here."

I had just finished speaking when Lucas appeared at the door with Adela holding his hand.

I jumped as if caught in the middle of mischief and turned my head towards Michael, but surprisingly, he was no longer there.

"What are you doing here?" I asked, looking at him. "Adela, still wandering around?" I added.

I walked towards the door with the intention of going out and closing it.

"I wanted Lucas to meet Simaco. Where is he?"

I smiled nervously.

"Simaco must have gone to sleep, it's very late."

"But you were talking to him..." she started saying.

I looked at Lucas, he turned on the light and entered, stopping next to the armchair.

"It's true!" he asked. "Where is Simaco?"

I looked at him in surprise. His tone sounded mocking. Was he making fun of me?

"We're going to bed right now, little one," I said, lifting her up onto my hip. "I'll be down in a moment," I added, addressing Lucas.

I walked a few steps, and when I realised he wasn't following me, I turned around.

He stood in the doorway of the library peering inside.

"Are you coming?" I asked.

He seemed surprised.

"No, I won't come back down. I'm going to my room," and approaching, he planted a kiss on Adela's cheek. "Goodnight."

He turned his back on me and walked down the long hallway to his room without even touching me.

I started to go downstairs with Adela; in the living room, I could hear the voices of the girls and Juan.

"You shouldn't bring people up here, Deli. Simaco doesn't like to be bothered, you know that," I said, tucking her back into the sheets.

"But Lucas is our friend, maybe he can become friends with Simaco too..."

"I don't think so, honey," I said. "Now promise me you won't get out of bed again."

I lay down next to her to make sure she fell asleep; we had had enough wandering and encounters for one night. Surely Michael would be furious.

I didn't realise I was sleeping until a noise from upstairs startled me.

I opened my eyes and looked at Adela, listening.

"Are you crazy, you son of a...!?"

It was Lucas' voice.

I hurriedly left the room and went upstairs. Indeed, as I approached, I could clearly hear the furious insults coming out of his mouth. They were coming directly from the library.

The scene that unfolded before my eyes left me bewildered.

Lucas, in the middle of the room, was shouting furiously at the shelf to the right, from which a book seemed to have fallen and lay open on the floor.

"What happened..." I began to say, but he interrupted me.

"He threw a book at my head!"

I entered and searched the room with my gaze, but Michael was not there.

"What are you saying?"

"Your ghost..."

"My ghost?" I said, approaching. "So now it does exist?" I asked sarcastically.

He touched his wound and looked at the blood on his hand.

"Did you see it?" I asked.

"I saw the book flying and..."

I looked into his eyes.

"What were you doing here?"

"I couldn't sleep, I wanted to read something," he said, touching his head. "Damn idiot!"

He was lying, I could tell by his evasive gaze, but I couldn't understand why he had gone to the library. I nervously looked towards the corner of the armchair and pushed Lucas to leave the room.

"Come on, let me clean you up, you're bleeding."

I turned off the light, and as I closed the door, I could see the glint of Michael's eyes in the shadows. We started going downstairs, and suddenly Lucas overtook me and, grabbing my arm with some force, something unusual for him, he cornered me against the wall.

"What's happening to you, Julia?" he whispered, barely containing his anger. "Don't you realise it's dangerous?"

He let go of me and paced a few steps in circles.

"God! I can't believe this is real!"

Leaning against the wall in the hallway, I looked at him in dismay.

"He's not dangerous, he's just..."

"Isn't it dangerous? Look at what it just did!" he approached, pointing at his forehead where a trickle of blood ran.

"You shouldn't have gone to the library, it's the only place in the house that should be respected..."

I interrupted myself when I saw his gaze.

"What are you talking about? Have you gone crazy? Respect what? Your ghost? Don't you realise it's the intruder?"

"He's not an intruder, this is his house, he has lived here for centuries."

"Julia, listen to yourself, please. You're talking like a madwoman."

"I know! I know it's insane!" I exclaimed. "But that's my reality now, whether I like it or not."

He looked at me with pity.

"It seems you rather like it."

217

The corridor light turned on, and we both turned around. Juan was walking towards us. In the doorway, I saw Marilyn looking at us, wrapped in her robe.

"What happened?" he whispered, and when he looked at Lucas, he added, "Is that blood?"

"It's nothing," Lucas said, moving away from me. "I hit my head."

Juan frowned, looking at Lucas's forehead.

"You hit yourself? With what?"

"I was going to the bathroom and bumped into a shelf..."

"I heard your screams, I thought there was someone in the house."

"I'm sorry, go back to sleep, it's nothing."

Juan looked at me, his sleepy eyes filled with concern.

"I'll clean his wound, he'll be fine," I said, forcing a smile.

I turned and continued down the stairs.

"Goodnight," I added.

Lucas followed me into the kitchen. I turned on the light and started searching for the first aid kit in one of the cabinets.

"Julia," he said, but I ignored him and kept checking the shelves. I was too angry with him and Michael to calm down.

"Julia," he said, taking me by the shoulders and making me turn around.

His face, a few centimetres from mine, showed me one of his tender smiles.

"I'm sorry."

I looked at him and sighed.

He held me in his arms and said again, over my head, "I'm sorry."

I slowly pulled away.

"Let me take care of you."

He sat down as I moistened a piece of cotton with antiseptic.

"It's nothing," he said. "It's hardly bleeding anymore."

Ignoring his comment, I started cleaning the wound.

We were silent for a few seconds. In my mind, I tried to imagine the reasons why Michael might have acted that way. Did he want to scare Lucas? Or did he just feel invaded in his privacy?

"You have to leave the house, this place is not safe for you and Adela."

Astonished, I paused for a moment in my task.

"Leave the house? No, I'm not going to do that."

"You can't put the child in danger..."

I was covering the wound with a small bandage, suppressing my frustration, and I secured it on his forehead with more force than necessary. Then I took a seat on the other side of the table.

"He's not dangerous, Lucas. What he just did was completely out of character."

I stared at him as I recalled the books flying off the shelves months ago.

"How do you know that? Do you know it that well?"

"Yes," I said, maintaining eye contact.

With a sarcastic grimace, he observed me for a moment.

"He was the one who helped me find Adela," I added.

He furrowed his brow, confused.

"When Adela disappeared, he showed me where she was. If it weren't for him..."

"You didn't tell me that. You said you found the hair tie in the library."

I nodded.

"Yes, but it was because Michael woke me up in the middle of the night and guided me there."

"Michael?"

He looked at me, somewhat uncomfortable.

"His name is Michael."

"Of course," he said, and didn't say anything else.

"Do you want coffee?"

He nodded and watched me thoughtfully as I busied myself in the kitchen.

"Samuel used to visit him in the library, and he adores Adela. They are very good friends. Well, you already know that..."

It was on when I turned to look at him that I realised I was smiling while he could barely contain his anger.

"He would never hurt us," I added.

"Do you trust it that much?" he asked, and in his eyes, I perceived a certain disappointment.

I nodded.

"I hope you're not wrong."

XXV

We woke up late and had breakfast together. I realised that I truly felt happy, with my best friends gathered around the table, enjoying and laughing. Even Lucas seemed to be in a good mood despite the bruise on one side of his forehead.

By nightfall, it was just the two of us again. Well... not entirely alone, Felipe, as she had decided to call her pet, was running around the living room, slipping on the wooden floor and growling at imaginary prey.

As I watched them play, relaxed on the couch, I understood how much my life had changed after the deaths of Lucía and Samuel. From the very beginning, I knew that nothing would ever be the same again, but now, after over a year, I saw that I myself had become a different person. My interests had changed, my way of seeing and facing life, even the things that used to make me happy seemed to lose their importance.

Without knowing why, my thoughts drifted to Michael. Was he now a part of my life too?

What he had done was unacceptable, and I would let him know that very night.

We had prepared a little bed for Felipe in Adela's room, a makeshift one made of a box and a blanket. The next day, we would go buy everything the puppy needed. Adela was thrilled with the idea of preparing a proper place for him in her room, and as long as the animal didn't grow too big, I would allow it.

Once the girl fell asleep, I went up to the library. My indignation had been accumulating, so when I opened the door and saw him calmly reading by candlelight, I felt even more furious.

"Hello, Michael, you look almost civilised, sitting there," I said, entering and closing the door behind me.

"Good evening," he responded without lifting his head.

I took a few steps and noticed that the book he had thrown at Lucas was still on the floor. I picked it up and placed it on the shelf. He didn't even flinch.

"Could you stop reading for a few minutes, please? We need to talk," I said, and seated myself behind the desk.

He ceremoniously closed the book and crossed his legs.

I looked him in the eyes, and he held my gaze without flinching. Although he remained serious, I sensed a hint of amusement that irritated me even more.

"I didn't like what you did, Michael. I thought we had moved past the poltergeist stage."

As he continued to remain silent, I added, "I understand that you were annoyed by him coming in here, but to hurt him..."

He let out a dry laugh.

"And he went crying into your arms, of course."

"He didn't come crying, but I don't understand that outburst of madness. He just wanted to take a book to read before bed."

He raised an eyebrow.

"Did he tell you that I simply threw the book at his head without any prior provocation?"

"Well, he didn't give me any explanations, but..."

"Then you shouldn't judge me so quickly," he argued.

I sighed.

"Fine, tell me what he did."

My condescending tone made him stare at me intensely.

"I don't like being threatened. I've never been a very tolerant person, but that really puts me in a bad mood."

"Did he threaten you? Did Lucas threaten you?"

He squinted his eyes, looking at me.

"You can believe it or not. Now, if you'll excuse me, I'd like to get back to reading."

And with that, he opened his book and fell into it.

I stood up and cautiously approached him. I saw that the book he had in his hands was "The Picture of Dorian Gray."

I sat on the windowsill, just a few metres away from the armchair.

"I don't know what kind of threats Lucas could have made to you, but you have to try to understand him. He cares a lot about Adela and her safety. You're a ghost, let's agree that it's not easy to accept," I said.

"It's not Adela he's worried about," he replied.

I tried to find the answer in his gaze, but his eyes were impenetrable.

"Do you know why he left after Damian's death?" he asked.

"What? What does that have to do with anything?"

"I thought you would have asked yourself that question many times."

I looked at him, confused, waiting for him to continue.

"Did you never realise that Lucas was in love with you?"

"What? No..."

He put the book on the desk.

"Well, you must have been the only one."

"What do you mean?"

"Damian found out shortly before he died, exactly on your birthday. Ask Lucas what gift Damian had bought for you. Maybe then you can understand."

Memories of those days overlapped in a jumbled mess.

I didn't want to stay there, I didn't want to keep talking about it with him.

I walked to the door.

"And make him understand that this is my house, and he's not welcome here."

Without turning to look at him, I left the library .

I walked to my room and sat on the bed without even turning on the light.

Disturbed by his words and everything he had insinuated, I took a deep breath, trying to calm myself.

I replayed that night in my mind, the night I turned twenty.

It should have been one of the happiest days, but it turned out to be unforgettable for the wrong reasons, due to the events that passed just 48 hours later which made it the absolute worst time of my life.

I had wanted to gather some of my friends, we weren't many, as there wasn't enough space in my tiny apartment, but the important ones were there, a handful of university colleagues, and of course, Lucas and Damian.

They both arrived late, I could remember that now, and Damian had been quiet, absent-minded throughout the evening. Lucas had left early, almost without saying goodbye.

When we were alone while I picked up the glasses and tried to tidy up the chaos, Damian sat on the couch, looking at me.

When I finally sat next to him and offered him coffee, he absentmindedly took it while listening to me talk. I remember he was lost in his own thoughts, not paying much attention to what I was saying.

"Why did Lucas leave so early? Do you know?" I asked.

He shook his head as he placed the cup on the table.

"We barely talked, I don't think he even congratulated me on my birthday," I added.

He looked at me without responding.

"Are you okay? You've been so quiet."

He smiled.

"But I did congratulate you on your birthday. In fact, I plan to do it again," and he leaned in, almost touching my lips, "Happy birthday," he whispered.

After kissing me, he stood up and went to the kitchen. He returned with two glasses.

"No, no, no more drinking..." I started to say.

"I want to toast to us," he said, sitting back down.

I took the glass he offered me.

"I didn't bring you a gift because..." he hesitated, "I had bought one, but I'm not going to give it to you just yet."

"What? Why? Show me, I want to see it."

"No, I don't have it here," he said, looking at me sadly, "I need to know something first."

Surprised by the seriousness of his tone, I straightened up in my seat.

"What's going on? Is something wrong with Lucas?" I asked, connecting the dots.

He looked directly into my eyes for a few seconds.

"Did you ever have something with him?"

"With who?"

He continued to silently stare at me.

"With Lucas?" I asked, astonished. "Why are you asking me that?"

"Just answer me, Julia. And please, tell me the truth."

I furrowed my brow, feeling upset, almost offended.

Lucas was his best friend, and my friend too. We had been inseparable for the past three years.

"Is this a joke? Are you really asking me that?"

He kept looking at me with that mix of sadness and hope that was so moving.

"You know I would never do something like that to you..." I clarified.

He approached and hugged me. I noticed he was taking deep breaths while holding me close to his chest. His heart was beating fast, eagerly.

I pulled away and looked into his eyes again.

"Aren't you going to tell me what happened?"

He shook his head.

"There's nothing to say. I just wanted to know."

"Come on, I know you well. Did you have an argument?"

He stood up and responded with annoyance, turning his back to me.

"It has nothing to do with Lucas, don't involve him in this."

"But..." I started, then he interrupted me.

"It's about us. Can it be just you and me for a moment?"

I was so surprised by his reaction that I didn't want to ask anything else. And, of course, I forgot about the matter.

Not even afterward when everything happened, when he disappeared and later when they found his body, not even in those terrible moments did I think about that conversation again.

The incident had remained tucked away in a corner of my consciousness until now, when Michael had brought it to light with his intriguing question.

"Ask him," he had said. "Maybe then you can understand."

And that's exactly what I was going to do.

XXVI

The next day, I left early for Lucas's apartment. I knew I would find him at home because, like me, he wouldn't have any appointments so close to the Christmas holidays.

His apartment was located downtown, a few streets away from his office. I parked my car in a private parking lot and walked the few metres that separated me from his house. As I rang the doorbell, I realised I was nervous. I hadn't even thought about how I would approach the conversation.

He was clearly surprised to hear my voice through the intercom, and for a moment, I wondered if he was alone. Our old camaraderie had disappeared a while ago, so obviously I wasn't aware of his comings and goings. Anyway, he let me in, and a few seconds later, I was standing next to him in the living room.

His apartment was modest, a clear contrast to the luxurious facilities of his office. The reason was that he himself was simple, and I smiled when I realised that hadn't changed.

I glanced for a moment at the two glasses on the coffee table next to the empty wine bottle. I hadn't been mistaken; someone had visited him the previous night, and maybe they were still there. Suddenly, I felt terribly uncomfortable, barging into his house like that, and I wished to leave quickly, but on the other hand, I needed an answer to the question that had been echoing in my brain since the previous night.

"I'll only be a few minutes," I said, not sitting down. "I don't want to take up too much of your time."

He came back from the kitchen with two cups and offered me one.

"Sit down. I just woke up," he said, standing next to the sofa. I sat down, and he followed suit.

"Do you have appointments today?" he asked while taking a sip.

"No, I came just to see you."

He raised his eyebrows in surprise.

"And since I don't want to distract you from what you were doing, I'll be brief."

"I was sleeping," he clarified.

I nodded.

He looked at me amused. Perhaps it was evident what I was thinking, and that amused him, or maybe he found my discomfort entertaining.

"I wanted to ask you something."

He placed the cup on the table and looked at me.

"On my birthday, Damian told me he had bought me a gift, but he wasn't going to give it to me, not at that moment."

His eyes widened in astonishment.

"Do you know what he bought? He probably told you something..."

He shook his head, still looking at me.

"Why bring that up now?" he asked.

"I've been remembering that night, and I realised that I never found the gift. It's true that I didn't even remember, but... I don't know, I thought maybe you knew something."

"No, nothing," he said. And knowing him as I did, I knew he was lying.

Our eyes met, and he quickly averted his gaze.

"Give me five minutes to get dressed, and I'll invite you for a proper breakfast."

And without giving me time to respond, he headed towards his room.

I stood up and sighed in frustration. There was something he didn't want to tell me, and that meant that maybe Michael was right.

He returned, and as he searched for his keys, I approached him.

"Lucas, you've been my best friend for a long time. I trust you more than anyone. Please, tell me the truth."

I noticed him becoming rigid.

"What do you want to know?" he said.

I looked at him, not knowing how to respond.

"More than eight years have passed, Julia. Why dig all that up? Don't you think you've suffered enough already?"

His gaze was sincere, the gaze of a friend who wanted to protect me. Protect me from what?

"What did you talk about on my birthday?" I asked.

"What? How do you expect me to remember that?"

"I know something happened that night."

He walked towards the door.

"Come on, we'll talk at the café."

I didn't move from my spot.

"Please, Lucas."

He sighed, and I saw a hint of sadness in his eyes.

"How is knowing that going to help you? Do you think it will make the pain go away?"

"I don't know, but I need to know."

He looked down, resigned, and ran his hand through his hair, pushing it back. He walked towards the window and began to speak.

"We argued, it was my fault. I said something I shouldn't have."

I waited for him to continue, but he fell silent, staring outside.

"What did you say?"

"Actually, it was what I didn't say."

I approached and stood by his side. My heart broke when I looked at him; his eyes were filled with tears.

"I was his best friend, and he came to share his greatest joy with me. But my selfishness prevented me from sharing in his happiness."

I placed my hand on his arm, he looked at me and smiled.

"You're going to hate me, Julia, because that's what killed him."

"What do you mean? It was an accident..."

"Was it an accident? You always had doubts about that."

"I know, and I blamed myself many times, just like you're doing now..."

He laughed bitterly.

"I've blamed myself for eight years," he said.

"What did he tell you?"

He turned around.

"He showed me the gift he had bought for you."

His gaze pleaded for mercy. Tears streamed from his eyes.

"What was it?"

"A ring. An engagement ring," he added.

I furrowed my brow, confused.

"He was going to propose to you. He was going to ask you to marry him on your birthday."

A kind of joy washed over me, like the distant confirmation of a love that had ended so long ago.

It was something I had never imagined, never even expected.

And then I remembered what he had just said.

"But you said you didn't share in his joy... Why?"

And as I looked into his eyes, I knew it. Not because of what Michael had told me, not because of what he was telling me now, but because of what I saw in his gaze. And it was so intense that I couldn't look away.

"I tried..." he said, and he moved away to the sofa, sat down, and rested his elbows on his knees, rubbing his eyes. "But he knew me too well, and the disappointment I saw on his face was such that I couldn't keep pretending."

He looked at me again.

"Why didn't you ever tell me anything?"

"Because I felt like garbage... The kind of garbage that falls in love with his friend's girlfriend"

"Lucas..." I began to say.

"What he didn't know was that I had started falling in love with you before, that I almost fell in love with you the first day I saw you..."

I sat down beside him.

"I'm sorry. I'm sorry for asking you this. It doesn't really matter what happened that night anymore. I'm sure Damian didn't commit suicide; it was an accident..."

"You don't know that."

"Yes, I do know," I replied, "now I know. If he wanted to marry me, why would he commit suicide? It doesn't make any sense."

He looked at me sadly.

"I wish I could believe you; you have no idea how much."

As I returned home, a whirlwind of emotions churned inside me.

Surprise at understanding that Michael knew what had happened that night, astonishment at Lucas' declaration of love, and sadness for the guilt he had carried all these years.

What would have happened if Damian hadn't died that day?

What would my life be like now? Would we still be together?

Of course, no one had an answer to those questions, not even Michael, who seemed to know everything.

Perhaps our relationship would have died after a few years, or...

Or maybe he would still be by my side, and a couple of little ones would have come to complete our happiness.

A distressed sigh escaped from my lips, so sad that it seemed to emerge from the depths of my soul. And for a moment, the same weight that had accompanied me for more than eight years tried to pierce my heart, like a parasite that threatened to suck the little joy I had left.

When I arrived, a delightful aroma welcomed me from the kitchen. Emilia was baking an apple pie, and she already had hot water ready for tea. I always enjoyed her care and confections, but that cup of tea comforted me more than ever that afternoon.

"Where's Adela?" I asked as I savoured the infusion.

"She's playing in her room. I went upstairs a while ago, and she had scattered all her toys on the floor."

I smiled and, leaving the cup, I went upstairs to greet her.

The silence on the first floor confirmed that she wasn't there, so following the murmurs coming from upstairs, I went up to the library.

She was in front of the desk, kneeling on the chair, drawing, and chatting animatedly. Felipe slept at her feet. Michael was reading in the armchair.

None of the three paid any attention to me when I entered, which instead of making me feel ignored, made me appreciate the trust they had in me.

I approached Adela and kissed her on the head.

"Are you going to eat apple pie?" I asked.

"Yes!" she shouted and jumped off the seat. "Felipe! Let's go!"

The little animal perked up its ears, surprised, and shaking its head, followed her.

Michael watched them run to the door, then his black eyes turned to me.

His gaze was intimidating, deep, and haughty, with his brow always slightly furrowed, as if implying that he didn't quite like anyone. However, I had learned to distinguish the different nuances, usually very subtle, that helped me understand where I stood.

That afternoon he seemed calm, almost relaxed, and I could even say he was glad to see me.

"Aren't you going to offer me a slice of pie?" he said, closing the book and leaving it on the desk.

I couldn't help but burst into laughter.

"I can bring you tea as well," I said. "With milk?"

"Black, please," he added, and his eyes sparkled with amusement.

I approached to look at the drawings Adela had left on the desk and gathered the pencils and returned them to their case.

"I talked to Lucas," I said, walking towards the window, "you were right."

Since he didn't respond, I turned to look at him. He averted his gaze and stood up.

"Can I ask you how you knew? How did you know Damian was going to propose to me?"

"Unfortunately, I know many things that I shouldn't know."

"What do you mean?"

He approached and looked me in the eyes.

"It's not what you think. I've never seen Damian. I told you he's not here..."

"He left? Yes, but he could come back, like you have..."

"I never left."

"But he could come back, right? If he wanted to..."

He shook his head.

"I haven't seen anyone come back. Maybe that place is so welcoming that no one wants to return to this hell on earth."

His sarcastic tone forced me to look at him.

233

"So, the ones who are here are the ones who decided to stay," I reasoned, and my heart sank.

"You don't choose to stay or leave. It just happens."

He moved away from me, as if ending the conversation, and began to fade into the shadows.

"Why did you stay? Was it because of your son?"

A few seconds of profound silence made me think he had left.

"He died. When you die, time stops, and nothing else matters."

I approached where his voice came from.

"Nothing matters? Don't you care about Adela or..."

I didn't dare to continue, but I imagined he understood.

But he didn't respond. Maybe he was looking at me from the dense gloom, or maybe he had already gone.

"...or me?" I added sadly.

XXVII

This morning I had to go to the city for shopping, Emilia and Adela accompanied me, and I took the opportunity to stop by my apartment and pick up some things. Despite having lived there for over five years, it felt less and less like my home, and slowly it was becoming almost abandoned, with covered furniture and empty closets.

Upon arriving at the mansion, I was astonished to find a car parked at the entrance: a black sedan. Instantly, my good mood vanished. I opened the door, and there he was, comfortably seated in an armchair, engaged in lively conversation with Pedro, who was looking at him in absolute silence. He turned and looked at me with a resigned expression.

"Inspector Sarabi," I said without greeting, "What are you doing here?"

He stood up and gave me a sly look.

"Good morning, Miss Vivanko," he said, taking a paper from his pocket and unfolding it carefully. "Here is what you asked for."

I frowned and approached to take the paper. Emilia glanced at me sideways and, holding Adela's hand, headed to the kitchen, followed by Pedro. I read the first lines.

"Judicial resolution authorizing entry and search of the property belonging to..."

"What is this?" I said, feeling furious. He simply smiled.

"...at the request of Inspector Máximo Sarabi for the purpose of finding objects or evidence that may be useful in clarifying the investigated crime..."

I handed him back the paper and, trying to remain calm, I looked at him.

"As you can see, I could turn your house upside down if I wanted," he said, still smiling, "but that's not my intention."

I sighed and sat down.

"So, what is your intention?"

"I just want you to show me that passage..."

"There is one that leads to the forest," I said, interrupting him, "when you were here, I didn't know about it, I discovered it a few days ago."

For once, his smile had vanished.

"Come this way," I said, getting up from the armchair.

He followed me to the living room and watched as I moved the bolt that opened the passage. The column slid aside, and I could see his astonished face.

We walked in silence until we reached the iron gate. Daylight penetrated through the bars, illuminating part of the dirt floor of the corridor and its damp walls. He passed by me and reached out his hands towards the door.

"It's closed," I said.

Ignoring what I said, he pulled firmly inward, and the gate gave way.

I looked astonished at the iron bars, searching for the padlock, but they had disappeared. I crouched down, searching for the chain on the ground.

"It was closed," I said, and my sigh seemed like a moan. "Oh my God! It was closed!"

"What are you saying?" he said, taking hold of my arm and forcing me to stand up.

"It was closed!" I repeated, tears of terror flooding my eyes. "Who opened it? It had a chain and a padlock!"

He looked around, searching for evidence of what I was telling him.

"A padlock? When did you see it closed?"

"A few days ago... Before Christmas."

I had started to tremble. I suppose that despite our differences, he felt pity for me seeing me in that state.

"Calm down," he said, "let's go back."

"I can't leave this door open!" I shouted. "Someone can enter the house!"

He took hold of my shoulders, forcing me to look at him.

"Listen to me, you need to calm down."

"Calm down!" I repeated, shouting. "You don't understand anything!" He looked at me, confused.

"Don't get hysterical. Maybe some teens were messing around in the forest and removed the padlock," he said.

"Teens? Is that the best the efficient English police can come up with? Mischievous children..." I looked into his eyes. "Do I need to remind you that you found a dead child just a few metres from this house, Lieutenant?"

Without waiting for his response, I turned around and began walking back to the living room. "It wasn't teenagers who killed that child," I whispered.

Pedro took care of securing the door with another chain, but that night, before going to bed, I searched through the bunches of old keys that Emilia kept in a kitchen drawer until I found one that locked the living room door. I knew it wasn't enough, but it was the only thing I could think of.

The next day, Pedro called a contractor who removed the gate and sealed the entrance with bricks. It wasn't until two days later when I went to see the result of the work that I could finally sleep peacefully.

I didn't go near the library for some time. Occasionally, I would hear Adela chattering or Felipe barking up on the third floor. I knew it was one of their favourite places, but I kept my distance. I kept away from Michael because I was afraid of what he might tell me. Some things were better left unsaid and recent confessions had only filled me with sadness.

One night, almost two weeks later, a terrible storm descended on us. Savage thunder heralded the salvo after salvo of torrential rain, while the unforgiving winds threatened to remove the windows from their rattling frames.

After making sure each window was securely closed, I went to bed. But my fear of thunder made it impossible for me to fall asleep. Several times, I got up to check on Adela. Luckily, she slept undisturbed, oblivious to the tempest that seemed to shake the very walls.

Suddenly, just as I had finally managed to doze off, Felipe started barking. Now it was highly likely that Adela would wake up since the little dog still slept in her room. So, once again, I hurried to the girl's room. I searched everywhere for the little animal, but I couldn't find him. The barks sounded somewhat muffled. Perhaps he had hidden in a closet, or maybe he was in another part of the house.

I walked through the rooms on the second floor, and when I reached the one that had belonged to Lucía and Samuel, I heard him again. I looked out the window and despite the wind, I felt sure that the sound was coming from outside. Sure enough, standing in the middle of the park was Felipe, drenched and barking incessantly. It seemed that something at the entrance of the forest had caught his attention. He walked a few steps in that direction, wagging his tail, then stopped and barked.

After observing him for a few seconds, I opened the window and shouted his name. The rain soaked me, and the wind completely took my words away. I closed the window and went downstairs wondering how the dog would have gotten out of the house. Before leaving, I grabbed a raincoat hanging next to the door and put it on, facing the storm. I pulled the hood almost over my eyes and tried to locate Felipe.

Now the little dog was at the entrance to the forest. He barked a couple more times and suddenly jumped and disappeared among the trees. "Felipe!" I shouted. "No, no! Come here!" But he was already gone. Cursing the foolish creature, I gathered my courage and walked decisively toward the grove.

Luckily, I had taken a flashlight as a precaution, so I turned it on and advanced slowly, carefully watching where I stepped. "Felipe!" I called again, but I saw no trace of the dog. I paused trying to decide where I should search. I knew he could have gone in any direction.

I took a few steps, and then I saw something about twenty metres ahead, something moving. My heart skipped a beat, and I became aware that being there in the middle of the night was madness. But on the other hand, I couldn't leave the dog abandoned in the woods during a storm. Surely, he would get lost and wouldn't know how to find his way back home alone.

"Felipe! Come here!" I shouted again. The noise of branches crashing together was terrifying, and the wind howled among the branches, creating eerie melodies. I walked a few more steps, and then I clearly distinguished the silhouette of a person walking along the path ahead. I stopped and aimed the flashlight beam towards the trees, trying to catch a glimpse of who it was.

My heart started beating faster, and my hand trembled, causing the light to dance and making everything around me blur. Holding the flashlight with both hands, forcing myself to keep it steady, I shone it forward again, and then I could see the figure disappearing into the thicket. The broad shoulders left no room for any doubt it was a man.

Likely alerted by the light, he stopped and turned. I couldn't see his face, but I knew he was looking at me. Suddenly gripped by an irrational fear I threw the flashlight to the ground and started running towards the house. The darkness was such that I stumbled once and then again, finally falling face-first into the mud. I scrambled to my feet as best I could, half-crawling, half-running, I finally reached the garden of the house. I walked backward, looking at the trees with fear that at any moment anyone could emerge from the forest and pounce on me.

Gasping for breath, I stopped a few metres ahead. The trees seemed like enraged giants, stretching their gnarled fingers toward the sky or toward me in anger, as if they wanted to pull me into their dark and sinister interior.

Suddenly, Felipe came running, whimpering, with his tail between his legs. He was so frightened that he didn't even stop to look at me; he passed by my side like a bullet, heading straight for the house. I watched him for just a moment and, casting a quick glance towards the forest, I started running after him.

We entered the house, and I locked and bolted the door. Taking Felipe in my arms, I approached the window and looked towards the forest once more. The poor thing was trembling, but I suspect it wasn't from the cold. However, no one came out from among the trees. Whatever had scared us stayed there, hidden, perhaps watching us, or perhaps just waiting.

XXVIII

After removing my muddy pyjamas, still in my underwear I rinsed Felipe under the jet of hot water. I rubbed him down with a towel and put him next to the bathroom radiator to dry.

He shook several times and curled up, making a circle with his body, getting ready to sleep. I took the opportunity to take a hot immersion bath with salts to relax and warm myself up. The cold rain had penetrated me to the bone, and it would be impossible to go back to sleep in that condition.

I kept wondering who that man could have been.

I couldn't believe that a normal person would be in the woods on a night like this and at that time. Except myself, of course, who was looking for a silly dog who had decided to go out and chase squirrels...

When the water began to cool, I lazily left the tub, dried myself, put on some clean pyjamas and, taking Felipe in my arms, went to bed.

I laid the puppy next to me, and while I was caressing him I looked at the shelf in front of me and something caught my eye.

I got out of bed, and turned on the light.

I approached and observed the books that Lucía had kept there: a thick volume of Evolutionary Psychology, some novels that I had left in her house and forgotten about, and Samuel's works. Everything was as she had left it.

I looked for the first volume of The Three Ladies, the trilogy that had brought my brother-in-law to fame. I took the book off the shelf and opened it. On the first page I found the dedication, in Samuel's unintelligible scrawl: "For my favourite sister-in-law." I smiled, caressing the blue ink, and leafing through the book I went back to bed.

I remembered something from the story that I had read more than six years ago: it was set today and the protagonist was a detective who began to work on a murder case.

After many comings and goings and more than three hundred pages, the young policeman discovers that those responsible for the deaths are actually three witches who have been terrorising the inhabitants of that region for more than 200 years.

I was reading, captivated once again by story, when without warning a particular paragraph stirred a feeling in my stomach, a feeling of fear. The offending paragraph contained a description that Samuel had made of them:

They were beautiful, however the clarity of their eyes laid bare the hatred they felt for him. He searched their faces for even a small difference between them and could find none. The three looked at him and smiled in unison, and his heart was paralysed.

Three witches... Three...

The image of the three women walking towards the house replayed in my mind forcing me to close the book and hold on to Felipe.

"It can't be them," I reasoned. Although I had not been able to see them up close, I remembered that they did not resemble each other, one of them was shorter than the other two and...

I went back to the book trying to find something else to confirm my denial. After reading several paragraphs I realised how much I wanted them to be ghosts, as Emilia said, and not witches...

I closed the book with annoyance when I realised that I was allowing myself to be disturbed by the story. "It's just a fantasy created by Samuel's prolific imagination," I said to myself trying to calm down, "Just a few teenagers wanting to annoy, nothing more." The police had assured me and there was no real reason for me to think otherwise. However...

Although everything seemed more than crazy, after having met Michael, the world held few surprises for me anymore.

I left the book on the small table and turned off the lamp. I tried not to think about them but the more I tried, the more terrifying ideas came to my mind.

Suddenly I opened my eyes in the dark when I remembered that Samuel had based the story of the witches on a book of legends that he had found in the house library. And that book still had to be there. I got up and without turning on the lights I went directly to the third floor. I opened the door slowly, and was surprised to see that everything was in the dark, Michael's lamp was unlit and he didn't seem to be around.

Almost on tiptoe, as if I could prevent him from hearing me, I approached the shelves and began to look for the book by the light of my mobile phone. I remembered placing it myself, the day we cleaned up after the disaster caused by Michael by throwing the books in the air, and I thought I had put it next to a collection of classics, on the ledge on the left.

This part of the shelf was divided in half leaving in the centre a space of just over three metres, where Michael's painting hung. While I was reviewing the books, flitting the torchlight here and there, I was conscious of those black eyes that seemed to follow me. Uncomfortable, I illuminated the face of the painting, and for a moment I stared at it in admiration. His face was really beautiful, curiously I had not found it so handsome the first time I had seen him but now, when I looked at him carefully, I realised that the he had a certain brooding nobility. There was something in his sullen gaze, and that subtle hint of sarcasm in the curl of his mouth, which the painter must have known so well to capture, made him look so masculine... so aloof. I sighed and laid my eyes on his: yes, that was him, as inaccessible as the moon.

I sensed movement behind me which made me turn quickly.

And I came face to face with him.

I took a step back, surprised to see him appear so suddenly, and so close, I was only a few inches away.

"Shouldn't you be sleeping?" he asked without preamble.

"Yes," I said, looking away, "I should...

He walked to my right, and looked up at the painting.

"Do you think I'm beautiful?" he asked, looking at me again.

Without looking away from the painting, I felt that I was blushing, luckily in the dark it escaped his notice.

"No," I answered safely.

I realised he was smiling, and I turned my eyes to him.

"Do you think you're beautiful?" I asked

"Some ladies have opined that this is the case.."

I raised an eyebrow and looked away.

I focussed on the book I was looking for while wishing he would stop looking at me.

"You shouldn't be ashamed, there's nothing wrong with it."

I redirected the phone light from the shelf and lit up his face.

"To your impressive list of qualities you can also add conceited" I said

He frowned and narrowed his eyes, annoyed. Then with his hand he lowered mine diverting the light. However, he kept his fingers on mine a moment longer than necessary and I felt a tingling in my stomach.

Disconcerted, I walked away and started looking on the other side of the shelf, while he followed me with his eyes.

"I don't think you're beautiful, besides I don't like men with beards."

He took two steps towards me until he was very close. He bowed slowly, as they did in times past, with his hands clasped on his back, and smiled.

"Liar," he said.

I looked at him open-mouthed without knowing what to say.

Luckily I had the book in front of me, so I took it, and walked to the door.

"Good night," he said behind my back, with more than a hint of fun.

I closed the door without looking at him, and went down stairs.

"Stupid ghost!"

I got to my bed, and sat in the middle with the book on my crossed legs. I was glad to know that he would not come to my room, because I was quite upset. Not only because of the direction the conversation had taken, but because of what I had felt in his presence.

It was crazy to feel that way because of a ghost!

I shook my head trying to dislodge these errant thoughts.

I opened the book, forcing any thoughts of Michael from my head.

The legends were grouped by year, and they all came from the north of England. There were several referring to witches, almost as many as werewolves. I reviewed them one by one, until I found the one that talked about the three witches who had lived in this region.

The story began to spread around seventeen hundreds when a series of infant disappearances had put the people of the surrounding area in a state of alarm.

Many accounts spoke of three women who appeared from the forest and took the small children with them. Although many of the testimonies were incoherent and exaggerated, several agreed on two things: the missing children were under seven years old, and all of them had lost their mothers a year earlier.

I stopped at that line feeling that a cold terror was invading my heart.

I kept reading with anticipation:

"Unlike other stories of witches of legend, these particular witches were distinguished by the description that the inhabitants made of them: they said that they were young and beautiful, not ugly with crooked noses. Their faces were angelic, their movement soft and graceful, their eyes beautiful, and their luminous hair, long even further below the waist. They looked like sisters, except that one was a redhead, the other blonde and the other brunette."

Some testimonies claimed that a group of locals had caught and drowned them upside down in a river that surrounded a small hill in the vicinity of the forest. Although there were those who said that the women who had died that day were mere innocent villagers and that the real witches still lived in the heart of the forest."

I wrapped both arms around my shoulders as if to give me warmth against a strange cold which was enveloping me. I didn't know how much truth there was in all that, but I had a bad feeling about it, which got worse the more I thought about them.

I left the book and took Felipe to Adela's room. Happy, he went to his bed, took about three or four laps and finally settled down to rest.

I looked at the girl, she slept deeply. I sighed in anguish, and it was only at that moment that I realised how helpless I felt. I put the blanket aside and lay down next to her. I couldn't leave her there alone, so hugging her, I settled in to keep watch over her dream.

XXIX

The dawn promised a fine day, with that exaggerated brightness that the sun has in winter.

There were still a few days of Christmas vacation left before restarting the work routine, so I decided to take Adela on an outing to take advantage of the good weather.

I called the girls and we decided to go spend the day at the lake that was only an hour's drive from our house. I went down to the kitchen to get some appetisers, and I found that Emilia had prepared three cups of tea and two dishes with pastries.

I smiled when I saw how she took care of me and Adela.

"Where is Pedro?" I asked.

"He's coming, he's finishing fixing something in the shed."

I drank a sip of my tea, but I left the cup on the table to wait for it to cool down.

"Look," she said, reaching the local newspaper, "look at what those children say they have done in the cemetery.

I took the paper and observed the photograph that showed the destruction in one of the tombs.

"How terrible!" I said. "Those tombs must be more than two hundred years old, how awful to graffiti them and spoil them like that. I can't believe anyone could do such a thing.

Pedro came in, greeted us and sat next to his wife.

"True, however I would not be surprised to find that they are the same ones who have been here, scaring you," Emilia said.

I looked at Pedro who seemed oblivious to our conversation.

"The ones that entered the park? If I remember correctly, you said they could be ghosts. I don't know, they didn't seem like naughty girls or ghosts to me. They looked too real and dangerous."

"Sometimes ghosts look very real..."

I looked up at the newspaper and looked at her. She was going to add something when Pedro's deep voice interrupted her.

"They are witches, not ghosts."

I looked at him, my eyes widened by surprise, when he saw them he hesitated and lowered his head.

"Witches?"

He didn't answer, he just kept his eyes on his cup.

"Another one saying nonsense!" Emilia murmured impatiently.

"Tell me what you think, Pedro."

"Don't say those things to the girl! Don't you see how scared she is?"

"It's okay, Emilia. Let him talk."

But Pedro had retreated even more, if possible.

"Do you think those three women are witches?" and I added almost in a whisper. "Witches like The Three Ladies, the witches of Samuel's stories".

Suddenly all the doubts disappeared.

"Samuel's books are fantasies!" said Emilia. "Are you not going to believe that...?"

He stopped in his tracks and looked at me. I looked at Pedro and he kept his eyes on me for a few seconds.

"What nonsense! You can't think that witches exist!" Emilia insisted.

Pedro remained silent with his eyes fixed on the cup in front of him.

"Samuel's story was based on a local legend..." I said.

Emilia took the cups from the table and took them to the sink.

"A legend is a legend. They are stories that people tell...

"But every legend always has a grain of truth," I insisted.

Pedro looked up.

"They are witches, they are the same witches who took Román's little brother."

"Pedro!" exclaimed Emilia, and her eyes clouded with a patina of terror.

"When did that happen?" I asked, and I felt a lump in my throat that made it difficult for me to speak.

"About fifty-five or sixty years ago, when I was small."

Emilia had sat down again and remained unusually quiet.

"How do you know they were? Did you see them?"

He shook his head.

"My friend saw them, when they were in the forest with the little one."

I was horrified and waited for it to continue.

"There were three, and young," and he added, slowly: "A blonde, a brunette and a redhead."

The last sentence rumbled in my head, like an echo: a blonde, a brunette and a redhead.

"Enough is enough!" Emilia said suddenly, hitting the table. "Stop the nonsense, Pedro! You know well that the boy was touched after his little brother disappeared. What about you, Julia? I can't believe that a young and intelligent woman believes in these things! Witches? Are you two listening to each other?"

She got up grumbling, and left the kitchen slamming the door as she went.

We were silent, both immersed in our own musings.

"Did you ever talk about this with Samuel?"

Pedro shook his head.

"In his book the protagonists are three witches, the three ladies as he calls them, and they... Well, they steal small children for... You know, to remain immortal.

I shuddered.

"Go with the girl," said Pedro, and I saw in his eyes a glow of pain. "It doesn't matter whether you believe what I told you or not, but take her away".

Without adding anything else, he stood up heavily and went out to the garden. I watched him go through the park, and get lost behind some trees, he was probably going to the shed again.

At eleven in the morning we left, Adela excited to take Felipe on her first walk away from home, I was hoping to be able to put aside the alarming thoughts that haunted me.

I went to pick up Marilyn and we went together to the lake where Janet was waiting for us. The talk in the car was one-sided as I was actually distracted. My attention strayed away from Marilyn's chatter and my mind returned again and again to the conversation of that morning and to Pedro's eyes full of fear. Once we arrived at the place, I finally began to relax. The sun shone relentlessly, transforming the wintry grey into a vibrant gold. Adela ran with Felipe, laughing as the little dog happily barked and ran playful circles around her.

In that place and at that moment, there was no room for scary women, whether they were witches or otherwise.

"Lucas called me yesterday," Marilyn said. I was carefully examining the appetisers that Emilia had prepared, trying to decide which one to pick. When Marilyn fell silent, I looked up. She simply stared at me, as if waiting for a comment. But I had nothing to say, or I didn't want to respond to the implicit question I saw in her eyes.

"What did he want?" Janet asked.

Marilyn smiled, still looking at me. "Basically, he wanted to know how Julia was. Of course, he beat around the bush before asking."

Now Janet fixed her eyes on me, expectant.

I looked at them both and shrugged, indicating that I didn't want to get involved.

"What?" I asked.

"What?" Marilyn said, handing me a glass of soda. "That's what I'm asking. Did you two argue?"

"No," I said. But they weren't going to be satisfied with that. So, after some evasiveness, I finally told them what had happened at their house a few weeks ago.

When I finished, they both looked down without saying anything.

"It was very strange and uncomfortable. I never expected him to feel that way about me, let alone hide it for so long."

"It was more than obvious to me," Janet said.

Marilyn simply nodded.

I looked out at the lake and searched for Adela. She was sitting a few metres away from us.

"And now?"

"Now? Well, I don't know..."

"Do you feel the same way about him?"

I pondered Janet's question.

Perhaps months ago, after the kiss and the events that followed, I would have answered affirmatively, but now...

Everything had changed. It wasn't just that my feelings had cooled off; someone else was starting to take possession of my heart, and realising this brought me a fleeting kind of joy.

"No," I said. "I care about him a lot, but..."

I didn't know how to continue, but they understood what I meant.

"And the ring? Who has it?"

"The ring?" I asked.

"The engagement ring... The one Damian was going to give you. Someone must have kept it."

I hadn't even thought about that.

"I have no idea, although it really doesn't matter anymore," I replied.

"No?" Marilyn said. "Wouldn't you like to have it?"

"Julie! Look! Come here!"

Adela's call saved me from answering and continuing a conversation that made me sad. I walked towards the girl and saw her putting stones into the little basket where she kept some toys. As I helped her choose the most colourful pebbles, I thought about Michael. How had he known about the ring? How did he know exactly what Damian and Lucas had talked about that night?

"I know many things I shouldn't know." That had been his response, but it wasn't enough for me. All of that had happened eight years ago, and somehow, inexplicably, he had found out.

We returned home before sunset. I bathed Adela and left her playing cards with Emilia and Pedro. I had promised Marilyn to accompany her to the movies, although I didn't really feel like it. Juan was away on a trip, and I knew she didn't handle being alone very well, so I decided to sacrifice my comfort and spend some time with her that night to cheer her up a little.

I came back very late, I took Marilyn to her house, and we stayed chatting so long that it was after twelve at night before I realised the time.

The forest road was deserted, as always, and I tried to travel it quickly, more than the reason advised. The forest was for me, after recent events, a place that I preferred to avoid, and that road made me tense and nervous.

I had chosen classical jazz in order to distract me from the darkness and keep the pervading silence at bay but it also distracted me from my driving which led me to take the next curve perhaps a little too fast.

What I saw when I rounded the corner made me hit the brakes, so abruptly that the car skidded a few metres, luckily coming to a stop before hitting the trees.

I stared at the forest to my right, it had not been my imagination, it was a woman I had seen entering the thicket.

What she held in her arms forced me to stop the car and start running towards her.

After only a few steps I was among the trees, walking almost blindly then I came to a stop. I stared into the darkness, into the silence, the kind of silence that bristles your skin.

The tears of despair had begun to fall and the anguish made its way to my throat in the form of a barely contained sob.

I kept moving forward until I saw them again. The three of them walked together, almost in sync, with their hair uncovered and their cloaks waving as they went.

My heart pounded in my chest, resonating in my temples, in my throat, a drumroll too fast, overlapping and creating a deafening rhythm: thump... thump... thump...

I couldn't stop, I couldn't let them get away. What I had seen compelled me to follow them and, even if, to try and stop them was madness. They were carrying a child in their arms, a child wrapped in a blanket.

And even though I had only seen them for a second, the fear that it could be Adela left me with no choice but to follow.

For a moment I lost sight of them, only for them to re-appear in the light of the moon briefly before finally disappearing completely.

I spun around, searching for them. I took a few steps to the left and then returned to the same spot. They were gone.

In helpless desperation, I felt tears streaming down my cheeks. I couldn't believe that this was happening, it couldn't be real, yet it had happened right before my eyes.

I wiped my tears with the back of my hand and turned to continue my search but was horrified to find the three of them standing behind me.

Though darkness shrouded their faces to the point where I could barely make out their features, I could feel their eyes on me.

Such was my horror that for a split second it felt like my heart stopped beating, then the spell was broken when one of them asked.

"What do you want?"

The tone wasn't threatening, but when I tried to speak, the words got stuck in my throat.

Closer now I looked at the bundle carried by the tallest one, it was a baby, just over a year old. A few strands of black hair peeked out from the blanket.

Relieved, and feeling guilty for it, I understood that it wasn't Adela.

"Give me the child," I said in a weak voice.

"Go away."

They looked at me for a moment, and then all three turned their backs to me.

I took two steps towards them, intending to follow them. Even if that wasn't Adela, I couldn't let them continue.

Two of the women continued their march while one of them turned to face me. Before I could say another word she reached out a hand toward my throat. A deep searing pain ran through me as her nails dug into my flesh. I stared at her in disbelief, searching for an explanation but she returned a look of indifference, not hatred nor cruelty, only the unconcerned look of someone swatting a fly.

Then something struck her hand, with such force that it caused her to release me and stagger back a few steps, and I fell backwards onto the ground. She did not continue her attack; instead she turned and walked in the same direction of her sisters, in that same elegant and measured gait.

I placed my hand on my throat and my fingers quickly became slick with blood. Another hand rested on mine as someone lifted me up.

"What have you done?" I heard, with a hint of sad reproach. "Why did you have to follow them?"

I searched for his face among the blurry images around me.

"Michael?"

He stood up, carrying me against his chest.

"Don't speak," he replied and began to walk.

I stared at his face, which was just inches from my own, and rested my heavy head on his shoulder. As we moved, the star speckled sky made random appearances through the black silhouette of trees.

I think I lost consciousness for a few seconds because when I opened my eyes again, I noticed the brightness of the park's lampposts, and I saw Michael's face glowing under the yellow light.

We were approaching the house. He pushed the door open so abruptly that it collided with the wall with a loud thud.

I heard hurried footsteps.

"Oh my God!"

"Call an ambulance," Michael simply said.

"What have you done to her?" Emilia's voice sounded scared and distant.

"Call an ambulance!" His booming voice echoed in the walls and seemed to rise through the staircase, spreading throughout the house.

His black eyes lowered to me.

"I'm here," he said, brushing the hair away from my face. "No one will hurt you anymore."

XXX

"When I came back to reality, I was in a hospital room. Despite the dim light, I could see Emilia sitting by my side. She stood up and approached, sitting on the bed.

"How do you feel?" she asked.

"Where is Adela?" I asked, trying to get up.

"Don't get up," she said, gently pushing me. "She'll stay with Marilyn tonight. I called Lucas, and he came to pick her up and took her to their apartment. I couldn't leave her at home after what happened..."

I looked at her, alarmed. "What happened?" I asked.

She shook her head. "I don't know, Julia, you tell me. Why were you with him?"

It was hard to follow the conversation, especially because Emilia seemed to speak in riddles. "Him?" I asked.

She made a face. "You know who I'm referring to."

I understood she was talking about Michael. "Did you tell Lucas?"

"No. What could I say?"

I closed my eyes trying to remember the events of the previous night. All I could recall was a patchwork jumble of images, but one thing was clear to me, that Michael had saved me from being killed by that woman in the forest.

"Lucas and Janet will be here any moment... And probably Juan. What are you going to tell them?"

I sighed. "No matter what I tell them, I can't tell them the truth, that's for sure..."

I looked at Emilia, who was watching me with concern. "I'm scared," I said.

She placed her hand on mine. "I told you he was dangerous," she whispered. "What did he do to you? The doctor told me that the cut on your neck was just a few millimetres away from the right carotid artery... You could have died..."

"It's thanks to him that I'm alive, Emilia."

She looked at me in surprise and started to say something, but the door opened, and Lucas entered the room, followed by Janet and Juan.

After greeting me and the routine questions, I saw the three of them looking at me with concern. Emilia was talking quietly with Lucas and Juan, while Janet sat by my side stroking my cold hands. I tried to listen to their conversation, anxious in case Emilia said something she shouldn't.

"So, you don't remember what happened?" Janet suddenly asked.

I shook my head.

Lucas approached. "Apparently, someone attacked her near the house, on the road," he said.

I looked at Emilia, who returned my gaze, raising an eyebrow.

"Poor thing, my dear," Janet replied, distressed. "I never thought something like this could happen to you..."

"If you're discharged tomorrow, you'll stay at home," Juan indicated.

"I can take care of her," Lucas interrupted.

"It's not necessary, she'll be fine," Emilia said curtly. "Until they find the culprit, the police said they'll send a patrol car to stay near the house."

"I can stay with her," Janet started to say.

I straightened up in bed and tried to speak.

"Guys..."

"Don't worry, I'll cancel some appointments for a few days, and I'll stay with her at the mansion."

"Pedro and I are at the house, we'll take care of her perfectly," Emilia added, somewhat offended.

"Listen, I..." I tried to say.

"Adela is already in our apartment, so I'll take her there," Juan insisted.

I sighed, annoyed. "Guys," I said, finally raising my tone. Everyone looked at me. "I don't need anyone to take care of me. As Emilia said, I'll be perfectly fine at home. What happened was an unfortunate stroke of luck, I'm okay, that's why they're discharging me tomorrow, so you don't have to worry."

I saw Janet about to say something, and I spoke up.

"I don't need you to take care of me," I repeated. "I feel a little tired right now, but I'll be fine tomorrow." I looked at Juan and smiled. "Thank you for taking care of Adela."

After another half hour of chatter around me that only made my head throb like a drum, they finally left. Only Emilia stayed, insisting on spending the night with me. I didn't even try to dissuade her.

The two of us sat there, and I had started to doze off when Lucas came back in, carrying two cups of coffee. Emilia looked surprised, and he handed her a coffee and sat down next to me.

"I'm going to stay for a while," he said. "Is that okay?"

I nodded, smiling. She stood up.

"Then I'll take the opportunity to stretch my legs," she said, and discreetly left us alone.

I watched her as she walked out and closed the door carefully, then turned my gaze back to Lucas. He placed the coffee on the table and took my hand in his. He looked at it intently while caressing it, then turned his eyes to me.

"What happened?" he asked.

I began to shake my head.

"I don't remember..."

He looked at me reproachfully.

"Tell me the truth."

I stared into his blue eyes, trying to decide whether to tell him what had happened.

"You wouldn't have doubted before..." he said, and those words touched my heart. It was true, I would have told him everything without even thinking twice before.

I sighed and closed my eyes, resting my head on the pillows.

"When Emilia called me, she was terrified," he added. "She asked me to take Adela because she was afraid for her. And you know Emilia isn't afraid of anything."

I opened my eyes and found that familiar look, the gaze of my friend from many years ago.

"It's crazy... Everything that has happened is crazy," I said.

Finally, I started talking, between sighs, with some tears appearing uninvited and long moments of silence when the recent memories overwhelmed me.

Most of the time, I kept my eyes on the window, observing the star-filled night. I didn't want to look at him, didn't want to see any doubts in his eyes or perceive what he was thinking of me.

When I finished, I finally turned my gaze back to him.

To my surprise, I saw an unexpected gleam in his eyes. He smiled tenderly and shook his head in pain.

"This is more than any person can bear, Julia. It has been a terrible experience, and I can't even imagine how helpless you must have felt."

When our eyes met again, he looked away and spoke again.

"I don't know how much of what you remember is real. I think the attack was unexpected and..."

"You don't believe me," I said, it wasn't a question.

"Of course, I believe you, but you must agree with me that some memories are unclear. You lost a lot of blood, it's impossible..."

"I shouldn't have told you," I replied, sincerely regretful.

"Julia..." he said, getting closer to me. "Listen to me..."

"No, you listen to me. I'm not crazy. I saw those women; they were carrying a baby in their arms... A baby, Lucas... What do you think they were going to do with him?"

"Julia..."

"And then she... She was just going to kill me. She didn't have a knife, nor even a blade, just her hands. I would have died if Michael..."

"No!" he said, raising his voice. "Stop right there."

I looked at him, astonished by his reaction.

"I can accept his existence, that you've seen him occasionally, but don't tell me he appeared in the forest to save you."

"You've seen him too; you can't deny it."

"Have I seen him? Maybe I'm as influenced as you are..."

"Influenced? Is that what you think? Do you think it's just my imagination?"

"Would you rather think a ghost saved you from death?"

"That's exactly what happened," a voice said from the door.

We both turned our heads and saw Emilia entering the room.

"I saw him," she added calmly, as she walked towards the chair and sat heavily.

He looked at her, with a furrowed brow of disbelief.

"He arrived at the house with Julia in his arms. She was covered in blood, and so was he. His white shirt..." Her voice broke.

Lucas stared at her, dumbfounded.

"I had never seen him before, I had heard footsteps on the third floor at times, but I had never ventured up there at night. But yesterday when I saw him arrive... I instantly knew it was him, I even thought he was responsible for Julia being in that state. I asked him what had happened, but he didn't give me any explanation, he just ordered me to call an ambulance, with that thunderous voice that left no room for arguments."

Lucas sat back down, lowering his head.

"He was furious," Emilia said, her eyes glistening. "I think if he hadn't been so worried about Julia, he would have gone out to look for them."

At that moment, Lucas looked up and looked at her.

"But he stayed with her, his hand on the wound, until finally, when he heard the ambulance siren, he let me take care of her..."

She looked at him, with a sad expression.

"Yes, Lucas, even though it's hard to believe, he saved her life."

XXXI

The next day I returned home. Juan came to pick me up from the hospital, with Adela, who kept talking and telling me everything they had done the previous day with Marilyn.

I felt tired, which was normal considering I had lost a lot of blood. But other than that, I was fine. The wound wasn't very big, although strangely deep. They had said that "the attacker had used an extremely sharp blade," but a couple of stitches had been enough, so now a small patch was the only sign left of the attack. That, and the tremendous dark circles that made me look vulnerable in everyone's eyes.

Emilia and Pedro moved into the house, into one of the rooms on the second floor, she would never sleep near Michael, she was very grateful to him but still afraid. They would stay with us for a few days, which gave me peace of mind, although, with my ghost at home, I wasn't afraid. Who could take better care of us than him?

Lucas came the next day, and I noticed he was somewhat distant and uncomfortable. He stayed for less than an hour, and spent most of that time playing with Adela. We barely exchanged a few words.

I couldn't quite understand his attitude. Was he feeling displaced by Michael, or perhaps jealous? That was ridiculous, but I was almost certain that's what was happening. I decided not to give it too much importance; I had more serious problems to think about. For example, taking care of Adela and keeping her safe.

She was completely unaware of what had happened. On the other hand, it was evident how much she had missed Michael. She had spent the whole afternoon with him in the library, chatting and playing. Late at night, I went up to get her. When I opened the door, I saw him sitting on the armchair. He quickly placed a finger on his lips and lowered his gaze to the girl.

"She just fell asleep," he said.

I smiled and whispered back, "She's been running around all day, and then here, with you, for almost three hours."

He looked at me silently while I picked up Adela's toys scattered around the room.

"How are you feeling?" he asked.

I made a gesture, wrinkling my nose.

"Tired... Not very well, to be honest," I finally admitted.

I was standing next to the armchair when I leaned down to pick up Adela. He reached out his hand to my neck and gently touched the wound.

I looked at him, surprised, but I didn't move away. His hand barely caressed my skin and then returned to its place. Our eyes met, and once again, I felt very close to him. Perhaps it was just gratitude for what he had done for me, and for what he did every day for my little girl. Or maybe there was something more, something I found hard to admit.

I placed my hand on top of his and smiled.

"Thank you," I murmured, and although that simple word was not enough to express the immense gratitude I felt, I didn't know what else to say.

He didn't move, he just kept his eyes fixed on mine with a deep, almost intimate gaze.

I removed my hand and took Adela.

At the door, I turned around.

"Goodnight."

"Goodnight, Julia."

My name sounded sweet on his lips, with an inexplicable joy I closed the door and went downstairs. After putting the little one to bed, I went down to the kitchen to chat with Emilia while she knitted. Pedro had already gone to bed, so I assumed she would take the opportunity to ask me questions and inquire about what had happened in the woods or talk about Michael since we hadn't had a chance to be alone since I came back from the hospital.

I realised that she was very superstitious, and although she made fun of Pedro's beliefs, talking about all that terrified her.

"Tomorrow you can go back home," I said, sipping my tea. "I'm fine now, it doesn't make sense for you to stay here. I know Pedro misses his things."

"Yes, he's a grumpy old man," she said, smiling. "Are you sure?"

"Absolutely, we'll be fine."

"I don't like leaving you alone..."

"I'm not alone," I said, and she looked at me for a moment.

She shrugged and got up to leave the cups in the sink.

"Whatever you want, anyway we're just a step away.

You call me, and I'm there."

When she returned to the table, I affectionately stroked her arm.

"You've already done enough, Emilia. You can rest assured that he will take care of us."

"Julia..."

"What?"

"I know you're alive thanks to him, but..."

She looked at me sideways.

"What's wrong? What are you worried about?"

She sighed before speaking.

"I don't think it's normal to trust so much in... in a..."

"...in a ghost?" I interrupted.

She nodded.

"He's dead, there must be some evil in him..."

She paused, seeing my furrowed brow and bewildered look.

"What does that have to do with anything? Do you think all the dead are evil? Lucía and Samuel too?" I asked, confused.

"They are where they should be."

And without saying anything more, she looked down at her knitting.

After taking two painkillers, I went to bed. The wound seemed to throb to the rhythm of my heart, and my head felt like it was going to explode every time I moved. I closed my eyes, praying for sleep or the painkillers to kick in; whichever came first.

But the chilling scenes that I had wanted so desperately to forget kept returning to my mind: the little boy with dark curls, snuggled in the blanket, her grey eyes shining with malice, her hands reaching for my throat.

Finally, I got up and, without turning on the light, approached the window. It was a clear night, and everything was calm. Just beyond the front door, I could see the police car. A red flash briefly illuminated the face of the officer they had sent to guard the house, who was leaning against the door, slowly smoking a cigarette. Above me, the floorboards creaked.

"Michael."

I felt a desperate desire to be by his side, to receive his comfort, and that sense of security that only he could give me, that everything would be alright.

I went out into the hallway and walked towards the stairs, hesitating as I climbed them, and opened the door. He turned to look at me as I entered, as if he had been waiting for me.

"Are you okay?" he asked.

"Yes," I replied, nodding, "I just can't sleep."

He approached, and to my surprise, he raised his hand, touching my forehead.

"You're burning," he said, sliding his hand down to my cheek.

"I'm fine," I replied, looking at him. "It's just that you're too cold."

"That could be," he smiled, and began to move away. I took his hand and stopped him.

"Michael, I don't know what happened the other night, I don't even understand how you ended up in the woods, but what I do know is that I'm alive because of you."

He looked at me in silence.

"Both of us owe you our lives," I said, moved by the memory that he had also saved Adela.

"You don't owe me anything," he began to say.

"Yes, but I don't mind being indebted to you."

For a moment his eyes met mine with intensity, then he took a step back, releasing my hand.

"Don't go," I began to say. It sounded like a plea, and I felt ashamed to beg like that.

For an instant, just a moment, his eyes showed something that made my heart leap. Something I had never seen until that day: tenderness? Affection? No, it was something else, something he quickly hid beneath his veneer of coldness, and I couldn't fully discern.

Though he didn't pity me. Without taking his eyes off my face, he slowly disappeared into the darkness, as if disintegrating before my eyes.

"Go to sleep, it's very late," I heard from the shadows.

I returned to bed as he asked, but I couldn't sleep.

It was impossible with the feelings burning inside me.

What was happening to me? When did gratitude and the sense of security I felt by his side turn into something else? For the first time, I could see clearly, and I felt horrified. How many years had it been since I loved a man? Eight years? And now, after all this time, did I want to give my heart to a dead man?

Tears threatened to flood from my eyes. We had to leave; I had to leave him. Pedro had warned me, and I hadn't listened. I had almost lost my life because of my stupidity. What was I waiting for? For a disaster to happen?

I didn't know if they were witches or just crazy murderers, but I wouldn't stay in the house to find out.

I fell asleep with the decision that we would return to my apartment and stay there for a few weeks.

On Sunday, we packed our clothes and all the things we needed to take. Of course, I didn't tell Adela anything; I couldn't explain what was happening. I didn't go upstairs to say goodbye to the library, even though I hadn't seen him for more than two days. Maybe he knew what I was going to do; he must have overheard me talking to Emilia, I was sure of it. But he wasn't about to approach me to ask why I was leaving; that's not who he was.

He was the kind of hero who remained in the background and only appeared when needed. He did what he had to do and then disappeared again. He never claimed anything, never sought to receive thanks or honours.

Late at night, while watching a movie with my little girl, I heard a car engine stop outside. I looked out the window and saw the policeman approaching the newcomer—it was Lucas. I rushed to open the door and signalled to the officer, who let him in when he saw me.

Crossing the threshold, he hugged me for a long time.

Then he bent down to look at my neck. I had removed the bandage, so the thin line, about three centimetres long, was clearly visible, still pink, and somewhat inflamed.

"Nice scar," he said, smiling.

"The doctor says it won't even be noticeable in a few months," I grimaced. "I hope that's true!"

He embraced me again and whispered in my ear, softly:

"I'm glad you're okay..."

His arms tightened even more around me, and finally, he let go and stepped back.

Adela appeared at that moment and jumped into his arms. While the two of them laughed and played, I watched them with tenderness. He loved me, he had always loved me, I could see it clearly now. His love had endured everything: he had loved me even though I loved another man, he had loved me even during the eight years we were apart, and he continued to love me without asking for anything in return.

After putting the little one to bed, he returned to the living room where I was waiting for him. We talked about trivial matters for a while, and then he got up from the armchair next to the fire and came to sit beside me. He put his arm around my shoulders and pulled me close.

"A few months ago, you asked me why I kissed you," he said, surprising me with such a direct statement, "but I imagine that after what I confessed to you a few days ago, you understand why now."

I had my head resting on his chest, unable to see his eyes, and perhaps it was easier for him that way.

"No, not really." I said.

A growl, half complaint, half laughter, escaped his lips.

"Yes, you do."

I waited without responding.

"I kissed you because, for once, I couldn't hold back."

I smiled.

"I had always known how to control myself, treat you like the friend you are, but that night... I don't know what happened to me."

I straightened up and looked him in the eyes.

"That night, you pitied me."

He shook his head as his hand reached up from my neck to my cheek.

"You've never inspired pity in me," he said, caressing my jaw with his thumb, "I love you, Julia."

I don't know if I expected him to say that, but it still took me by surprise.

He took my face in his hands, and his lips slowly opened, gently caressing mine.

Then a door slammed shut upstairs. A gust of cold air enveloped us, and the two doors of the room we were in slammed shut, startling us.

Lucas let go of me and stood up. Without speaking, he headed towards one of the exits. Before reaching the door, it slowly swung open, and then the other one.

He turned and looked at me, a gesture of confusion in his eyes.

"I think it's best for you to go," I said.

"What?" he asked, confused.

On the first floor, the doors began to close, one by one, with increasing violence.

"Go home, Lucas," I said, heading towards the door. He took my hand and stood in front of me.

"I'm not leaving you here alone with that madman," he said, shielding me with his body.

I let go of his hand and walked out of the room.

"I'll be fine, just go."

"Julia..."

"Please! Can't you see that all this is because of you?"

I could sense his helplessness preventing him from speaking. He looked at me once more, his jaw tense, and then he grabbed his jacket and left.

I quickly climbed the stairs, furious with Michael for behaving like this. When I reached the first floor, I saw that all the doors were wide open again.

I started walking towards Adela's room, but before reaching the first door, it slammed shut. I continued walking slowly, and the same happened with the next one, and the next one, as if he were walking ahead of me, angrily closing the doors as he passed.

When I reached Adela's room, nothing happened. I entered and approached the bed, making sure she was fine. I couldn't believe she was sleeping so peacefully with all the noise.

I left the room, and I almost had a heart attack when I saw all the doors wide open again.

I headed for the stairs, and as I walked, each door closed again, just like the first time.

"Enough, Michael!" I muttered angrily, "That's enough!"

I went up to the third floor, determined to find him in the library. As I walked, the doors closed one by one, shaking the walls.

When I reached the library, the door was still open. I hesitated for a second as I surveyed the darkness, trying to make out his face. I was about to reach out to turn on the lights when the door slammed shut in my face, making me jump back.

I had had enough!

I opened the door and entered.

"What are you doing?! Do you want to hurt me?! Have you gone mad?"

The room seemed empty, but I knew he was there.

"Come out and show your face!" Then, I added something that undoubtedly only increased his anger, "Coward!"

The lights were still off, but the brightness coming through the windows allowed me to see the empty room.

Something brushed against my hand, and I began to feel the temperature drop. I looked to the right, trying to distinguish his figure. And then his hand took mine, and I felt his chest against my back.

I wanted to turn around and see his face, but his hand prevented me, encircling my throat. I held my breath, waiting. I didn't know what he was going to do, yet I wasn't feeling fear.

I felt his cold breath on my neck, next to my ear.

"Do you think I'm a coward?" he murmured, "Or are you the coward?"

I turned myself around and faced his gaze.

"I don't hide, nor do I go around trying to scare people."

His brow was still furrowed, but there was something in his eyes that forced me to keep looking at him, even against my will.

"Are you scared?" he asked.

"No."

"Do you fear me?"

"No."

He took another step towards me until our bodies were almost touching. His hand still held mine.

Enchanted by his black eyes, I thought he was going to kiss me. However, he only said:

"Or do you fear that I'll hurt your boyfriend?"

"He's not my boyfriend," I said, withdrawing my hand and stepping away from him.

His quiet laughter fuelled my anger.

"And even if he were, it's none of your business," I said, and I stormed out, slamming the door behind me.

I went to bed still furious, knowing that leaving was the best decision I had made, not only for Adela but also for myself.

XXXII

We settled in my apartment once again. Although Adela wasn't very convinced, the excuse that she had to start school again and that I had to go to work persuaded her to some extent. As my physical wound healed, so did the non-physical ones, fears, and suspicions. Adela started enjoying her classes and activities again, and I enjoyed my work and social life.

Of course, the girls were happy that we were in the city centre, as they had me closer and visited me every week. However, Lucas hadn't come to see me even though we had been in the city for two weeks already.

But both of us missed the house and Michael; almost every day, the girl persisted in asking me when we would go back. And even though I tried to distract her and postpone the possible return, I myself couldn't wait to be there again, not only because my apartment no longer felt like home, but because being away from him was killing me.

During those fifteen days, I had spoken with Emilia several times, and she assured me that everything was calm. Although the police still had no leads on the suspect of my attack, this time they were taking it seriously and had started a thorough investigation. A police car still passed by at night to check that everything was in order.

For my part, I had provided the most accurate description possible of my attacker, although I had omitted some details such as the fact that she had slit my throat with her own nails and not with a knife, or that she was carrying a child in her arms. However, I did clarify that there were three of them.

One night, as I was getting dressed after taking a shower, something fell from the pocket of my clean pyjamas. When I bent down, I saw that it was the brooch that Adela had found in the gazebo, the small golden brooch with the name Joseph delicately embossed on it.

I had completely forgotten about that object, and I was surprised that it had remained in the pocket of my pyjama pants even after several washes. Nevertheless, there it was, and as I held it in my hands again, I felt the same uneasiness I had felt that morning when Adela showed it to me. Perhaps it was because I understood that it had belonged to a young child, or maybe it was because Adela had found it, as if someone had intentionally left it in the gazebo for her to find.

I didn't want to think about it anymore; I opened my jewellery box and dropped it in, hoping that one day I would discover who it had belonged to and why it had come into our hands.

But that night, I had a dream, strangely sad and intensely realistic.

I was walking through the gardens of the house, our house. Suddenly, I began to hear the crying of a child, and I knew that child was my son, but I didn't know where he was. Desperate to find him, I started going through each room, but the crying grew more and more distant. Still, I kept running from one room to another, going up and down the stairs, until finally, exhausted, and crying, I went up to the library.

When I opened the door, there was Michael, looking out the window. As he saw me enter, he turned slightly and smiled. My heart leaped with joy knowing that he was there, and the love I felt for him was so intense, so deep and true, that tears filled my eyes once again.

Then he turned completely, and I saw that he had a child in his arms, my child. I approached to kiss him, and then I looked down at the little one with black hair and eyes, just like his father. He stretched his chubby hand to hold mine, and I could see, almost hidden among his clothes, a golden brooch with his name: Joseph.

Confused, I raised my gaze to look at Michael, but he wasn't looking at me; he was looking at someone who had just entered the room. His eyes were shining with love and admiration, and then I turned and saw her: a woman with light hair, who was also smiling at him.

As if I wasn't there, they approached each other until they were united in an embrace with the baby between them. And in that instant, in that tragic moment, I understood that this wasn't my child, and Michael wasn't mine.

Then I woke up.

Anguish clung to me for several hours after waking; the sensations of perceiving Michael's love for another woman had been so real. And although I knew it had only been a dream, I kept thinking about every detail, and it felt more and more real. For example, what was Michael's child's name? I didn't know; I had never asked.

The dream could be just that, a dream, but the brooch was something real, and the child to whom it had belonged was real too.

Suddenly, everything fell into place: if that brooch belonged to Michael's son, the little boy who had supposedly disappeared, and if the witches were responsible for that disappearance, then they could have left the brooch in the gazebo as a warning, or as a threat... or as a taunting gesture towards Michael.

If I thought that leaving the house would make me feel safer and more tranquil, I was mistaken. In my apartment, I felt terribly alone. The worst part was the nights; it was difficult for me to fall asleep, knowing that he wasn't upstairs watching over our sleep. With time, I realised that being in the city didn't make me any safer because the only one who could truly take care of Adela and me, was Michael.

What happened in the fourth week confirmed all my fears.

On Tuesday, I took Adela to school and went to work as usual. Around noon, I went back to pick her up, and to my surprise, one of the teachers told me, with a smile, 'Your sister came to pick her up."

I stood there paralyzed, looking at her.

"What?" I said, my voice trembling.

"Your sister. She said she would take her to the park and wait for you there."

I didn't even stop to ask for an explanation from the stupid woman who kept smiling at me, nor did I shout at her that my sister was dead. I simply ran out of the school, desperately searching for Adela among the people who hurriedly walked down the street.

The park was two blocks away from the school. We used to go there with the girl at noon when the day was sunny.

I ran through the crowd, ruthlessly pushing surprised pedestrians who got in my way until I caught sight of the trees rising above the buildings.

I crossed the entrance gate and began to walk along the main path, looking left and right. The place was almost empty; the threat of rain had scared off the mothers, and the fine drizzle had driven away the few brave ones who had dared to go out for a walk in the garden.

My heart was beating so fast that I thought I would have a heart attack. In my mind, I didn't even dare to analyse what was happening.

Half walking, half running, I reached the playground.

I stopped, looking at the swings where she loved to play until she exhausted me, but they were empty.

Further on, by a fountain with several water jets, I saw a woman sitting on the edge. She was facing away and seemed to be alone. I quickly started circling the fountain to approach her and ask about Adela. But suddenly, the woman stood up and started to walk away.

"Excuse me!" I shouted, but she didn't even turn around.

And I was completely alone again; the park was deserted.

I leaned against the cold stone, trying to catch my breath and calm down. The drizzle had started falling again, and the cold water washed away my tears.

Suddenly, I heard footsteps behind me. I turned around and saw her; she was walking along the path covered in white gravel. She was alone"

I ran towards her and took her in my arms.

"Adela! My love! What are you doing here? Who did you come with?"

She looked at me, surprised. I held her in my arms and sat on a stone bench, ignoring the dampness that instantly soaked through my clothing.

"Your friend came to school," she calmly replied. "She told me we would wait for you here."

I looked at her in horror. Almost in a whisper, I asked:

"What friend, my love? Victoria? Janet?"

She shook her head, her brown curls dancing.

"Honoria," she said.

XXXIII

It had been them. I didn't know how or why they hadn't taken her, but I was sure it had been them.

The idea that they were toying with me made me shudder; they wanted to demonstrate their absolute power over me. I realised that no matter where we were, if they wanted the girl, they would come for her. And even though everything seemed to indicate that returning to the mansion was crazy, I knew it was the only place where we could be protected. That was where we would find the only person who could truly take care of us.

Two days later we returned to the house.

Adela couldn't contain her joy, and although I was still scared about what had happened, I felt as happy as I could under the circumstances.

The first thing she did was go up to the library, but I decided to wait. After what had happened in our last encounter, I didn't know how to face him.

When night came, I accompanied the girl to bed, and while waiting for her to settle in, she asked me:

"Julie, why does Simaco live in the library?"

"Because he really enjoys reading," I absentmindedly replied.

"But there's no bed there. Where does he sleep?"

I was gathering her toys, and I turned to look at her. Her questions surprised me; it was the first time she had started to inquire about Michael.

"I don't think he sleeps much," I said.

"And he doesn't eat either?"

"I don't know..."

"We could invite him to eat someday. I'll ask him tomorrow," she added, and very pleased with her new resolution, she finally settled down to sleep.

I waited for her to fall asleep and went to my room. With the nightstand lamp on, I stayed awake, staring at the ceiling, waiting to hear him upstairs. However, there was absolute silence. Without realising it, I fell asleep.

"Julia, wake up."

In my dream, someone touched my face with a cold, pale hand, a dead hand.

My heart, racing with fear, thumped in my chest as I blindly searched the shadows for the owner of the voice.

"Damian? Is that you?"

"Wake up."

"I'm awake. Tell me what's happening. Where are you?"

"Wake up."

And then I understood that the one calling me wasn't Damian; that wasn't his voice. It was the familiar voice of another. A feeling of calm fell over me; knowing that I was no longer in danger because of his presence.

"Michael?"

"Wake up."

I sat up in bed, realising it wasn't a dream.

"Michael?"

Suddenly, he was by my side.

"Get up." I looked at him astonished; what was he doing outside the library? Then I realised that something was happening, something really bad.

"What's going on?" I said and started walking towards the door. "Is Adela okay? Is she safe?"

"She's fine..." As he hesitated to respond, I brushed past him and rushed out into the hallway.

I ran to the girl's room and quickly opened the door.

There she was, sleeping, with the blankets falling to one side of the bed. I approached and carefully covered her.

"You must get her out of the house."

I turned around; he was standing by the door. I looked at him in confusion, but before I could ask anything, he added.

"You don't have time, Julia. Get dressed and call Lucas to come pick you up. Stay at his apartment; he will take care of you."

I left the room, closing the door.

"At his apartment? What's going on, Michael?"

The hallway was dimly lit; some of the doors were open, allowing a little light to filter through. He was in front of me, very close, so close that I had to tilt my head to look into his eyes. And his eyes, those eyes that usually showed no emotion, now looked at me with concern.

"You're scaring me. What's happening?"

"You must get her out of the house."

"Why?"

He started walking towards my room. I followed closely behind. He approached one of the windows and discreetly glanced through the curtains.

"Call Lucas," he turned around, and as I stood there doing nothing, he added, "Now!"

I took out my cell phone and made the call. Lucas answered instantly.

"I need you to come pick me up. Something has happened, please hurry."

Only after hanging up the call, did I realise how much I had trusted Michael's request. Without understanding what was happening, I never doubted what he was telling me, not even for a second.

"Is it them? Tell me!" I shouted as I packed some things into a bag.

He turned around and looked at me intensely.

"Yes. You must hurry. They have returned."

"But..." I said as I moved around the room. "You said they wouldn't enter the house..."

He looked at me without responding.

I gathered a few more things and put on a coat over my pyjamas.

"They're coming to...?" I couldn't continue.

"They're coming to take Adela," he calmly replied.

Despite the alarming statement, my brain accepted it as something that I knew would happen sooner or later.

I returned to Adela's room. Carefully, I wrapped her in a blanket and took her in my arms.

"Michael!" I called out as I walked through the dark hallway toward the stairs. "Don't leave me alone, please."

"I'm here," I heard him from the end of the corridor.

"Where are they?" I asked as we descended.

"I don't know, but they will arrive any moment."

When we reached the living room, I stopped and turned to him.

"I'm scared," I said, realising that tears were welling up.

He brushed my face with his fingers and smiled, with that strange smile of his.

"I know."

We went to the door, and before opening it, he looked through the glass.

"They're already here," he said, and I felt my heart freeze.

I looked outside and saw them, just like that night, slowly walking towards the house.

Trembling, I looked at Michael.

"You must go to the road, find Lucas on the way, go through the forest."

"I can't, they'll catch up with me," I sobbed.

"Julia..." I looked at him through my tears. "You can do it," he said. "You must do it. You're all she has," he added, gently stroking Adela's head.

I took a deep breath and nodded.

"Leave through the kitchen door," he said, opening the door.

"What will you do?" I asked, terrified.

"I will talk to them. Go!"

I crossed the kitchen in complete darkness using only my familiarity to guide me and slowly opened the back door, looking into the small courtyard at the rear of the house.

Despite the shadows, I could see that it was empty. I ran the few metres remaining to the gate that led outside, unlocked it, and opened it.

The forest stretched out before me, hundreds, thousands of black giants watching me from above. I suppressed a whimper and walked forward with determination.

It wasn't the first time I walked in the forest in the middle of the night, but now I was there with Adela. I had no idea what time it was, but I imagined it was around three in the morning, as I could see a pitch-black sky overhead, still devoid of the clarity of the red dawn.

I knew where I had to go. The road curved, approaching the house, and that's exactly where I had to wait for Lucas. But although it was no more than two hundred metres, traversing them in the dark, on damp ground covered with leaves and branches, was not easy. Not to mention the burden of the sleeping child and the terror that gripped my heart, making my legs feel heavy.

Adela started waking up, and I had to stop to adjust her position.

"Julie? Where are we going?" she asked, pulling the blanket off her head.

"Lucas is coming to pick us up. We're going to his house," I said, as if it were the most normal thing to do in the middle of the night and on foot.

She looked around, confused.

"Why don't we go in your car? I'm cold! Where's Felipe?"

"He's sleeping, he'll stay to take care of Emilia. Don't worry, love, we're almost there."

I sat her on my left hip and covered her again with the blanket. I allowed myself two deep breaths to calm down and continued running.

Suddenly, I heard a car approaching. I started running, half stumbling over roots I couldn't see.

If Lucas reached the house...

I didn't know what would happen, what they would be capable of doing to him if they found him there. I tried to sharpen my hearing to perceive how close the car was, and in my heart, I raised a desperate plea. Just thirty more metres.

The car was approaching too fast; I wouldn't make it in time.

I started climbing the embankment that surrounded the road, using my free hand for support.

Then the car sped past me.

"No!" I screamed. "Lucas!"

I finished climbing and stood by the side of the road, and took out my mobile phone.

"Please, please, answer the call."

With the phone to my ear, I started running along the road toward the house.

"Julia?"

"Lucas, I'm on the road, turn around."

"What?"

"Turn around!" I screamed hysterically.

Adela had started crying, but I didn't have time to calm her.

Then, a sound akin to the roar of a furious beast rose into the night and echoed through the forest. Then all fell silent as if the forest itself were in shock. A silence just as terrifying as the roar moments before took hold of the night, only to be broken by a deafening crescendo of all manner of animals scurrying fearfully into the night. Adele and I covered our ears trying to block out the cacophony.

Then the world went white. It took me a second to realise that we were being blinded by the car's headlights as Lucas had turned around and was approaching us. The passenger door flung open providing us with an escape we gratefully took.

With screeching tyres, we fled from there. I leaned back and looked through the rearview mirror at the road; I could see the animals still crossing, terrified, moving in the opposite direction of the house.

"Michael."

I turned around in my seat, but at this point the house was completely obscured by the forest.

Tears, which I had managed to hold back until now, started to stream down my face. I wiped them away with the back of my hand while still looking in the direction of the house.

My ghost was there, alone, facing them. A thorn of remorse for leaving him behind pierced my heart, and if it weren't for Adela, I wouldn't have hesitated for a moment to get out of the car and run towards him.

I turned my head and looked at the road. Taking a deep sigh, I closed my eyes, and I felt Lucas placing his hand on mine.

XXXIV

As we were travelling to the city, I clumsily answered Lucas' questions. My answers must not have been very coherent because I realised he had to repeat each question several times, but he finally managed to understand what had happened to some extent. Fear made my voice tremble, and constant glances backward, examining the road, forced me to start the story repeatedly.

When we arrived at his house, I refused to take Adela to a room. I laid her down next to me on the couch and cuddled up with her under a blanket.

"You'll be more comfortable in bed, you can rest for a while..." Lucas tried to convince me.

"I'm not going to sleep," I said firmly.

He looked at me for a moment and then added,

"Then I'll make coffee."

We drank our coffee in silence, in the dimness of the living room, illuminated only by a single lamp. I held the cup in my freezing hands, hoping to warm them. Michael's dark eyes, looking into mine, wouldn't leave my mind, and the anguish I felt not knowing if he was safe was unbearable.

"We should call the police," Lucas suddenly said.

I shook my head.

"It wouldn't do any good. I've talked to the police many times, and you saw what happened," I straightened up on the couch and added, "I have to go back."

"No, Julia. I'm not letting you go back. You've seen what they can do."

"I can't leave him there alone..." I began to say.

"You have to stay here," he approached and squatted next to me. "He knows how to take care of himself. You know I don't sympathise with him, but..." and he reluctantly added, "This time, I think he's right."

Fatigue was overpowering me, so I decided not to argue. I couldn't go back in the middle of the night, but I would do it the next morning, and with that resolution, I fell asleep almost instantly.

I woke up startled by the ringing tone of Lucas' mobile phone.

"Yes, she's here," he said, "I'll pass her the call."

I looked at him as he handed me his phone.

"It's Emilia," he clarified.

I looked at the time on the screen, it was almost nine in the morning.

"Julia! Oh my God! Are you okay? Is Adela okay?"

"Yes, yes, we're fine. What's going on? Did something happen?" I said, feeling myself tense up.

"What are you asking me, Julia? Of course, something happened! The police are here!"

"The police?!" I shouted, startling Lucas. "Are you okay? And Pedro?" I got up from the couch, moving away from Adela so as not to wake her. "What happened, Emilia? Did someone break into the house?"

"I called the police because when I got up this morning and saw your car parked, I thought one of you might not be feeling well, and that's why you didn't go to work. But then when I entered the house..." she paused, and as I waited for her to continue, I held my breath, terrified. "I called you, searched for you both throughout the house, then Pedro came, and we started calling your mobile phone. I was really scared, we thought... something bad had happened to you," I heard her sigh, and I sensed a suppressed sob. I checked my mobile phone in my bag and saw six missed calls from Emilia.

"I'm sorry, I should have called..." and I didn't know what else to say, I didn't know if I should tell her what had happened.

"Why did you leave? Why did you leave the car?"

"Lucas came to pick me up."

"Lucas? Last night...?"

"Did the police find anything?" I asked, interrupting her.

"They were looking for you, in fact, they're searching the area around the house right now."

"Last night... they tried to break into the house, that's why I left with Adela," I said. For a moment, she fell silent, surprised by my comment.

"Why didn't you call us?"

Lucas was looking at me from the end of the room.

"I don't know, I panicked," I sighed, remembering the events of the previous night. "Tell them that someone tried to break in, ask them to search the house, check all the rooms for any signs that someone was there. Especially in the Library..."

"In the Library?" she asked slowly.

"Yes," I answered confidently. "Especially there. Please, Emilia, make them do something. I'll be there in fifteen minutes."

When I hung up the call, I saw Lucas shaking his head disapprovingly.

"You can't go back, Julia. Remember what happened last night, what we saw on the road..."

"I have to go and talk to Michael. I need to know what we're up against and what I should do."

"What you should do is stay here, at least for a few days."

I looked at him. His eyes searched mine, worried. I could see all the unease in his heart through them.

"I'll just go and get our things, we'll stay at my apartment," I approached and placed my hand on his arm. "I need to go, and I need you to take care of Adela."

He shook his head.

"No, I'll go with you..."

"I can't take her, Lucas, only you can protect her until I come back," and as he still hesitated, I added, "Please..."

I quickly got dressed and approached Adela. She was sound asleep, her chubby cheeks were rosy, and her hair covered her forehead. Tears welled up in my eyes, threatening to overflow at any moment. I didn't want to be apart from her, but I had to go back to find the answers to the millions of questions I had.

A taxi took me to the mansion in just a few minutes. I stopped on the driveway in front of the entrance gate and looked at the house. I looked up at the window of the library, hoping to see him looking at me, like so many times before, but he wasn't there.

Emilia opened the door, and to my surprise, she hugged me.

"How you've made us suffer!" she said as she let go of me and stepped aside to let me in. "Come, I have hot tea."

"I'll go get some things from my room and be down in a moment," I said as I walked towards the staircase.

I quickly went up to the first floor, almost as I always did. But this time, more than just haste urged me to run up the stairs. Without hesitating, I continued up to the third floor and stopped in front of the library. The door was closed, a deep and almost unfamiliar silence enveloped the whole house.

I rested my hand on the doorknob and gently pushed. The door slid open with a mournful creak.

"Michael?" Despite the light coming through the window, the room seemed dark and cold to me.

The empty armchair...

The lamp turned off...

Books meticulously arranged on the shelves...

"Michael?" I searched for his slender silhouette, his shining eyes, in the darkness.

He wasn't there. Had he left, or had they...?

And then sobs shook me from within, rising through my chest and throat like a claw scratching my heart and soul.

I approached the tall armchair and touched the rough fabric with trembling hands.

A faint murmur of footsteps, barely perceptible, and that scent, which I could now recognize as his, made me turn around.

Standing in the centre of the room, he was looking at me.

Motionless, I gazed at him through my tears. Then he took a step, and I closed the distance between us in a second.

I stopped, hesitating, and perhaps a little abruptly, I threw myself into his arms. Just as I was about to pull away, aware of what I was doing, he wrapped his arms around me. For a few seconds, precious seconds, our souls transcended barriers, merging the world of the living and the world of the dead.

When I regained awareness, he was looking at me with a faint smile.

"Why are you crying?" he asked. I sighed and moved away.

"What happened last night? What happened to them?"

"They left."

I looked at him, confused. "They left? They simply... left?"

"They left in fury," he said with a crooked smile.

"They didn't do anything to you? Did they... Did they try to...?"

"Kill me?" he asked.

I looked at his hand, which still held mine, and curiously observed his long, pale fingers and the ring with intertwined initials.

"How is it possible that I can touch you?"

"I don't know," he said.

"Can you feel me?"

"Of course, I can," he said, smiling.

I gazed into his hypnotic black eyes.

Emilia's scream made me jump.

"Julia! The tea is getting cold!"

I smiled and said, "I'll be back as soon as possible," and walked towards the door. There, I turned and looked at him. "Don't disappear..."

"I'll be here," he added in his husky voice.

As I descended the stairs, I realised I was smiling. For a moment, I was surprised to feel that kind of happiness amidst everything that was happening. Feeling so close to him even when my heart was beating and his was not.

Emilia was waiting for me, sitting at the kitchen table. She was alone; Pedro was probably working in the garden or fixing something at his house.

I sat in front of her, and for a moment, I had a déjà vu. I saw myself in that same place, sharing tea with Emilia, and when she spoke, she said exactly what I knew she was going to say.

"Why did you come back? If they came looking for the girl last night, if they are so dangerous... Why did you come back?"

She was scared, afraid for us, and that scared her. It also made her furious.

"I came to talk to Michael. I want to know what I should do."

She snorted. "And you think he can advise you?"

"Yes, he knows what's going on."

She got up from the table, impatient. She went to the counter and started drying the dishes with quick movements.

"You're obsessed with him," she said, turning to look at me, "and he's obsessed with you."

I looked at her, not knowing what to say.

She sat back down and added sadly, "You two are... You're like our family."

"I know," I said, caressing her hands.

"Listen to me and leave here, even for a few days, until everything calms down."

The phone rang, and I jumped in my chair, spilling some of the tea.

"Julia?" It was Lucas.

"Did Adela wake up?"

"She's watching a movie. Have you talked to Michael yet?"

It sounded strange to hear Lucas calling him by his name.

"Not yet. Don't worry, I'll be back in about half an hour."

"Okay."

"Lucas?"

"What?."

"Thank you for coming to pick us up last night and..." I paused, moved, "Thank you for always being there for us."

"That's what friends are for," he said, and his voice sounded sadly resigned.

XXXV

We had been sitting in silence for over fifteen minutes. I had gone up to the Library and sat in the chair behind the desk, while he observed me from his armchair.

"Tell me the truth, Michael, even if it's terrible," I finally pleaded.

"They are witches. They are the witches who took my child, and the ones who have taken dozens of children in the last hundred years."

Although it was what I had been fearing for some time, that confirmation, so abrupt and direct from him, startled me. I brought a hand to my mouth, stifling a gasp, feeling that even the last hope of being wrong disappeared.

"There are three of them. They have lived in these parts for centuries. Their longevity is due to their witchcraft. They are sorceresses and they use the blood of children to stay young and strong."

I stood up and took two steps, then leaned on the desk.

"Oh my God! I can't hear this," I said, feeling my stomach churn and everything spinning around me.

Michael fell silent, looking at me.

I struggled to breathe for a few seconds until I felt the blood flow normally again. I walked around the room in silence, trying to understand what was happening. Although all I wanted to do was scream in frustration, I forced myself to calm down and think. I had to be strong, I had to forget my fears and fight for her.

I turned to Michael, our eyes met, and as if he knew exactly what I was thinking, he said, "I'm sorry."

I smiled sadly and returned to my armchair, replying, "Tell me everything."

And he did.

He told me everything, leaving in all the distasteful detail that anyone else would have omitted, with that hint of indifference in his voice that made it even more personal and painful.

The witches had taken his son.

It had happened before, other children had disappeared, and although no one dared to name them, everyone knew they were responsible. Michael knew it too, he had seen them lurking in the forest, watching the house, monitoring his movements. But he also knew they wouldn't enter the house unless he let his guard down. That's why he had watched over his little one's sleep every night, always with a lit lamp, until that fateful night when he fell asleep.

When he woke up and saw the empty crib, he believed he would die from the pain.

Guilt, combined with despair over such a loss, made him completely lose his sanity. For three days, he searched for the child in the forest, shouting his name, begging the witches to have mercy on his son.

Unable to bear it any longer, two weeks after the child's disappearance, he took his own life.

But to his surprise and dismay, he found himself trapped in that house, alone, without his beloved child, and with the same pain gripping his dead heart. As the days went by, the suffering became more and more intense, until it became unbearable.

The Library was his dwelling. He saw the horrified townspeople, staring at his decaying corpse, then saw them lower him, wrap him in a sheet, and take him out of the house. Then solitude and oblivion took hold of the mansion and his consciousness.

One day, he noticed that a thick layer of dust had formed on the books and shelves, and realised that he had no idea how much time had passed, it could have been months or even years. Some things were still fresh in his memory, but he had forgotten many others. For example, he couldn't remember how or why he was still there, whether it had happened for no reason or if it was something he had done or failed to do.

But there was one thing that could not be forgotten; one thing forever burned into his memory. He remembered with perfect clarity waking up at dawn and seeing his little one's cradle empty. Every day he relived the pain and utter desperation as he searched the house in vain. He could recall the agony of knowing without doubt that they had taken him.

"That day was the beginning of everything," he said, looking into my eyes. "I realised that time had passed and I was still here, that I had been dormant all these years and had become a wandering being who couldn't fully die. Because death cannot be this, Julia, death should not hold pain or consciousness."

I maintained his gaze, not knowing what to say, feeling his profound sorrow.

"And a new feeling took hold of me, almost to the point of obsession: vengeance. They had stolen what I loved most in the world, so that day I decided that I would destroy them. It might take me years or centuries, I didn't care, I had time, sooner or later they would return, and I would be prepared to make them disappear forever."

Our gazes met again, and once again I remained silent.

By chance, he had discovered some of his "abilities," such as moving objects. That had allowed him to return to one of his most cherished pastimes, reading, and it had also opened the door to a wealth of knowledge about witches that he had never expected or desired to acquire when he was alive.

During the first months, he devoured all the books about supernatural beings he found in the collections of the old mansion, searching for information about sorcerers, necromancers, magicians, and fortune tellers. Most of them were fictional stories about fantastic creatures, but he came across an old tome that immediately caught his attention. It was a compilation of ancient stories, especially about witches and wizards. It seemed to be the result of extensive research since many of the stories were supported by real testimonies or by verbatim quotes from allegations made in trials against witches or in local hearings.

The things he discovered in that book went beyond his imagination, but he decided to follow the threads of the ones that seemed most logical or had more substance.

"For example, it's not the blood of infants that prolongs their lives, it's the death of the innocent."

As if he didn't realise the impact his words had on me, he continued with his explanation.

"Many believed that witches drank the blood of children to stay young, but that's not true. What extends their lives is the spell they perform, which includes the sacrifice of an innocent, meaning a child under seven years old whose death must be painless..."

He looked back at me, and I don't know what he saw, perhaps my terror filled eyes because he paused in his narrative.

"Maybe it's better that we don't talk about this anymore," he said.

"No, go on... I need to know everything. I need to know what they can do," I cleared my throat as if I was being strangled, preventing me from speaking or even breathing. "Why Adela?" I asked. "Why your child?"

"Because their mothers died. A mother's love is something they cannot overpower."

"But..." I began to say and felt that knot constricting me again.

"I know. I loved Joseph as much as his mother did, just like you love Adela... But that's how things are. We're not their mothers. When they die, a door is left open."

I watched him with pain, without confessing my secret. Someday, I would give him the brooch that I now knew had belonged to his son and that I kept in my jewellery box. And now I understood who had left it in the gazebo and why.

After all, I couldn't take care of my little one. My tremendous love for her wasn't enough. The pain was accompanied by an unsettling fear and the dreadful certainty of being incapable.

"Isn't there anything we can do, Michael? There must be something..."

"Keeping her away from them is the only thing you can do."

"But you spoke of destroying them, you said that's what you've been trying to discover all these years..."

He stood up and approached the desk, then turned and looked at me.

"I never thought it would be so hard for me to tell you this," he lowered his gaze and moved one of the books on the desk by a fraction. "You must go, get away from this house as far as you possibly can. Leave everything behind, start a new life with Adela far from here."

"No..." I knew he was right. It was madness to stay, and especially madness because what kept me from leaving wasn't my attachment to the house or the life Adela had had there with her parents, no, that had become secondary. What made the idea of leaving unbearable was what I felt for him. And he knew it.

"You will be able to return, you just have to keep her away for a few years, until she is a little older. When Adela grows up, they will no longer have any interest," he smiled and added, "I will be here taking care of the house."

I tried to smile and held back the tears.

I nodded, as if convincing myself.

"I will do it. I will stay at my apartment for a few weeks and make preparations for leaving."

"No," he said, "you must leave today."

Our gazes met, my eyes were moist, his were not.

My mobile phone started ringing.

I looked at the screen, it was Lucas.

I answered the call.

"I'll be there in a while," I said almost automatically.

"Julia," the tone of his voice made me shudder, "Adela has disappeared."

XXXVI

The phone slipped from my hands, and my eyes locked onto Michael's.

"Adela!" I shouted, and he understood immediately.

"No..." he began to say.

Anger boiled behind his eyes like a volcano on the edge of eruption.

"Not again," he repeated, and for a moment, his face seemed to start fading away, like mist dissipating in the sunlight, or perhaps it was just my tears hindering my clarity of vision.

I crouched down and picked up the phone with trembling hands while Lucas kept talking.

"...the police are on their way. I don't know why I called them. I'm sorry, I'm sorry..." and I noticed his voice breaking.

"I'm going to find her. The police can't help us," I said and hung up.

I looked outside. A joyous morning had transformed into a despondent afternoon. Angry clouds threatening deluge hung from the sky, keeping the sun from view, while the night crept impatiently on before its time.

The forest appeared even more ominous, and a similarly dark feeling gripped me. I couldn't explain how, but I knew Adela was there, among those twisted trunks. There, where she had played with her mother so many times, close to the sorceresses unknowingly, surrounded by an invisible shield that prevented them from touching her.

Surely, they had watched her with a dark desire to claim her, wishing for her to become an orphan so she could finally be theirs. But they never approached, for the halo of love that surrounded her was too powerful, even for them. But now Lucía was no longer there to protect her.

I looked at Michael; he was observing me. We gazed at each other without asking or explaining anything, it wasn't necessary, we both knew what we had to do.

I sighed and approached the door, to my surprise, he followed me.

"Let's go," he said. "I know where to find her."

He offered his hand in a quick gesture, I took it, and we hurriedly went down the stairs and out.

He walked fast, so much so that I almost had to run to keep up with his pace. Amidst the despair I felt, I found myself wondering how he managed to leave the house.

As if he knew what was on my mind, he said, "I've been there a thousand times. I know exactly where they are and what they're doing."

An icy claw of dread dug into the base of my spine, and sent a shiver running through me right to the top of my head.

But that was it; I didn't allow discouragement to overwhelm me. There was no time. I couldn't afford to cry or scream; I couldn't even allow myself to think too much about what was happening at that very moment.

Michael walked with astonishing confidence through the almost completely darkened forest. I don't know if it was due to a natural ability in him resulting from his knowledge of that place or his condition, but the truth was that he seemed to glide along the blurred paths of the forest while I hung onto his hand, stumbling, and swaying like a rag doll in his wake.

We reached a point where there was no longer a trail, only thick undergrowth, and dense vegetation at our feet. I looked up at the sky; I could barely make it out among the tangled branches, but I realised that night had finally won the battle.

"When we get there, we must act quickly. The element of surprise will put us at an advantage. You must take Adela and run; I will deal with the witches."

"How?" I asked, panting.

"Don't worry about me, there isn't much they can do to me," he said, shooting me a quick glance with his crooked smile. "Don't be afraid," he added. "They will try to stop us, but together we can get her out of there."

I blinked nervously as some chilling images came to mind.

"If they're not that powerful, why have people feared them for centuries?"

"They are incredibly powerful, but they don't love Adela... You do."

He squeezed my hand, not looking at me, in a gesture of trust and protection. He slowed his pace, and I did too. We stopped, partially concealed behind a thick oak tree, and following the direction of his gaze, I saw with astonishment an ancient building rising in a clearing. At first glance, it appeared to be a house, somewhat narrow, until I realised it was a mausoleum, and then I saw the scattered graves across the terrain.

"Is this a cemetery?"

He nodded.

"This used to be the cemetery of my county. It's older than the one at the town church, but it was abandoned because of the stories told about it..." He looked at me, raising his eyebrows.

"About them?" I inquired.

He nodded again, gazing at the mausoleum.

"How many times have you been here?"

"I don't know. I've followed them hundreds of times. At first, they seemed to vanish when they arrived there, but by repeatedly coming back, I finally found the way in."

"Have you entered?"

"Yes."

"Have you seen them, while...?"

"Yes."

He squeezed my hand.

"Don't think about that," he said.

I raised my head to look at him.

"I'm scared, very scared. I don't know if I'll be able to do it. Maybe I'll freeze while they..."

"We'll do it together."

"Okay," I responded, nodding, trying to muster courage for myself, "Let's go".

He started walking decisively towards the crypt. As we approached, it seemed like the door was slightly open.

My logical side, that part of me that could still think, told me not to enter there. But it wasn't just the normal reasoning in the face of an unknown danger; it was a visceral and profound feeling, an absolute certainty that inside there, I would come face to face with death.

Michael pulled the door with some difficulty, creating a gap of just a few centimetres through which he slowly slipped. He held the door for me to enter and then closed it.

He looked at me, waiting for my reaction, the answer to the question that I could see in his eyes.

"Let's go." I said.

"You know that once we get there, there's no turning back..."

"There's no turning back, not for me." I replied.

He nodded and started walking into the darkness. I followed him, trying to sharpen all my senses, but not only was I almost blind in the unfathomable darkness, but the silence was also absolute.

It felt like we were descending; the stone floor became more and more slippery, and the slope steeper. The corridor we were in forked, and Michael chose the right passage without hesitation. As we turned, I looked to the left and in the distance, I could see a faint glow. Michael walked quickly, and I hurried to catch up, avoiding the small puddles that dotted the path. Thin threads of water ran down the walls, seemingly coming from somewhere above our heads.

A barely perceptible tremor made us stop.

"It has started," said Michael, looking ahead.

As a lump rose in my throat, Michael started running, and I followed him. I didn't dare ask him what that meant because I didn't really want to know the answer.

We ran through that never-ending hallway, and when we reached the next fork, he stopped, extending his hand for me to do the same.

He turned and leaned closer to my ear, whispering softly.

"This is the place; the room is to the right. Don't look at them, don't listen to them. I will take Adela in my arms, they don't expect that, and I will give her to you. Then you must run and get her out of here. Can you do that?"

I nodded and gripped his arm, sighing.

He kissed the top of my head and stepped back to look into my eyes.

"Don't let them win," he said, a glimmer of light in his eyes.

Without giving me time to respond, or even to think, he turned and walked with determination.

"Good evening, ladies," he said, and upon hearing him, surprise overcame my fear.

I peered in, and there they were, the three of them.

Michael walked across the granite floor of the centre of a hexagonal chamber which was surrounded by walls of stone.

In the centre of the room, from a hole roughly three metres in diameter, the flames of a strange fire emerged, flickering, and spreading in every direction seemingly of their own will.

The walls were decorated with what I thought were stones, forming peculiar designs. Higher up, there were openings where, to my horror, I could see dozens of tiny coffins.

Desperately, I searched for Adela, but she wasn't there.

I took a few steps towards them, inadvertently casting my shadow against one of the walls, drawing their attention and causing all three of them to turn and focus on me.

"What are you doing here?" asked the blonde, and a deep echo repeated the question.

"Where is...?" I began to say, but when I looked at the redhead, the words got stuck in my throat.

She was beautiful, stunningly beautiful. I remembered Pedro's words: "the most beautiful woman I had ever seen in my life." Her grey eyes, the colour of steel, shone with such malice that it stopped me in my tracks and slowly forced me to retreat a step or two. The memory of what she had done to me in the forest was still an open wound.

She shook her head as she walked towards me, and her red hair swayed as she moved.

"Have you come to watch her die?"

"Where is she?" I repeated, finally mustering some courage.

She extended her white and delicate hand playfully towards the fire.

"She's sleeping," she said and smiled.

I clumsily walked towards the hole, feeling an indescribable pain in my chest as I did so, that almost took my breath away.

Then, I became aware of a cradle a little further ahead.

It was an old, unpolished wooden crib, without any decorations, completely unremarkable. And inside, in her teddy bear pyjamas, lay my little girl.

I took two steps towards her, and a hand stopped me.

"Let her sleep," said the woman with golden hair.

Michael stepped forward, shielding me with his body.

"I'm taking the child. This time you won't stop me; you'll let us leave without a fuss.

The witch started laughing. Her laughter echoed off the stone walls. She looked at me and then turned her icy stare to him.

"Fine," the smile did not leave her face, "we'll exchange the child for her."

And she looked back at me.

It took me a few seconds to understand what she was saying.

"I won't make any deals with you, Sancia. You'll give me the child because if you don't, I'll bring the whole town down on you tomorrow," she observed him without flinching, "I promise you that," he added.

Sancia approached me. I tried to remain calm, although fear made my legs unsteady, and weak.

"Why are you helping her? " She asked, narrowing her eyes.

And quickly, her hand closed around my throat.

Michael reached out to pull her away from my neck, but he failed to even touch her. I looked at him, terror widening my eyes, and I saw to my horror that his face had changed: his skin seemed to become more and more translucent, and now I could see his bones through it; his head a skull, with dark and empty eye sockets, the bones of his fingers moving uselessly toward Sancia's hand but never quite reaching.

Our eyes met mine bulging and red and his empty and skeletal.

"If you want the child, take her now. I won't give you another chance," said the witch.

My consciousness seemed to fade away under the pressure of the steely grep of her fingers, but even though tears blurred my vision, I could see Michael making his way towards the crib.

"Why are you crying? Are you scared? What would be more painful, seeing her die or dying for her?"

Then, she brought her mouth close to my ear and added:

"Perhaps we can enjoy both today."

And she released me.

I fell to my knees, coughing and gasping, sucking the air back into my lungs.

I looked around and realised that Michael had left with Adela, that was the only important thing. Now I had to think of a way to give them more time to escape, even if it was the last thing I ever did.

Maybe Lucas would come to look for her to take her away. Yes, that would be best. I didn't have to worry; Michael would know what to do.

The three of them had approached the circle of fire. They spoke in low voices, or perhaps repeated some incantation. After a few seconds, Sancia approached me, looking down at me as she walked around me.

"Stand up," she finally said.

I got up, with some difficulty, and once again faced her gaze.

"No one has ever before entered this place, you're the first in hundreds of years. When you see what we're going to do to your girl, you'll finally understand who we are and why we are here."

The ground began to shake, as before, but now a deep sombre sound began to emanate from the fire pit. A sound without words that seemed to rise from the depths of hell that spoke of an unquenchable yearning; a sonification of dark hunger. The sound got louder and closer as each moment passed, until I was forced to cover my ears with both hands.

The fire changed to an intense red colour and rose, brushing against the vaulted ceiling.

As I watched in horror as it began to slide down the walls in crimson waves, I remembered the roar I had heard in the forest the night I fled from them with Adela. It was the same terrifying, furious, powerless shriek that had scared the animals. And now I knew where it came from.

The silence came upon me so suddenly and absolutely that it pained my ears.

"Bring the girl," the woman said, and the blonde headed towards one of the exits. "And finish him off once and for all," she added, looking at me. I looked at her in astonishment as she walked away.

"No! You have me! You promised..."

"I promised? What did I promise?"

"Do whatever you want with me, but let them go..."

Her eyebrows rose as if my words amused her.

The brunette slowly approached me.

"You already know what you have to do, Honoria," the other one said, never taking her eyes off mine.

Fear and helplessness clouded my thoughts. I had to do something urgently, something that would prevent them from carrying out their plans. I was about to throw myself at her in a crazy and desperate attempt to destroy her when the sweet little voice made me falter.

"Julie...?"

She was coming, holding hands with the witch, almost smiling as if none of what was happening surprised her.

"My dear!" I fell to my knees, crying, as I extended my trembling hands. "Come here, sweetheart!"

The little girl ran into my arms, and as I held her against my chest, I looked around, foolishly hoping to see Michael entering the room.

"Let her go," the witch ordered me. Invisible hands took hold of me, and I could no longer move or speak. My body stopped obeying my commands, and to my horror, I watched as the redhead walked towards the fire with the little girl following obediently.

The three of them formed a circle around the bonfire with Adela in the middle. The girl stared at the flames, mesmerised. The women murmured, their gaze fixed on the fire, as if they were speaking with something or someone inside it. The flames seemed to respond to their pleas, and if I kept my gaze fixed long enough, I could see strange demons dancing to the rhythm of their prayers.

And suddenly, the ground began to rumble again.

The torch light flickered and went out, but the intensity of the bonfire kept the crypt illuminated as if it were daylight.

I shuddered, knowing that the moment had come. What I had feared so much was about to happen, and I cursed my helplessness.

Waves of burning flames rose and spread again on the walls, reaching the floor, and two thin scarlet rivulets approached from both sides towards the circle of fire, plunging once more into that scorching abyss.

I suddenly became aware of an ominous, ancient hypnotic chant which slowly began to rise. I thought it was coming from the witches until I realised that their mouths were closed. It was strangely sublime but terrifying at the same time. It not only made my skin crawl, but it also reached the depths of my soul, filling my heart with anguish and pain, with the destructive hopelessness of evil. Just hearing it made me desire death. Those few notes that reached my ears made me feel the horrors of hell.

I averted my gaze from the fire and focused on Adela. With all the strength of my devastated will, I searched for thoughts and memories that would pull me out of the abyss I was sinking into because now I knew that hell was real. I felt its power in every fibre of my being.

And if hell existed, then heaven must exist too.

So many times, I had doubts. I had wanted to believe, but doubts always outweighed my insignificant faith, especially after so much loss and suffering. But now I no longer needed to believe; because I now knew the truth. And with this certainty in my heart, I prayed like I had never prayed before, asking that evil would not overcome me and seeking help from my forgotten God to save my little one.

And, of course, in my hour of need, He came to my aid.

I felt as if a breath of fresh air filled my lungs, and my whole body was filled with an energy I had never felt before. The invisible chains that held me captive released their grip, and I stood.

I walked towards the circle, and the girl saw me. As if awakening from a bad dream, she looked at the women, confused, and then at the fire. She took a few steps back and began to run towards me.

Sancia saw her and started to turn, but the hand of the young brunette stopped her.

"Let her go," the girl said, without releasing her grip.

"Adela, come here, my darling." I approached and took her in my arms.

I took only two seconds to settle the little girl on my hip, and with one last look at the witches, I started running towards the exit.

But the woman in red had no intention of allowing me to escape.

This time not only did the ground shake with her scream, but the entire cave did too. The ceiling cracked open, and large chunks of stone fell, while the entrance walls crumbled with a thunderous noise of dust and rocks, leaving the door through which we had come completely inaccessible.

I didn't dare look back; I didn't want to see her.

The triumphant laughter was the only sound that echoed once the stones stopped falling. I looked down at Adela, who stared at me with her eyes wide open.

"I want to go home," she said, and started to cry.

XXXVII

"Come here," whispered the lady with red hair. The woman turned, still holding the child in her arms. The little girl cried, curled up against her neck. Ignoring the command she began to walk toward the other entrance with single-minded determination.

"Come here!" roared the witch with such force that the walls began to crack.

"Enough, mother! Let them go." Said the brunette.

Both the red witch and the woman turned to look at her. The witch in fury and disbelief, and the woman in surprise and incomprehension.

"That's enough," the young witch added.

"Don't you dare..." Sancia began, hissing through clenched teeth. "Don't you dare defy me, Honoria."

"I can't keep doing this!" Honoria exclaimed, and the walls trembled with her scream.

The red witch looked at her, eyes ablaze, her hair moving as if it had gained a life of its own.

"I am doing this for you!" she replied as she closed the distance between them. She moved like a snake stalking its prey.

"Stop lying, mother! You do it for yourself!" the other shouted, extending her hand. The redhead stopped abruptly, as if something was holding her back.

"Do you really think you can stop me?" she asked, as she raised a hand to her lips and blew a kiss in her direction. The kiss became a breeze, and the breeze became a wind raising dust and stones. It increased in strength and intensity enough that it lifted the young witch off her feet and sent her crashing into the stone wall behind her. The force held her at the point of impact prostrate in the shape of a crucifix.

"Don't deny what you are!" Sancia hissed her warning. "This is our nature..."

"Our nature?" the girl replied, unable to move. "Do you think we were born this way? No, mother, this life was a choice,"

And for the first time in her long existence, Sancia felt something that men had often talked about: regret...

She, the all-powerful, the one most feared, regretted.

Not for choosing to be who she was, or for taking so many lives. She regretted choosing this girl; this stolen girl, and wanting to have her forever, to love her. She regretted turning her into something the young woman despised. How long had she hated herself? Years, decades? Centuries?

She cursed the day she took her from her crib and brought her back to life. She cursed the day she killed her mother, sealing her fate to love her forever, with love that was almost human. And above all, she cursed the fact that her heart fluttered with fear for this ungrateful creature who now stood before her in defiance.

She took a few steps and observed the human woman clutching the child with chestnut curls in her arms, looking at her with terror. Why feel compassion for that little girl? She was just another child, one of many.

Then she remembered the words her sister had spoken to her just a few months ago:

"Her mother's blood is changing her." She turned and looked at Honoria, observing the long dark mane floating against the cave wall. It was just like that of her mother, her real mother.

She averted her eyes avoiding the accusatory gaze of her daughter which threatened to pierce her heart and turned to the blonde witch.

"Let's not waste any more time. A soul has been offered, and a soul is claimed."

A voice sounded behind her.

"A soul is claimed? Then we'll deliver yours."

She quickly turned to find the ghost with his natural elegance, calmly walking toward them. She threw a furious look toward her sister.

"I ordered you to destroy him," she said.

"You can't destroy a dead man," the blonde replied grimly.

"No," he said, and with a barely noticeable smile, he stole a glance at the woman and the child.

"But you can destroy a witch, it's easier than you'd think," he added, taking a few more steps towards them.

The red witch eyed him suspiciously, her face painted with undisguised anger, hands clenched on her crimson dress, and attentive eyes calculating the next move.

"This secret was only ever known to a few," the ghost continued, "but when it was revealed, men found it so simple that they thought it a deception."

He walked around the circle of fire, cautiously looking into the well. Then he stopped a few steps from the witch.

"Men try to destroy a witch's body because they think it contains her soul but that was a mistake many didn't live long enough to regret." His words were clear and confident.

"Search for her amulet, they say. She will keep it hidden, close to her heart. It is a token that belonged to the one who gave her life, and she will guard it with savage intent because it contains her soul," he smiled, looking into her eyes. The sorceress slowly brought her hand up to her chest.

The ghost's eyes narrowed with fury, and his skin suddenly became more and more ethereal.

"Take away their amulet, and you take away their immortality, their power. They will become ordinary women, stripped of all artifice, and then..." He approached until he was inches away. "Then you can kill them however you prefer."

In a movement so swift that it left her no time to react, he reached for the witch's necklace, but his fingers seemed to pass through the woman's flesh. She began to laugh as her anger turned to amusement. He looked at his hands, confused and enraged, and reached out again, trying to touch her. But his fingers seemed to have lost all of their substance, he noticed that his body also had begun to lose its consistency.

She looked at him, triumphant, and laughed again as she walked away from him as if he no longer mattered.

"Poor wretch! You don't even know what's happening to you."

She walked towards the woman and took the girl. The young woman looked at her helplessly, tears streaming down her cheeks.

"You are a thing of death and corruption, the worms took your body hundreds of years ago, perhaps this tomb holds some of your bones, or maybe just your dust."

As she spoke, she walked with the child in her arms.

"It is love that makes you strong. Love for this girl, and love for her," she said, pointing in the vague direction of the woman who had fallen to her knees against the wall, bereft of all hope.

"And it is hatred that weakens you, your hate and fury lessens your link with this world, until you become nothing... less than nothing."

She put the girl down and led her by the hand towards the circle of fire.

"It is obvious that your hatred for us is much greater than your love for them," she added, turning her back on him.

The child remained holding Sancia's hand, once again in silence mesmerised by the flames.

"Don't you dare harm her!" Michael shouted. He shouted, and the more he shouted, the fainter he became until at last he disappeared completely.

The woman sitting against the stone wall watched what was happening with a look of resignation. The tears had stopped, her eyes were dry, sunken, and weary.

"Let me die."

Sancia looked up at the young witch, who remained motionless, still helplessly fixed to the wall.

"Please, mother..."

The witch extended her hand as if moving invisible threads. Then in response Honoria began to descend along the wall, in the same tortured position, until she reached the ground and fell to her knees.

She placed both hands on the ground and began to cry.

"Kill me, go ahead and do it."

"Stand up. Come closer to the fire," the red witch commanded.

"I want to die! I beg you mother!" Honoria shouted, then she put her hands on her chest and remained motionless.

For a few seconds, silence descended on the cave. It seemed that even the roar of the fire had fallen silent.

"Did this belong to my mother?" Honoria asked then, climbing to her feet.

Sancia looked at her. The young woman held a medallion in her hand with a thick chain hanging from her neck. It seemed to depict an eye from which a tear in the shape of a purple gem was falling.

"Did she give it to me before you killed her?"

The witch looked at the young woman, and her expression transformed, perhaps because she was remembering that day.

"Was it before or after you separated me from her forever, mother?" The contained anger shone in her dark eyes.

"Do you think that's true? It's just the gossip of ignorant and stupid men."

The young woman tore the amulet from her neck and looked at it once again.

"Do you mean that if I throw it into the flames, nothing will happen?"

Sancia's eyes widened, but she said calmly, "Of course, nothing will happen. You're a witch, you're more powerful than you know."

Honoria walked towards the fire and extended her hand over the flames, with the medallion gently swinging from its chain.

"Why did you do it? Why did you kill her? Were you going to use me too, like the other children?"

"No!" Sancia replied quickly. "No..." she added, "you were always my daughter..."

"I was never your daughter!"

"You were dead the first time I saw you. Your mother begged me to breathe life back into you."

Honoria shook her head as she slowly circled the fire, moving toward her mother.

"How could you do such a thing?"

"Because I loved you! Because I loved you from the moment I first saw you!" She approached the young woman and caressed her face. "Because that day, I knew that nothing would ever be the same for me..."

Her beautiful eyes looked tenderly at the young witch.

"Give it to me," she said, extending her hand. "Give it to me, please."

Honoria looked at her, her eyes filled with tears.

"And I loved you, mother. I have always loved you. You are the only mother I have ever known."

320

She extended her hand to gently caress the cheek of her beautiful mother, then pausing to stroke the majestic mane of red hair.

"That's why I have to stop you, and I'm the only one who can."

Then Honoria stepped back, her expression a strange mix of triumph and regret.

Then she brought her two hands together over the fire, one holding her medallion and the other a rustic leather cord with a dangling rune.

Sancia looked at the pendant and then brought her hand to her chest to confirm its absence.

"Honoria..."

"Mother, let's go together," she said and dropped both amulets into the circle of fire.

Both talismans danced for a moment before slowly sinking into the pyre. A new chant began to be heard, and the flames turned a pale blue colour. They grew wild and then abruptly disappeared. And then they emerged again, hotter and with more fury than ever.

The blonde witch stepped back, taking the child's hand.

"What have you done?" Sancia asked, her voice filled with pain and confusion. "I gave you everything I had, I have always given you everything..."

Two tongues of fire flickered in the air like two crimson snakes, dancing and painting themselves orange, golden yellow, before turning into a dark crimson. Then they descended and, crawling gently along the ground, began to wrap themselves around the long dresses of the women.

"I love you, mother," the young woman said, and staring into the deep abyss, she took a step into the void, disappearing into the flames.

"No!! Honoria!!"

Sancia sank to her knees as the flames began to consume her with chilling rapidity.

The ghost did not lie; without her amulet she was mortal, stripped of her spells, devoid of power. A mere mortal. She felt the searing pain of the flames but it was dwarfed by a yet greater pain, greater than any she had ever borne in her long life, which tore at her heart; a heart that had become almost human many, many years ago.

The witch with golden hair had disappeared through the only remaining exit, leaving the child alone in the centre of the room. The woman seized her chance and ran toward her.

She lifted her up and buried the child's head into her shoulder then turned once again to look at what remained of the witch. A shapeless mass of smoking flesh and charred bone continued to smoulder next to the hole. The flames appeared much calmer now, perhaps after two deaths its unnatural hunger had been sated.

Before the woman even had time to feel the relief at the conclusion of her nightmare, the room began to shake violently.

The fire went out, and a huge gaping crack appeared the length of each of the six walls. The ceiling collapsed, disintegrating into hundreds of pieces of sandy rock, the walls crumbled, revealing the bones that formed them.

Julia looked in horror at those tiny bones, which she had mistaken for rocks −the bones of hundreds and hundreds of innocent children stolen over the centuries and sacrificed on that macabre altar.

Turning her back on the monstrous sight, she began to run.

XXXVIII

Adela was no longer crying, but instead screaming, terrified by noise of the destruction of the cave. The passageways were collapsing behind us giving me no time to decide which path to choose.

I ran aimlessly until I reached the end of a corridor but the way ahead was blocked by debris.

The noises echoing through the tunnels and caverns were truly alarming, and I was so terrified that I couldn't even think. Adela had calmed down, so I set her down to rest for a few seconds. The girl turned, staring back at the tunnel we had just traversed.

"Simaco!" she shouted and started running.

"Adela! Come here!" I called, looking in the direction she was headed, but the way was deserted.

"Adela! Wait for me!" I pleaded, and she stopped. "There's no one there, sweetheart," I said, leaning down and embracing her. "Simaco isn't here."

The girl looked at me, furrowing her brow.

"He's over there! Can't you see him? He's waiting for us," she said and started walking. She stopped and turned. "Come," she said, taking my hand. "He knows how to get out."

I took Adela's hand and tried to make out Michael in the darkness. Perhaps I simply couldn't see him, and this idea filled me with pain. She walked quickly, and when she reached a junction, she turned left without hesitation.

"Is he... Is he okay?" I asked hesitantly.

"Yes," Adela replied after a few seconds.

"Do you hear him when he talks to you?"

The girl nodded, looking at me.

"Don't you?" she asked.

I smiled without answering.

"He says 'don't worry about it'," the little girl added, pulling my hand.

Indeed, we had a bigger problem. The rumbling was getting closer and closer. Clearly, the caves and labyrinth of connecting tunnels beneath the forest were collapsing, and if we wanted to stay alive, we had to hurry to avoid being trapped inside.

I began to notice that we were ascending along the long corridor, and hope was rekindled, along with my certainty that Adela was really seeing Michael and that he was guiding us.

Finally, I could make out the torches at the entrance, and pushing the heavy door, we stepped outside.

The forest was dark and silent. I looked back at the corridor one last time; now there was complete silence.

It was all over.

Time stands still when we die, and nothing else matters.

Memories fade, and we begin to forget.

What irony! The dead forget about us while the living do everything possible not to forget them.

Despite being alive, despite having recovered Adela and knowing that no one would harm her anymore, melancholy overwhelmed me. And I knew I was selfish and ungrateful for not feeling completely happy. But I couldn't.

Michael was gone.

He left without saying goodbye, without even allowing me to say thank you.

I tried to resume our activities, especially to immerse Adela again in her routines to help her forget. Fortunately, she didn't remember much; it was as if she had been in a kind of trance that night.

However, everything was etched in my mind and soul, and perhaps I would never fully heal from it.

As the days went by, she also started to forget Michael. She stopped going to the library, stopped asking about him, and finally stopped mentioning him. I felt happy for her; the last thing I wanted was to see her suffer from his absence.

One Sunday morning, almost two months later, we were having breakfast when Emilia arrived. She made herself a cup of tea and sat with us at the large kitchen table. Adela gave her a quick kiss and ran to the garden to play with Felipe, who was already frolicking around Pedro. We could hear Pedro protesting, yelling at the little animal to stay away from the flowers.

I looked out the window and saw the old man carrying some tools in his hands.

"Is Pedro working on a Sunday?" I said, making a grimace.

"You know him, he can't stay still."

But I noticed that she avoided my gaze.

"What is he doing? Some repairs in the cottage?"

"In the mausoleum," she said casually. "Would you like more tea?"

But I was fixated on the garden, watching the two crouched next to a cluster of primroses. My mind had flown back to those unwanted memories.

"Julia," she looked at me, "are you okay?"

I nodded.

"Yes, I just... I had forgotten. I had forgotten that I asked him to seal the mausoleum."

She approached and caressed my face.

"The best thing you can do is forget, forget everything," she said.

I smiled.

"Yes, you're right. There are many things I want to forget, but... not everything."

As if she knew what I was talking about, she withdrew her hand and went to sit again.

"It's all over. You shouldn't think about it anymore."

I looked at her and asked, "Do you think he's gone? I mean... gone forever."

"Yes, thank God."

"He didn't even say goodbye to Adela," I said sadly.

"He left, and it's for the best. He has got what he wanted after all these years; there was no reason for him to stay," she replied gravely.

"What do you mean?"

"He wanted to avenge his son's death and wanted to destroy the witches. Well, he did it. Why would he stay?"

She was right, it was so obvious, yet...

"The poor man had been wandering around here like a spectre for over a hundred and eighty years. It was time for him to rest in peace."

I hid my eyes, which were welling up, looking at the almost empty cup. And what she added afterward plunged the dagger into my heart.

"You must let him go."

The following week we stayed at my apartment. The excuse was an easier commute to work, but the truth was that the old house wasn't the same without him; I missed Michael so much. On Wednesday, Lucas came to see us, we had dinner together, and after putting Adela to bed, we stayed and had coffee. It had been a long time since we had talked until midnight, actually, it had been a while since our last friendly chat, the ones we used to enjoy so much years ago. After a few minutes of silence, he asked:

"Are you okay?"

I nodded as I took a sip.

"Don't lie to me," he added.

I sighed.

"I'm as well as one can be after what happened."

He nodded, looking at me tenderly.

"It's incredible how well Adela is handling it. Does she sleep well? Does she have nightmares?"

"No, she's doing very well."

He nodded again.

"And you?"

"Me?"

He was looking at me. I tried to stay calm, but I felt tears welling up in my eyes.

"I'll survive," I said, getting up and picking up the cups, heading to the kitchen.

He followed me and approached from behind, making me turn around. He saw my teary eyes.

"What's wrong, babe? What's going on?" he asked gently.

"Michael is gone..." I stammered.

His smile faded, and he squinted at me, trying to understand.

"What do you mean?"

"I can't see him anymore. He doesn't respond when I call him, maybe he's not at home, I don't know..."

He looked away.

"I didn't know you were so close," he said mockingly.

"He saved my life, and Adela's. I'll never be able to thank him enough for what he did."

He looked me in the eyes, clearly upset.

"What do you feel for him? Is it just gratitude?"

I averted my gaze, distancing myself from him.

"He's my friend, even if it's hard for you to understand..."

"Friend? You mean the one who throws things at your head and gets furious when another man kisses you in your own house?"

"Don't judge him, Lucas, you don't know him!" I shouted.

"What does it matter if I know him or not?! He's dead! Once again, you're wasting your life on someone who's dead!"

I looked at him with sorrow.

"I can't believe you're saying that... Damian was your friend!"

"And he's dead, we buried him, and you cried for eight years over him!"

He was right, there was nothing I could say against that.

"What grotesque irony of fate makes me keep loving you while you cling to the memory of a dead man?"

I didn't dare to look at him, I didn't want to face his eyes again. He stood still for a few seconds, perhaps waiting for an explanation, but I had nothing to give him.

That same night, I made a decision.

The next morning, we returned to the house, and in just a few hours, I packed our clothes and some of Adela's toys. I talked to Emilia and asked her to close the house. She didn't ask any questions; she could probably see the suffering in my eyes. The girl was with me the whole time, for a moment I thought she remembered something and that maybe she would want to go to the library to see Simaco, but she didn't.

And neither did I.

The sun had already set when we left. Although I knew we wouldn't be back for a long time, I didn't linger on farewells or foolish sentimentality. After a quick hug to Pedro and Emilia, we got into the car and left.

As we travelled the winding roads that led to the highway, I looked at the forest. Strangely, that gloomy place no longer scared me, perhaps because now I knew what was hidden there, and imagination is almost always more terrifying than the truth. Almost always.

Adela had fallen asleep in her car seat. I looked at her through the rearview mirror, and a surge of tenderness tightened my throat. My baby, how was it possible to love someone so much?

I could already hear the echoes of cars racing on the motorway, just one more turn ahead.

I stopped the car by the trees, made sure the little one was still asleep, and got out. We were on a hill, a few hundred metres above the forest. The trees extended downward until they reached the house, where the park suddenly began, illuminated by the yellowish glow of streetlights. The mansion stood out, tenebrous and imposing, dark and looming. I looked for that familiar light in the window and waited, hoping that it would suddenly shine, showing me that he was still there.

But everything remained still, sombre and silent. The breeze carried lamentations whistling through the branches of the trees, which resonated with my soul. I sighed and turned, walking the few steps that separated me from the car.

A cold gust of wind jostled my hair but something about it felt unnatural, so much so that it made the hairs on my arms prickle.

Even without seeing it, I knew that danger was lurking. I placed my hand on the door handle, and just as I was about to open it, she moved, and I saw her.

The keys fell from my hand, and an exclamation escaped my lips.

"What are you doing here?" I asked, unable to move.

The woman advanced, slowly pulling back the hood of her cape as she advanced, revealing her long golden hair.

"You know why I've come. I need the child."

My hands trembled, and my whole body did too. I leaned against the car to avoid falling.

"You were the one who let her go. Why did you come back?" I whispered.

"It wasn't the right time to stay..."

I crouched down, frantically searching the gravel with my hands for the keys.

"Give her to me. If you do, I'll let you go."

I ignored her request and kept fumbling blindly through the gravel.

She continued walking toward me. Sobbing finally found its way out, and I began to whimper while murmuring an unintelligible plea.

"Oh, God, no... Don't let her take her, please..."

I lifted my head and saw her closer to the car than I expected, and I realised I had run out of time.

Abandoning the search, I ran to the other side and stopped in front of Adela's door, extending a trembling hand, as if by some inexplicable means, I could stop her and prevent her from taking my little one.

"Don't touch her," I threatened through gritted teeth.

She stopped and looked at me, almost pityingly.

"There's nothing you can do. You're alone."

You're alone.

Alone.

The words seemed to resonate in the vastness of the night, like a sad and dark echo, a litany of death. I was alone, completely alone. And the only thing I had was about to be taken away from me.

How had I supposed I could defeat them? How, even for a second, had I imagined that we could escape from them and their evil? I looked at her through my tears as my shoulders slumped; defeated. I was alone, and there was nothing I could do against her. But when I thought of Adela, an inexplicable strength filled me completely. She wouldn't take my child. I was going to fight until my last breath.

And if it was necessary, I was going to kill her with my own hands. I braced myself, waiting for her attack, then something moved a few metres away. It took me only a second to understand what was happening.

"No, I'm not alone," I said, finding an ember of hope.

She turned her head, following the direction of my gaze.

I couldn't see her face, but I could imagine the annoyance drawn on her countenance.

"I thought I had seen the last of you," she said.

"And I of you," he replied.

With tears of gratitude, I watched him approach with his hands clasped behind his back, his elegant and measured gait. She cautiously walked sideways, ensuring that she didn't turn her back on either of us.

"I see you haven't learned the lesson, ghost," replied the witch..

"On the contrary," Michael responded, "I am a keen student, and I have learned everything I need to know to defeat you."

"Oh, I understand," she said smugly, "the amulet."

She opened her dress to reveal her bare neck.

"Where is my amulet?" She asked, and she started laughing. "You'll never be able to find it."

My heart skipped a beat.

Michael took two quick steps, closing the distance. She moved away, and I saw her raise her head, looking at the sky.

What initially seemed like a light breeze rotating high up in the trees which quickly grew into a wind approaching a gale, agitating the leaves and clacking the branches together. As the tornado descended as it grew in strength, I had to lean against the car to protect myself.

The wind pulled incessantly at Michael's hair and clothing but he himself remained unmoved. The whirlwind hit the ground behind him ingesting plants, earth and other forest debris as it turned.

Micheal started to move toward the witch ignoring the roaring violence of the wind, unstoppable.

The woman extended her arms and began moving her fingers tracing rapidly, intricate patterns in the air; the preliminary for the casting of a spell. A spell never completed as Micheal brought the previously hidden sword skilfully down on the witches arm. A precise blow which completely severed her arm from her body. The witch screamed in pain but more in rage, as the useless limb fell to the dirt.

"It's true, the best way to hide something is in plain sight." Said Michael as he delivered another powerful blow, not to the witch but to the bloodied arm laying on the ground. He had cleaved his way through the hand splintering bone and scattering blood and chunks of flesh into the surrounding area.

"What you've forgotten is that I know all your secrets. I've been listening to them for decades."

She screamed again with such force that birds took flight in fright.

"You'll regret this!"

He knelt down and picked up what appeared to be fragments of a ring, then put them in his pocket.

"I see you haven't learned your lesson, sorceress," he said, his black eyes twinkling, "you can't destroy a dead man."

He took a few steps toward her and looked at her for a moment, confidently resting the tip of the sword on the ground.

"But you can kill a witch," he added, bringing the tip of his sword up in a single movement and thrusting it deep into Lena's chest.

Before the witch sunk to the ground her face was painted with four distinct expressions. First surprise, of what had come to pass then came confusion, next was understanding and lastly horror of her rapidly approaching fate.

Michael dropped the sword and walked towards the car.

I remained leaning, supporting myself with my hands, to keep from falling to the ground as my legs could no longer support me.

He stopped a few inches away and looked at me.

"Thank you for coming back," I said.

He furrowed his brow in an inquisitive gesture.

"Coming back? I never left."

I looked into his eyes, trying to understand what that meant.

And then something happened. He turned quickly and shouted.

Without fully understanding what was happening, I opened my mouth to speak, and then I felt something cold penetrating my side, making me shudder. I turned my head, confused, and saw the witch standing next to me, looking at me with her clear eyes. The triumphant expression on her face reminded me of Sancia.

Slowly, she withdrew the sharp blade she had plunged between my ribs, and a stream of warm blood began to trickle down my clothes. I looked in horror at the dark stain forming on my shirt and staggered, seeking support against the car.

I searched for Michael with my gaze, but he seemed to have disappeared. I made my way around the car attempting to reach the passenger side door where Adela was seated . I began to feel dizzy, and my clumsy movements became slower and slower.

"Yes, ghost, I'm going to die, but I will have some company," I heard the witch say. Her voice sounded distant, confused.

The effort of standing became too much and I let myself fall to the ground in a sitting position with my back against the rear wheel. I lowered my head and looked at the wound , and realised there was too much blood on the ground and on my clothes.

The witch crouched in front of me; she too was bleeding, not only from her arm but also her chest, her yellow dress had turned almost completely crimson.

"I won't be able to have your child, but neither will you," she said, raising her healthy arm, from which the bloodied dagger protruded.

A malevolent smile played on her lips momentarily before transforming into an expression of surprise, her mouth opened in a silent question. And without me understanding how, her head slid to the side and fell to the ground, leaving her body in exactly the same position for a fraction of a second: her knee on the ground, her raised hand with the knife shining in the darkness, her dress still fluttering in the wind.

Then her body collapsed like a suddenly abandoned marionette, and even more blood pooled the road.

The head had rolled a few metres and stopped, swaying rhythmically, while its still open eyes seemed to be fixed on me.

A final spasm twisted her mouth into an expression of astonishment and left it open, with a ridiculous and yet terrifying expression.

I remained fixed on those lifeless eyes as I felt my own life slipping away.

Michael, with the sword still in his hand, walked towards me.

"Julia!" he said.

And although I knew he was by my side, I could no longer see him.

"Michael? Where are you?" I asked.

My eyes were closing. I forced myself to keep them open and tried to clear my vision, which seemed to be fading quickly.

"Michael, don't leave me alone..."

I stood up and walked around the car.

"Michael?"

I looked at Adela through the window; she was still asleep.

"Where are you?"

"Julia," I heard.

The voice seemed to be coming from the forest now. Confused, I started walking towards the edge of the road.

"Julia, come," I heard again.

The slope was steep; it looked dangerous in the darkness and with the wet and slippery ground. Sitting on the damp earth, I began descending, using my hands for support. I slipped a couple of metres, but quickly regained stability with some effort. My hands were injured and dirty, but I didn't care.

The leaves from last autumn still covered much of the ground; I could hear them crunching under my feet. Sometimes they caused sudden slips, forcing me to hold onto tree branches or whatever was within reach.

After a few minutes, I could make out the path that led to the house in the darkness. I ran the remaining metres and entered the park. The mansion was completely illuminated; it seemed that there wasn't a single room without a light on. It shone majestically, filling the night with a familiar beauty. I pushed the door open and went inside.

"Michael?" I called, running upstairs.

I opened the door to the library and then stopped, astonished. He wasn't there, but the room wasn't empty.

My heart stopped for a moment, absolutely dumbfounded, and then it accelerated, pounding in my chest.

I walked to the desk, seeking support, while my eyes were locked onto his.

"Hello, Julia," he said, and then I recognized the same voice that had spoken to me in the forest. It was his voice, the voice I had dreamed of hundreds of times... How had I confused it with Michael's?

I placed my hand on my chest, trying to calm my heart, but its erratic beats prevented me from speaking.

"Damian?" I said in disbelief, and wiping my eyes that were already filled with tears, I added, "Is it really you?"

Then he smiled, and his smile illuminated the room.

"It's me," he said.

I clumsily walked towards him, with my trembling hands extended.

I stopped, not knowing what to do. He took the few steps that separated us and enveloped me in a hug. I hadn't even had time to think about what it would feel like to touch him, whether it would be like touching Michael or something different, but that moment in his arms surpassed everything I had experienced and everything I had imagined.

It was peace, warmth, love...

An infinite and perfect love, and happiness, so much happiness that I had never felt in my life and never imagined I could feel. And an immense feeling of security and protection.

I was motionless, I don't think I was even breathing, when he said, "I have come, as I promised."

His promise, made so many years ago.

I lifted my face and looked into his eyes, beautiful, golden, with long lashes.

"Not everything ends here, Julia. There is more," he smiled, "so much more."

The happiness I saw on his face forced me to smile.

"Julia, let me tell you, what comes next is the best."

I laughed, realising that only Damian could say something like that, even in a moment like that.

"Then... Are you happy?"

"Do you want to know if I'm happy about dying at twenty-one? No, I think I would have liked to live a little longer, enjoy a few more years with you," he caressed my face, "but I'm happy to keep 'living,' learning, and growing."

I observed him, trying to understand the incomprehensible, trying to imagine the life he was talking about. And then, it suddenly struck me like a ray of light illuminating my mind. I stepped back.

"Why did you bring me here?"

He kept his eyes on mine without answering. I lowered my gaze and lifted my blouse. A deep cut extended about ten centimetres below my left rib, curiously not a single drop of blood was flowing.

I looked at him again.

"That's strange..." I began to say, "I thought it would..." and I left the sentence unfinished.

I kept my gaze fixed on his eyes, trying to understand what was happening.

"I'm dead..."

He smiled.

"I'm dead," I repeated.

He took my hand in his.

"No, you're not dead," he said, caressing my cheek, "not yet," he clarified.

"If I'm not dead... where am I?"

"At the gates."

"The gates...?"

He grimaced.

"...of paradise, the afterlife or whatever you want to call it."

I opened my mouth in a gesture of surprise and disbelief.

"Am I going to die?" I felt a lump in my throat that prevented me from speaking.

"I don't know," he responded calmly.

And I realised that I didn't want to die.

Even if Damian and Lucía were in that world, and my parents... I didn't want to die.

"I don't want to die," I said, "I'm not ready..."

And I thought of Adela.

"I have so much to do..."

And I thought of Lucas.

"I need to learn to be happy..."

A twinge of pain in my side made me wince and I took a step back.

I looked at Damian, pleading.

"A second chance..." I said in a whisper, "to do things right. I need a second chance..."

He approached and held me in his arms.

"I love you, Julia," he said. I closed my eyes as he gently kissed my lips.

"Julie!" I heard, and my whole body tensed, "Julie! Where are you?" The plea, which contained a note of desperation, forced me to open my eyes.

"I'm here, love," I said, finding myself sitting on the road once again. The car door opened slowly, and I saw the little brunette head poking out.

"Can I get out?"

Without waiting for an answer, she jumped from the seat and approached me.

I tried to focus on her face, but despite my efforts, consciousness was slipping away from me. I searched for Damian through the shadows.

"What's wrong, Julie?"

"Deli, look for my cell phone, it's on the car seat. Call Lucas..."

"Why are you sitting on the ground?" I noticed her frightened voice, she was almost crying.

"Call Lucas, love. Tell him to come and find us..."

With desperation, I noticed that it was becoming increasingly difficult for me to breathe.

"Damian..." I pleaded softly, "don't take me, not yet..."

I felt Adela's warm body next to mine.

"Lucas is the first one, right?" she asked, and I suppose she was pointing at my contact list.

I nodded and smiled.

I heard her talking to Lucas, she seemed calm.

I stretched my arm as much as I could and pulled her closer to me. She sighed, taking refuge in my chest.

I tried to stay conscious, desperately holding on to what little life I had left.

"Lucas yelled at me," she said, sobbing. "He was angry."

"He's not angry, my dear... He's just scared..."

"Why is he scared? Are you scared too, Julie?"

XXXIX

I opened my eyes; the feelings of anguish and despair had not left me.

I couldn't see where I was as my eyes had not yet become accustomed to the dazzling light. That beeping sound repeating every one or two seconds, I realised that I had been hearing it long before I had woken. My mouth was like sandpaper and my eyes stung until tears came. The sharp pains in my legs and ribs reported with every movement and breath.

If I was dead, if this was "the afterlife," it seemed closer to hell than to heaven.

I scanned the room with my eyes, taking in everything I could see without moving. Close to the bed, in a chair way too small for him, was Lucas. He was asleep, his head hanging against his chest, and a lock of hair covered his eyes.

He looked so young! As he slept, I could almost see the little boy I had met ten years ago: sweet, gentle, with a huge heart full of kindness. Why had I never seen these qualities before? Yes, I had, but I failed to appreciate them as much as I should have.

He was almost the only one who could make me laugh when I was sad, console me when I felt lonely, listen to me when I didn't even know what was happening to me. He was the one I trusted the most, the one who had always been there for me, at any hour of the night and under any circumstances.

I felt a tear roll down my cheek, understanding that the great loneliness that had consumed me when Damian died would have disappeared much earlier if Lucas had been with me. Because he would have known how to heal me.

Lucas was what I needed to heal my soul; he was my balm but I was the only one who didn't realise it.

I sighed, and he did too.

I tried to move my head, but a sharp pain stabbed my side, eliciting a moan, and he woke up. He looked at me, confused, and immediately stood up, approaching the bed.

"Don't move, I'll call the nurse," he said, starting to move towards the door.

"No," I said, extending my hand, "come here."

He sat down beside me and placed his hand on mine.

"Adela?" I asked.

"She's with Marilyn now. She and Janet have been taking care of you every night since the accident."

"Accident?" I asked, raising my eyebrows.

Lucas looked at me, furrowing his brow.

"Adela called me, and when I arrived, I found you next to the car, you were almost bleeding to death."

"My little girl..."

"It was lucky; that call saved your life."

"Did they find anything?" I asked, pondering.

"Find anything like what?"

I looked at him, assessing whether I should reveal what had really happened that night.

"Was there someone else with you?" he asked, looking at me deeply. "What happened, Julia?"

"It was the last desperate attempt to take Adela away from me."

His eyes widened, astonished.

"I thought everything had ended long before..."

I nodded.

"So did I."

"Was there someone else with you?" he asked again.

"Yes, Michael was with me."

He didn't say anything more, as if he had understood everything without needing an explanation.

"I'm glad he was there," he said finally.

I squeezed his hand affectionately, and tears welled up in my eyes.

"I'm glad you were there, Lucas."

A few weeks later, I returned home. Adela would still stay with Marilyn and Juan a while longer until I could fully recover, so Lucas took me home and helped me settle in the living room, where Pedro had set up a bed so I wouldn't have to climb the stairs.

After organising everything, Emilia went home, leaving us alone in the kitchen.

"Milk? Tea? Coffee?" Lucas asked, taking the cups from the cupboard.

"Milk with honey."

"Oh, how spoiled you are! 'Milk with honey,'" he said, imitating the tone of my voice.

"I'm convalescing," I replied.

He laughed as he went to the fridge.

His laughter stirred something within me, and I stared at him trying to understand what I was feeling. He didn't look at me; he was heating the milk.

"It's true, you need to be taken care of," he said.

And as I remained silent, he turned his head towards me.

I don't know how transparent my gaze was, or how much of what I was feeling he could guess, but his eyes locked onto mine long enough for my heart to change its rhythm.

"Are you okay?" he asked.

I nodded and lowered my gaze.

"I was thinking... How long have we known each other? Fifteen years?"

"Sixteen."

"That's a long time," I said, and I arranged the napkins to hide my embarrassment.

He handed me a cup.

"I could say that you know me better than anyone," he commented.

"Really? Actually, we were separated for half of those years..."

"But still, you know me better than anyone," he insisted.

I sighed and looked into his eyes again.

"I would love to believe that."

He frowned.

"Do you doubt it?"

"I don't know," I said, avoiding his eyes, "but I would love to believe it."

"It's the truth."

I raised my gaze and tried to smile to lighten the mood.

His eyes anchored onto mine. I stayed there, trapped in the deep blue sea of his warm gaze. And I saw once again the love, his love, that so many had talked to me about.

And unable to resist, I said, "Don't leave me, Lucas. Please, no matter what I do or whoever you're with, don't leave me," and I was ashamed of being so selfish.

He smiled, with a sad smile.

"I'll never leave you, I can't," he simply said.

I stood up and took refuge in his arms, resting my head on his shoulder.

I sighed, and he sighed too.

And then he decided to do what he had been holding back from for so long. He tilted his head slightly to look into my eyes again and gently placed his lips on mine.

And I was surprised by everything that this timid and tender kiss awakened in me. Too many sensations at once, and too intense.

A warm current ran through me from head to toe and settled like a burning fire in my stomach, and then I had the absolute certainty that this was my place, right there, in his arms. I raised my hands and caressed his face; he opened his lips and softly enveloped mine. And we kissed as we should have done a long time ago.

And I knew. What I was feeling was love.

And I knew he felt the same, I didn't need to ask. Because love is a language between souls, and my soul knew what his felt with total and absolute certainty.

And I pressed closer to him, wishing to merge my essence with his.

Then, gently, he took my face in his hands and looked into my eyes.

"How could you, even for a second, believe that I would be capable of abandoning you?"

"I love you, Lucas," I said, looking at him through my tears. And my heart leaped for joy at this confession. "I love you," I repeated, smiling.

And I couldn't speak any further; silenced by his kisses.

And for a few precious minutes, I could feel the same peace, the same infinite love, and the same sweet protection that I had felt in Damian's arms just a few days ago.

The first thing I did as soon as I could climb the stairs was head for the library.

I needed to talk to Michael. He had saved my life and Adela's more than once, and even though there was no way to repay such a gift, I wanted to try.

I walked slowly to the door and stopped before opening it. Grief overwhelmed me as I saw the empty and dark room; I had expected to find him sitting in his armchair with the lamp on and his head in a book, but instead, everything was in darkness.

I walked to the bookshelf and glanced around, trying to see if there were any books missing. I searched for his favourites, but they were all there neatly arranged on the shelf.

I approached the desk, lit the old oil lamp, and noticed something at the foot of the antique candle holder.

It was an envelope with my name written in elegant masculine handwriting. I opened it and began to read:

"You are reading these lines wondering why I didn't say goodbye, why I didn't embrace Adela one last time, why I chose to write instead of speaking..."

"The explanation is straightforward: it's just simpler this way. I avoid the necessity of meeting your gaze and witnessing the silent search for answers within my eyes."

"Coward," I whispered.

"I had wondered many times why I stayed in this house, waiting without knowing what I was waiting for. I thought that hatred and the desire for revenge kept me tied to this world, but when I finally got my revenge, nothing changed. All these years, there was nothing but hatred in my heart, and when the hatred finally disappeared, I was completely empty."

"But you brought something new into my life, something I never thought I could feel, especially with a withered and bloodless heart.

"I am writing to bid you farewell because I wouldn't be able to say it if you were in front of me."

"This way, I can only imagine you looking at me with your big eyes, that mixture of fear and adoration that I had started to become accustomed to."

"I love you, Julia, and I will love you always. I have an eternity to love and remember you. But you have a whole lifetime to forget me and be happy.

"And it's because I love you that I am letting you go."

I stood up with the paper in hand, tears streaming down my face.

"Where are you?" I asked.

I threw the letter onto the armchair and walked towards the corner where he used to hide.

"Don't hide from me, Michael."

I violently drew back the curtains and shouted, "Where are you?!"

But only the echo of my own voice answered me.

I approached the armchair and sat down once again. I rested my head and closed my eyes, caressing the fabric of the armrests.

"You're here," I said, trying to calm myself. "No matter what you try to make me believe. I know you too well."

So profound was the silence that my whispers filled the room. The distant wind whistled mournful accompaniment.

"Life is very short, Michael, and eternity is very long. Too long to be alone."

I opened my eyes and searched the darkness for his.

"I could never forget you so don't ask me to try. You sealed your heart with mine the day you saved my life for the first time."

Finally, I stood up and walked towards the door. When I reached the threshold, I turned back.

"But you're right. Thanks to you, I have a whole lifetime to be happy."

Life is strange, so full of joy and pain, laughter and suffering. It is never as we expect it to be, it surprises us at every turn.

It never seems to go as planned, even though at times it seems to have been personally designed for us with all its twists and turns, ups and downs; moments of light and darkness; a pinch of joy here or a sprinkling of sadness there. It's only when we look in the rear view mirror that we realise that those moments were exactly what we needed to find ourselves.

It seemed to me that my life had been overburdened with adversity, leaving no room for happiness as if I had no right to the joyous part of my life. I had grown accustomed to sadness because hoping for more only made it worse. But the worst of it was that I had dragged someone with me into that misery.

When I finally loved and let myself be loved, only then could happiness follow.

EPILOGUE

A long sigh escaped the shadows, a faint gleam flashed in the darkest corner, and he emerged from the darkness. He looked at the closed door, and a smile formed on his lips. She was stubborn alright, too stubborn for his spiritual peace and his dead heart.

He knew that staying there was a bad decision, perhaps the worst decision he had made in his long existence, but he couldn't leave, he couldn't abandon her. It was as if an invisible bond connected his withered heart to her beating one, a tie impossible to break.

He ran his hand over the dusty volumes, lingering over the one she had touched. Then he took it and approached the window. He brought the book to his face; it still had her scent. He sat down and opened it.

He caressed the yellowed pages with the same delicacy as if they were her skin, and he felt the bond tightening even more, squeezing his heart until a groan escaped him.

He shook his head, forcing himself to think of something else, and approached the lamp and lit it.

The dim light grew until its soft golden glow filled the room. His silhouette was outlined in the third-floor window.

An owl gazed down on the forest from its tallest tree, it turned its head toward the glowing window and emitted a mournful call. It turned its head toward the thicket and called again. On receiving a distant response it took to the air.

Then quiet fell and a thousand hidden eyes of the forest watched, expectancy hung thick in the air like a hammer waiting to fall.

Another window lit up, just below the first, only for an instant, like a flash of light in the night. And then silence.

The man not reading, the woman not sleeping.

And the bond remained unbroken.

A few minutes later, the mournful hooting was heard again, and with a quick flap of its wings, the owl perched on the pine tree, on its preferred branch. Its beak opened in another sharp call, and its head rotated one hundred and eighty degrees, gazing at the house. Its large, hypnotic eyes fixed on the window just as the light went out.

As if that were the signal it had been waiting for, it lowered its head and nestled into the hollow that served as its nest. Its eyes slowly closed, and the stillness and peace, long yearned for, finally reached the sinister place.

THE END

FOR YOU

Dear Reader

Thank you for reading my book. It is my sincerest hope that you have enjoyed reading The Three Ladies as much as I have enjoyed writing it.

I hope that this story resonates with you and that you have been transported to a new world every time you have picked up my book. Even if it brings only one person a moment of joy it would be worth all of my efforts. If you did enjoy it I would ask that you take a minute of your time to rate it on Amazon to help other readers find what they are looking for. Thank you and I hope we meet again in my next book.

OTHER WORKS

Saga Las Tres Damas

Vol.1: LAS TRES DAMAS
https://amzn.to/46Nx03J

Vol.2: EL REINO DE LAS ALMAS ERRANTES
https://amzn.to/3QI5S1i

SOL DE PLATA
https://goo.gl/NwCzkw

AQUÍ TE ESPERARÉ POR SIEMPRE
https://goo.gl/UqCbcB

REFLEJOS
https://goo.gl/S78kQC

SOCIAL MEDIA

BLOG
http://laescribiente.blogspot.co.uk/

AMAZON
http://goo.gl/FGaV9x

OBRAS
https://goo.gl/6IWMCe

INSTAGRAM
claudiacortez_autora

FACEBOOK
https://www.facebook.com/claudia.cortez.la.escribiente/

TWITTER
https://twitter.com/CEscribiente

E-MAIL
claudialaescribiente@gmail.com

Printed in Great Britain
by Amazon

39376232R00198